THE CLAY MESSIAH

Karen Rae Levine

To Betty
My good good friend
and a wonderful person
I love you
Karen

HALESITE
PRESS
HUNTINGTON, NY

Halesite Press LLC
PO Box 2011, Huntington, NY 11743

ISBN 978-0-9885615-0-2

Cover Design by Karen Rae Levine

Image, front cover: "The yellow star that nine year old Vera Bader had to affix to her clothes," Artifacts Collection of the Yad Vashem Museum, Gift of Vera (Bader) Weberova

Image, front cover: "Dog tags and mezuzah worn by Lawrence Luskin." (1920-1973, US Army 11th Armored Division), from the Lawrence Luskin family collection. Photo courtesy of the Museum of Jewish Heritage – A Living Memorial to the Holocaust

Photo, back cover: United States Holocaust Memorial Museum, courtesy of K. L. Rabinoff-Goldman, Photograph #19402, Dachau, [Bavaria] Germany, April 29, 1945. "American soldiers view the Dachau death train."

Image, p. 71: Letters, Harold Porter to his parents May 7, 10, 13 and 15, 1945 [World War II Participants and Contemporaries Papers, Porter Harold: Memorabilia]; World War II: Holocaust, The Extermination of European Jews; Dwight D. Eisenhower Presidential Library

Details of the Jewish service at Dachau from *The GI's Rabbi: World War II Letters of David Max Eichhorn*, permission of Mark S. Zaid (ed)

I WANT TO BE HAPPY (from "No No, Nanette") Words by IRVING CAESAR Music by VINCENT YOUMANS © 1924 (Renewed) WB MUSIC CORP. and IRVING CAESAR MUSIC CORP. All Rights Administered by WB MUSIC CORP. All Rights Reserved Used by Permission of ALFRED MUSIC PUBLISHING CO., INC.

With the exception of Rabbi Eichhorn, all characters are fictional.

For Matthew,
my light in the darkness

9th of Tishrei, 5705

(26 September 1944)

Avrum sunk the blade of his shovel into the river mud and leaned his thin frame against the wooden shaft. His water-logged boots sank into the muck and the autumn water seeped between his toes.

Hours ago, during the march from the camp to the river, he had been thankful for the boots. Those who didn't have them were forced to slip and shuffle in canvas clogs. But now the boots seemed a great weight; an anchor that would pull him into the frozen underworld of the lapping green current.

Avrum ticked off his days in a succession of painful labor. The day before it had been sacks of cement heaved on his back, to be carried gasp after agonizing gasp from the cart to the construction site and then back for another. Today it was heaving shovelfuls of brown mud into a bucket that another tortured soul would drag up the steep wooded path from the riverbank. Avrum didn't know why mud was needed and hardly cared. Grasp with blistered hands. Lift with wasted muscles. He wanted to cry or scream or just collapse, or do anything but lift one more useless glob from the shore.

The lunch whistle blew high and shrill. It alerted the only guard in Avrum's sight, a plump German soldier with a long overcoat and dry boots who had been half dozing against a tree. Avrum loosened his grip and let his arms relax. An hour's respite.

The blue-striped prisoners spaced along the river's edge shouldered their shovels and found their way up the forested paths, sidestepping around the unfortunate few who had to complete the journey laden with buckets of sludge.

The anticipation of a slice of bread renewed Avrum's energy. But his boots were too heavy to lift. He stood as still as stone.

The guard stared at Avrum as if he was an organ-grinder's monkey who had decided not to grind the organ.

Avrum stared back.

The guard pointed his rifle.

Avrum wondered how it would feel to have a bullet penetrate his skin, his skull, his brain. Would the pain last for a moment or would it accompany him forever? A bizarre curiosity had squashed his mortal fear. Could that speeding scrap of metal put an end to his misery? He had lived fifteen years. He had witnessed fifteen times fifteen deaths. Was today the day? Was today *his* day to die?

He waited for the answer.

The guard glanced up at someone approaching from the road. An emaciated prisoner slipped and stumbled through the brush. Against his chest, just below the yellow star, he clutched a brown paper package. This he held out to the guard, who still had his rifle aimed at Avrum's head.

The guard lowered his rifle, grabbed the package and brought it to his nose. He inhaled and smiled and waved away the provider of his lunch.

The prisoner removed his cap and bowed from the waist. He bowed again and again as he backed away from the guard, down the hill towards Avrum.

The guard, now more transfixed with his meal than with Avrum, settled down against the tree to eat a sandwich heavy with thick slices of meat.

"Sit," whispered the man, now standing shoulder to shoulder with Avrum. Without turning his head, he tugged at Avrum's sleeve. "Sit."

Avrum lifted one foot and then another. The river had released his boots. He took a few determined steps, sat on a log beside the stranger and leaned his shovel between them.

"I knew your father," said the man.

Avrum stared at the river, still puzzled by the mystery of a bullet to his head.

"He was a good man."

Avrum thought about his father every day. In his nightmares he relived the panic of waking to his father's cold, dead body on the wooden shelf they shared for sleeping.

"And a great Kabbalist." The man produced four slices of

brown bread from his jacket and handed two to Avrum.

Avrum chewed.

"We've met once before, you and I."

The guard snorted. Avrum turned to find him fast asleep against the tree.

"A lazy one, that," said the man. He turned his eyes skyward. "Baruch HaShem." *Blessed is God.*

Avrum tasted margarine. He hadn't tasted that in months. He forced himself to chew slowly.

The man dropped to his knees and dug his hands into the mud. "Your father," he said. "I was his teacher."

Avrum noted the profile of the man. A long, slender nose. Gray eyes.

The man formed a mound of the mud on the brown strip between the lapping water and the brush. "Yes," he said. "A good man." He reached for Avrum's shovel and began to dig. He formed a large mound beside the smaller one. With the shovel, he cut lines in the larger mound.

Avrum saw the man had created a child's sculpture of a head and a torso with two arms. "What are you doing?"

The man, sweating now, dropped to his knees and began molding a nose. "I don't think your father would want you to give up just yet."

"You're crazy. I don't know you."

The man sat up and rested dripping hands on his thighs. "Please, there isn't much time. Come here and help me."

Those fingers. Long and bony and paper white. Yes, he had seen those hands before. A man with those hands sat with his father in the closet of an apartment his family had been forced to occupy. He had a dark beard then, streaked with white, and a felt hat pushed to the back of his head. He and Avrum's father drank tea from glasses and talked in whispers while Avrum's mother, a radiant flower who had wilted in the dark of the ghetto, mended a shirt in the murky light of the only window. Avrum didn't know his name, but when the man left, his father had called him Rabbi.

Rabbi? The title meant nothing here. With his shaved face and scalp, striped prisoner's cap and yellow star, he was just another despised and dispensable Jew.

"Come. Come now," said the rabbi.

And a crazy one at that. But this man, this rabbi, was also a witness to Avrum's existence. He had memories of Avrum's parents. It was as if Avrum had uncovered a forgotten photograph. It brought him to a time before this time, when he belonged—when he was cherished.

Avrum dropped to his knees and felt the wet cold creep into his legs. He couldn't fathom why he should do this. Except that if this didn't make any sense, then neither had anything else that had transpired since his mother sewed the first yellow star on his jacket half a lifetime ago. And if he was ready to give up his life a few minutes ago, he might as well die helping a rabbi make a man out of mud.

When they were finished Avrum relaxed his tired hands and stared at their creation. The rabbi had made wells for the eyes and inscribed a mouth. Avrum had done his best with the legs and feet.

"Well done." The rabbi studied the sculpture and stroked a beard that wasn't there.

Avrum checked on the guard, still sleeping under the tree. "If you say so." He sat on the bank, too tired to lift himself. "Is this supposed to be somebody?"

The rabbi focused his gray eyes on Avrum for a moment before turning away. "Who do you wish it to be?"

Avrum almost laughed. A wish was as unreal to him as a pastrami sandwich or a feather bed.

But in spite of himself, Avrum wished. He wished it was his father—Papa, who would wake up and say, "There's my good boy. There's my Avrumel." But no. Avrum couldn't even begin to imagine that this lump of drying clay could transform itself into the bright and complex being who had been his Papa.

Avrum wished again. He wished this was a monster that would rise up from the earth with bloody, dripping fangs—a monster that would dig its claws into the heart of every Nazi in the camp, leaving each one white and lifeless in a puddle of his own blood. But not just the Nazis—also the Kapo who had whipped him during roll call because he had swayed with hunger and fatigue and the Block Elder who had tried, more than once, to slip his tobacco-stained fingers into Avrum's pants. Evil wore both green wool and blue stripes. It wore the broken crosses of the Nazis, the yellow stars of the Jews and the red triangles of the political prisoners.

Avrum spoke to the cold earth he squeezed between his fingers. "I wish—"

The rabbi leaned closer.

"I wish I didn't have to be afraid all the time. I wish—I wish I had someone to protect me—to care for me. Is that too much to ask?" Avrum grunted a laugh. "If I live in shit and sleep in shit and smell like shit, do you think it's too much to ask that I might close my eyes and pretend, for an hour or two, that I don't live in a shit-hole? Do you think this lump of clay can do that for me? Do you, Rabbi?"

Avrum looked at the man squatting beside him. The rabbi's body rocked back and forth, back and forth, swaying like a branch in the wind. With his eyes closed and his lips barely moving, he chanted. He chanted Hebrew words and letters that formed a long and droning prayer. Had Avrum heard it before? An image flashed, of Papa reading from a worn and ancient book as Mama whispered that he should put it away.

Avrum erased the memory. He erased everything. He leaned forward and back. He closed his eyes and rocked. Back and forth. Back and forth. Again and again. Only an hour for the midday meal. Only an hour to rest. But time had no meaning. The ache of hunger seemed far away. Avrum let the empty feeling carry him. For how long? He didn't know. The singsong chant of the rabbi embraced him, lifted him and set him down again on a cushion of silence.

Avrum opened his eyes. The rabbi had a stick and he was writing in Hebrew, from right to left, across the forehead of the muddy sculpture. Three letters. Aleph. Mem. Tav.

The whistle blew, signaling the end of their break. Avrum turned his attention to the guard who cursed and fumbled clumsily for his rifle. Avrum sprang up, grabbed his shovel and began to dig. A fellow inmate slid down the hill with a bucket in time to catch Avrum's second lob.

He didn't dare turn his eyes to the man-shaped pile of mud. There were no comments from the other laborers. The guards seemed oblivious as well. The pain of Avrum's labor was swept into the whirlwind of his thoughts.

A golem. Avrum had heard stories of golems. They were creatures molded of clay and brought to life through secret recipes of Jewish mysticism. Sometimes the golem, a lumbering creature that couldn't speak or reason, was meant simply to serve the synagogue of the rabbi who created it. In the greatest and most fearsome story, a golem was created by a revered rabbi in Prague in order to save the Jewish citizens within the walled ghetto, attacked by the neighboring townspeople after being accused of using the blood of Christian children to make their matzos. The golem, an invincible giant, slew the invaders, saved the village and was returned to clay by its creator.

Avrum searched his memory for the legends told to him. Each tale had a teller, and each story conjured a memory. On the knee of his father. A rainy afternoon in the attic, listening to his cousin Eliyahu tell a story. Memories and legends intertwined, his past as surreal as a folktale. And his present more ghoulish than any tale of horror.

A whistle brought Avrum back to his reality. Cold. Wet. Aching. Consumed with hunger. The workday was at an end. He turned for the first time to where the man of mud had rested but found only footprints and puddles. Someone else must have dug it up or perhaps it had been trampled. On the way up the hill and during the weary march back to the camp Avrum looked for the rabbi but saw no sign of him. Avrum couldn't find him among the ragged groups consuming their evening meal of watery soup or among the masses of prisoners who stood at attention throughout the drawn-out roll call. He began to believe he had dreamed the entire episode.

Limp with exhaustion, Avrum crawled onto the shelf he shared with four others. But sleep did not come easily. Memories bore memories. And each lump of remembrance, no matter how sweet or how pungent, was soured by loss. Confusion and grief consumed him. And through it all, there flashed the three letters the rabbi had inscribed on the forehead of their golem. Aleph Mem Tav spelled *Emet.*

Truth.

29 April 1945

From the town, they followed the railroad tracks. Daniel tucked his rifle in his armpit and huffed hot breath across the fingers of his left hand. Gloves made him more clumsy, and he was clumsy enough as it was. He ran his eyes across the weedy patches of snow and scanned the woods. Just because the war seemed to be coming to a close didn't mean he still couldn't get killed. A somber little jingle, whispered across divisions during the course of the long winter, had become every soldier's private mantra: *Stay alive in '45.*

A whistle, vague and tuneless, drifted from behind. The sergeant broke the single-file line to glare back at Whitey, whose nervous whistle disrupted every no-talking-no-smoking formation. Ahead of him, Daniel watched the handle of a folded shovel tap in rhythm against the pancake backside of Alabama. He couldn't imagine what Alabama expected to dig. Since crossing the Rhine, warfare had gone from trench-by-trench to town-by-town. It wasn't necessarily any better, but at least they covered more ground—for the most part.

Daniel had spent the entire week of Passover caught in the brutal battle for Aschaffenburg. Hopes for a quick sweep through Germany were almost dashed in a town that put up a fanatical resistance, and had to be seized building by building. On the first night of Pesach, Daniel sat entrenched with his squad in the basement of a half-demolished bakery. Beneath the rumble of artillery fire as he munched his matzah (procured through the Catholic chaplain) the ceiling puffed clouds of flour. Daniel, tired to the bone and scared, laughed at the irony of attempting to eat an unleavened meal in a fog of forbidden chometz. And so, in a basement that reeked of sweat and exhaustion (and bread), and in a nation whose pillars were cemented in a foundation of anti-Semitism, Daniel chanted the Four Questions—the same song that would probably be sung a few hours later by the eight-year-old son of his cousin Alvin, and given the rapt attention of all those assembled for a Seder in the overheated dining room of his Aunt Esther's house in Sheepshead Bay, Brooklyn. "Mah nishtanah halailah hazeh mikol halaylot?" Daniel began. *Why is this night different from all other nights?* When he was finished, Turk said, "Not a bad tune, there, Dan." Even Baxter, who referred to Daniel as "the heeb," nodded his sleepy-eyed approval.

Not that Daniel had been worried about their reaction. He'd already earned the respect of his platoon—although he couldn't think how and his eagerness to live up to his army training aside, he assumed it was simply because he was the only January replacement still alive. But even his survival did not seem to have been achieved by any degree of skill. He considered it an accident, pure and simple. Daniel had deduced that beyond the diligent practice of a few basic rules, whether or not he'd live to twenty was completely in God's hands—and God's hands, it seemed, worked within a framework of surprising randomness.

In the weeks since Aschaffenburg the progression of Daniel's regiment east through Germany had been swift, but not without cost. The only break in the approach-and-seizure of town after town was the tedious process of crossing the Danube on a pontoon bridge.

This morning, I-Company was supposed to be waiting in reserve as K and L-Companies, supported by a tank battalion, pushed through the German resistance toward Munich. During any battle, "in reserve" was a relatively safe place to be, but Daniel's pleasure at his company's status was short-lived. They were assembled early and informed of new orders: to attack and capture a nearby concentration camp.

Concentration camp. Daniel had heard the words before, but hardly knew what they meant. A prison? A POW compound? Heavily guarded? Abandoned? Nobody knew. But it didn't matter, really, what you knew or what you guessed. This engagement was like any other—you forced yourself to take that first long stride into the unknown, and step after boot-clad step, pushed on from there.

Up ahead, Daniel watched the First Platoon disappear around a line of railroad cars that curved with the tracks. The crisp air

creaky rumble of rolling metal. Boxcar doors were
'd. Daniel tensed, waiting for the pop-pop of rifle
_ɘ came. Good. The cars were abandoned. Not a
_at.

Daniel and the three dozen men of the Second Platoon advanced. There must have been thirty or forty cars snaked along the tracks. Beside the cars the obedient line of olive-drab ants (single file, five paces apart) had dispersed into a dazed and listless swarm. Big Butch McMurphy was bent away from the group, vomiting at the tree line. The Platoon Leader, a quiet little lieutenant from Kansas, had his helmet off and scratched his head as if the itch would never go away. Like a warning bell, the song of Daniel's sergeant, repeated at every approach and attack, rang clear in Daniel's brain: *Spread out, goddamn it. Keep moving.*

Why were they bunching up, hesitating? Daniel's shoulders tensed and he wrapped long fingers tight around the wooden stock of his rifle.

The first car was still sealed. The second car was an open box, its disjointed, snow-spotted cargo barely discernible through the opened side door. Daniel had an impression of what it was, but told himself it couldn't be.

A GI Daniel didn't know stared inside the third car. With his head cocked and his mouth open, he looked as if he were about to emit a question of profound importance. Daniel stepped in front of the yawning doors and in a wave of dizziness felt the GI's question become his own: Why were they sleeping?

Propped up against the splintered walls and sprawled out across the floor, people. But not quite people—human frames with taut, gray skin, gaping mouths and close-cropped hair. Dozens. Men. A woman? One child. Another. Not sleeping. Dead. But not killed. Obviously left to die of cold and hunger. Hands clasped or arms flung wide. Dirty. Inert. Like some giant madman's idea of a shoebox diorama. Only it wasn't an Indian village made of matchsticks, or a coral reef with paper fish. Here was Agony, carefully and meticulously boxed for presentation to the class, constructed with a most abundant material—the deflated shells of discarded human beings.

Soldiers drifted past as Daniel, who had lived with Death for months, studied it now in a form that had not yet been catalogued.

Someone said, "What the...?"

And someone said, "Jesus."

And someone said, "Holy Mary Mother of God."

And someone said, "Fuckin' Krauts. Those fuckin' fuckin' Krauts."

Bit by bit, the putrid stench invaded Daniel's senses. The foul gasses of decomposition pushed tears to his eyes. He wanted to turn away, to run into the woods and gulp air scented with life and growth but he couldn't move.

He let his eyes rest on the soles of two feet, stained and swollen, and followed the line of the legs to the torso of a man sitting against the back wall. His jacket, made of the same blue-striped material as his trousers, was buttoned up to his neck. Perhaps against the cold. Perhaps in a final attempt at neatness and dignity. His hands, large and out of proportion to his skeletal body, rested on his lap. The stranger's cheeks were sunken and his eyes wore the thick film of death. His head leaned slightly forward and when Daniel looked into the man's face, it seemed almost as if the stranger had lowered his head in order to return the gaze.

At the yeshiva, when a tract of the Talmud was especially difficult to understand, Daniel might converse with one of the ancient sages. Rashi, Rambam, Ramban—each had a face in Daniel's mind, and even a personality. It was an exercise of the imagination but sometimes Daniel would be rewarded with a tiny clue that might lead to a higher level of comprehension or more rarely, revelation. Now, in a haze of confusion, Daniel begged for revelation from the stranger on the train—who was surely not a sage, but who, with his jacket branded with a grimy yellow star, was most certainly a Jew. *Where did you come from? Why are you here? What does it mean?*

In the stranger's silence, through his smoky, lifeless eyes,

Daniel sensed a spark of accusation. It startled him, and Daniel responded in defense. *How could we know? We've been fighting. Dying. We're here to free the world.*

A break in the clouds sent a shaft of light into the car. It crossed the stranger's eyes and for an instant the mist of death lifted and the eyes blazed with light and this lightning bolt of consciousness—it struck at Daniel's core. And the eyes cried out, *Too late.*

Daniel backed away and walked on. Had to watch his feet. Corpses dotted the train-side gravel. In car after car the nightmare repeated. Anguished death in bundles of blue and gray. Here and there, a muted patch of yellow. Everywhere, hollow, staring faces. Everywhere, skin stretched tight over protruding bones.

His mother's voice boomed in his ears. Skin and bones! That's what she shouted when he pushed away the potato latkes or the apple cake. Skin and bones! You'll waste away to nothing, my Daniel, and what will be left for your poor mama? Skin and bones!

"Mama."

Maybe he said it out loud. He wasn't sure. Right then he wanted her. Wanted his face between her pudgy hands. Wanted to go home. He would. That's what he'd do. Go home. He stepped back from the tracks. Which way? Stepped over a blue-striped cadaver sprawled on the ground, a cleft in its skull the width of a rifle butt. The other way. Home was the other way. He walked the other way. Heard the sergeant. "Move out." Didn't sound like the sergeant. Sounded like, maybe, the sergeant's little brother. Gray face. Loose jowls. Didn't look like Sarge either. The man who was like the sergeant lifted his hand above his head and turned around. And Daniel followed the hand and followed the sergeant and joined the plodding stream (single file, five paces apart) that flowed past the tracks and the railway cars and the skin-and-bones people who were not sleeping. Daniel wiped a sleeve across his eyes and then his nose. He gripped his rifle and scanned the woods. It wasn't over. They still had to take the camp.

Stay alive in '45.

Daniel got a boost and followed Turk over the eight-foot brick wall. The barbed wire on top had already been cut. He crouched and ran along the manicured backyards of a row of pretty houses. He found it hard to marry the quiet, residential scene to the images from the train—but he didn't have time to think about it. His five-man squad took a house and went through the rooms, one by one. At each doorway Daniel's heart stopped and it didn't start again until he found himself blissfully alone. Turk shouted, "Clear!" and it echoed off the books and the children's toys and the potted herbs on the windowsill.

Next, running low, they skirted paved streets. Offices. Warehouses. Rose gardens. Clear. All clear.

"Kraut."

Daniel followed the line of the pointing finger through a row of slim trees to a long barbed-wire fence ticked with a series of guard towers. Visible through the window of the closest tower was the unmistakable curve of a German helmet. Daniel raised his rifle and filled his lungs. The steel sight circled around the broad back of his target and Daniel struggled to bring it to center.

"I got this one, Dan." Turk slid up beside him, his rifle already to his cheek.

Daniel swallowed mixed droplets of irritation and confusion. Normally he would have been more than happy to relinquish the kill. From the moment he'd first felt the weight of a rifle in his hands Daniel had been in a moral panic. Then soon enough, on the battlefield, came the fear and the anger and Daniel found himself in abandoned prayer for the death of the enemy—because this was a world of kill-or-be-killed. Still, each time he took a life, it was like another needle in his soul.

Turk took the shot and the guard in the tower slumped.

More shots. More dead guards. Rifle fire. Friendly. No return fire.

A GI herded eight enemy soldiers, hands on heads, west towards the secured area.

Daniel's squad jogged north on a paved road that paralleled

the barbed fence as men of the First Platoon took control of the two-story guard posts. A German guard toppled down the length of a white tower. The hatless, rag-doll body thumped on the grass and rolled into the cement moat that flowed between the fence and the trees. From the upper window, McMurphy spat down on the corpse.

Movement beside one of the barracks—one of a long, neat row of identical one-story buildings, perhaps twenty yards behind the barbed wire—halted Daniel's steady scan of his surroundings. He blinked. Another fleshless human in filthy blue stripes. But this one was standing. Watching. The man swayed and lifted an arm to brace himself against the whitewashed building.

Whitey gave Daniel a little push from behind. "Whaterya doin', Danny? Sightseein'?"

"Right, Whitey. Sightseeing." Daniel quickened his pace.

His boots pounded. His calves ached. When would this be over? He followed Turk through a treed and shaded section to a long brick building topped by a stout chimney. The stench crept into Daniel's consciousness. He recognized the gut-churning odor of decomposition tinged with the acrid sting of burnt flesh, encountered a time or two before in his war-time experience. It was stronger here, almost overpowering.

Whitey's whistles grew shrill and unnerving.

Alabama gagged and spat. "Jeee-sus H. Chraast!"

Beyond Alabama's gap-toothed grimace lay the reason for his outburst: A stack of white corpses against the red brick. Skin and bones. Naked. Piled like cordwood. Organized. Meticulous. Death in perfect order. But not quite perfect. A twisted foot here. A protruding arm there. Limp genitals at wayward angles.

Bile burned Daniel's throat. His thumb found the safety latch on his rifle. He clicked it on. Then off. Then on. Then off again. Like his mind, his senses. On, then off again.

They swept the building—stepped cautiously around man-high piles of ragged clothing in the yard... nervously through steel doors marked with a skull and crossbones and

14

the word *GASKEIT*... quickly past storage rooms jammed with naked corpses... numbly across a large room that housed four giant brick ovens.

Daniel paused at a doorway over which the word *BRAUSBAD* had been painted in large black letters. Whitey stood in the center of the twenty-foot-square brick-floored room with his head back and his mouth open, contemplating the rows of showerheads in the ceiling. Daniel's command to "Come on!" echoed within the windowless chamber and Whitey snapped out of his daze.

Machine gun fire tat-tatted in the distance.

Daniel was the last one out. He thought he heard a muffled clink behind him and turned, but he was alone. Only distant and intermittent rifle fire broke the graveyard silence. He had to investigate—it was one of those basic rules.

Around the corner of the building, clear. But at the bottom of a steep cement staircase that hugged the brick wall, double doors were slightly ajar. Baxter was supposed to have cleared the basement.

Daniel pressed the butt of his rifle into his shoulder, aimed the barrel down the stairs and said, "H'raus." He'd heard others use this gruff command before, but from his own mouth, it sounded weak and school-boyish. Anyway, he was probably talking to himself.

The door creaked and a handkerchief fluttered at the end of a hand. Daniel gripped the stock tighter and forced himself not to jerk his index finger. He swallowed and repeated his command. "H'raus!"

A German soldier in camouflage field clothes emerged, his hands in the air. "Nicht schiessen." His voice shook. "Bitte, nicht schiessen "

Daniel stepped back and motioned with his rifle for the soldier to ascend. The German's hobnailed boots clumped up the cement steps. Daniel switched his attention back and forth between the soldier and the basement door.

"Ich bin allein, ja? Allein."

The fright in the enemy's blinking eyes was enough to convince Daniel that he was telling the truth—that he was indeed alone—and so Daniel narrowed his focus on the prisoner.

The double-lightning-bolt insignia of the SS decorated the collar of the attractive young blond with his hands in the air. Daniel knew from the Yiddish papers how the SS—Hitler's elite and brutal Death's Head squads—had terrorized Jews in Germany before the war. In combat also, the Waffen SS units had a reputation for merciless fanaticism. But at the moment, this green-eyed teenager didn't look particularly brutal or merciless. He looked scared.

Daniel eased the rifle from his cheek and let his shoulders relax.

The prisoner sighed. "Lieber Gott." He dropped his hands to the top of his head and interlaced his fingers. And with worry still knotted between his eyebrows, in a manner that was almost flirtatious, he grinned.

Grinned. The simple expression shook Daniel. A smile on this well-fed face, against the backdrop of a building crammed with the starved and tortured. It was too much. The past few minutes... hours... months...

Daniel's shout exploded into the putrid air. "You think it's funny?"

The corners of the Nazi's mouth dropped and his eyes flashed fear.

"Did you smile at them when they begged for food? Did you laugh when you smashed their brains? Did you—how do you live with yourself? You're a monster. That's what you are. A monster!"

Daniel experienced a darkness he had never known before—as if the Angel of Death had infiltrated his soul, squeezed out all the hope and pity, and also all the grief and pain, until all that remained was blessed emptiness. And in this hollow darkness, a new strength grew. He became a powerful machine. Expendable. Lethal. Righteous.

Daniel squeezed the trigger and the crack of the rifle stung his ears.

A patch of red blossomed across the brown and olive swirls of the camouflage jacket. The German's eyebrows lifted

in surprise. His fingertips, released from their lock a.
head, grazed his ears. He thumped back against the brick.
Eyes fading, he blinked.

When Daniel was small, he'd watched the man at the street
market cut the neck of the chicken his mother had selected. The
legs and wings had twitched for what seemed a very long time.
"Make it dead, Mama," he had cried. "Tell him to make it dead!"

Daniel squeezed the trigger again. A second blossom
appeared on the jacket.

A cold film washed the emerald eyes and, with liquid
deliberation, set them in a frozen stare. Boots planted, the lifeless
body scratched down the brick, where it remained—knees up,
head dropped, seated.

What had he done?

Whitey's voice. Far away. "Shit, Danny. Shit."

An arm weighed across his shoulders. Alabama. "It's aw-right,
Danny. Don't you worry 'bout it. It's aw-right."

Baxter. "Looks like the heeb's gone off his rocker."

Turk. "Na, he's okay. Aren't ya Dan? Come on, Dan. Come on.
Let's go."

A shaft of stray sunlight illuminated the dirty feet of the man
sleeping next to Avrum. The usual early morning siren
summoning them to roll call had not blared. The blessing of
chance to rest longer was marred by the ill-boding of a break in
the methodical routine of his efficient jailers.

Avrum heard voices in the overcrowded room, somewhat
more animated than usual. Too exhausted to lift his head, he
simply listened.

"Deliverance."

"Americans."

"Blessed be the Lord."

Avrum had little patience for such wishful thinking. He
reached under his striped shirt and into the hair of his armpit.

ewhere along the line, through one camp after another, had become a man. Or perhaps, at the age of sixteen, only half a man. A haftling, as the Germans called it. Avrum pulled out a louse and crunched it between his fingers.

Avrum's movement jarred the leg of a bunkmate he didn't recognize and the man's knee thudded on the wooden platform. Angry that this bag of bones was crowding him in a bunk that offered precious space, Avrum gathered his strength and pushed him away. The man rolled flat on his face. Not for the first time, Avrum had been sleeping beside a corpse.

He wondered where Vladik was.

The distinct creak of the barrack's double doors pushed a sluggish wave of silence down the center aisle. It washed past his bunk and caught the last speaker, at the end of the barrack, in mid-sentence. At a funeral pace, the haphazard cadence of heavy steps clumped along the wooden floor.

Avrum caught his breath and shrunk behind the dead man. By the time he could see them, a second wave of sound had begun—the hollow thud of fleshless hands brought together in applause.

They wore funny bubble helmets and disheveled uniforms. Both cradled rifles. One of them pressed a handkerchief to his mouth and nose. The other, loose-jawed and wide-eyed, caught Avrum's eye and looked away in horror.

Herman, in the bunk across from Avrum's, reached out and touched one of them. Startled, the soldier turned around, then backed up into the other. Both faces conveyed disgust and revulsion. They retreated from the barrack.

The hollow applause died into heavy silence.

Avrum saw himself through their eyes and the gush of a forgotten feeling filled his emotion-starved consciousness. It found him unprepared and shook his tortured body. Unable to escape it, Avrum could only curl up in a ball.

He had never felt such shame.

Avrum watched Vladik roll the dead bunkmate off the and drag the corpse away. Avrum's mute friend and protector had appeared the day after Avrum had been digging near the river with the gray-eyed rabbi. That had been months ago in Maidenek, before their long march to Dachau.

Vladik shuffled back inside and climbed into the bunk next to Avrum.

As soon as Vladik had settled into a stony position with his back to Avrum, a soldier's steps thudded on the plank floor. Those who were able stood. Those who weren't inched their heads to the edge of their bunks.

"It's real," said Herman, leaning on a wooden post. "I thought I'd dreamed it."

Avrum lifted his face above Vladik's body.

The soldier paused in front of Avrum's bunk. This one was dark-haired and carried his helmet under his arm. For a moment, the glazed eyes of the soldier met Avrum's. Avrum ducked out of sight.

The soldier coughed. Cleared his throat. "Shalom," he said. "Shalom Aleychem."

A soldier greeting them in Yiddish? How absurd. Who taught him to say that?

The greeting was not returned.

"Ich bin a Yid."

A Jew? In the Army? Too impossible to believe. From behind Vladik's shoulder, Avrum dared to watch.

The stranger shifted the rifle slung over his shoulder. "Ich heys Rabinowitz. Daniel Rabinowitz."

"Aleychem Shalom!" shouted Binyamin from the bottom bunk. "Aleychem Shalom!" He collapsed into gasping sobs.

Herman flung his arms around the man's shoulders and kept repeating, "A mal'ich von Gut. A mal'ich von Gut." An angel from God. Someone knelt and kissed the Jewish American's hand. By the sobs and shuffling, Avrum sensed others kissing his feet and embracing his legs. Hands stretched from the bunks and bony fingers reached out for this young Messiah.

Tears streamed down the face of Daniel Rabinowitz. "Nain. Nain. Bi'teh. Ich bin—gornit vert."

Confident this man was far from "worthless," Avrum yearned to touch him and cursed his own weakened body.

Vladik never budged.

30 April

He woke up afraid. The kind of fear that slides into your belly, reaches up behind your sternum, and grips your throat so hard you can't breathe. The kind of fear that consumes your body—shakes it. The kind that empties your brain of reason. Daniel waited. Through the panting. Through the trembling. Through mind-numbing panic. With his heart pounding in his ears, Daniel waited until finally, and by degrees, he could harness the painful rhythm of his breath.

He let loose the blanket that had been clutched in his hands.

It hadn't been a dream—at least not one that he could remember. Probably just a noise outside the barrack—something that had the sound of the whine of a shell or the hiss of shrapnel. Inside, it was quiet—the post-dawn quiet of a dozen sleeping men—a snort, a cough, a sentence murmured through sleep.

The smell of dried sweat and damp wood permeated the air. Daniel took a long breath of it. He told himself it was over. The war was over. Not officially, but at least for him. Just about the whole of the 45th Infantry Division, on its push into Munich, had left him behind.

Almost fully dressed, he rose from the narrow cot in his new home—a barrack in the large SS compound they had seized the day before. He reached under his shirt to scratch between his neck and shoulder. He always washed as best he could, but he hadn't taken a shower in weeks, and the plumbing here was still out of commission. Daniel pulled his boots on, made a quick run to relieve himself into a ditch behind the building, and returned shivering.

He never got used to the cold. Nearly an entire winter living under the trees, and he never got used to it. Just endured it. At least now he had a roof over his head. That was the good news. The bad news was outside—across the moat and behind the barbed wire. The bad news was the reason he had made the request to stay behind. But he wouldn't think about that—not yet. As he made his way back between the two rows of sleeping soldiers he scratched the same itch and in the dim light, focused on locating his pack.

Daniel found his musette bag and reached inside. He could almost feel his fingers warm when he touched the pouch. He'd had few opportunities in the past months but now it seemed right—now he craved it.

He slipped the kippah onto his head, then secured the band and small leather box to his forehead, pushed up his sleeve, and wound the straps of the tefillin around his left arm. Daniel had found that a morsel of treasured solitude in a world devoid of privacy could be salvaged through davening. He closed his eyes and in murmured Hebrew, began the morning service:

...Blessed are You, Lord our God, King of the universe, who has formed man in wisdom and created in him many ducts and organs. It is known that if but one of these be opened, it would be impossible to survive and stand before You...

Someone coughed. A lighter clicked. Daniel tried to retreat into the prayer but a quiet communion eluded him.

...O my God, the soul that You placed within me is pure; You created it, You fashioned it, You breathed it into me, You preserve it within me; and You will one day take it from me, and henceforth restore it to me...

"What the fuck are you doin'?"

Daniel didn't recognize the voice. In order to stay behind, he'd had to accept a transfer to L-company, brought back from the front and assigned to guard the camp. Most of the men were strangers to him.

The nasal reply and high-pitched guffaw belonged to Kopeki. "Taking his Jewish blood pressure."

Daniel felt a blush of irritation. It wasn't what Kopeki had said, it was that Kopeki had said it. Tony Annunziato had blurted those same words on the first morning in boot camp—as Daniel prayed just as he did now—and with that single retort, had diffused the tension of a situation that could have escalated into an ongoing fight. Daniel and Tony, a jovial teen from a close-knit farming family in California, became quick friends. Since then, more times than he could count, Tony's friendship had been, in one darkness after another, Daniel's only light.

Kopeki, who had latched onto Tony and Daniel in the replacement depot back in France, must have heard Tony repeat his little joke, and was now, apparently, trying to help. But the words had opened a gate in Daniel's mind.

They had been walking at the edge of the woods—cradling their rifles and talking. Daniel had glanced behind him in order to get the full effect of the punch line of Tony's newest joke. "What's the difference between a pregnant lady and a light bulb?" But the punch line never came. Daniel looked down to his friend, sprawled out on a blanket of snow, his head resting on a pillow of blood. A tiny wisp of condensation rose from the black-red hole where Tony's right eye had been.

Daniel couldn't pray. Maybe later. In the evening. What day was it anyway? Monday. Well, at least he wouldn't have to spend another Shabbos wondering if he was going to die. Maybe he would light the candles.

"Hey, mac. I asked you a question."

Kopeki's quip had fallen flat. If Tony were here, tough and funny...

Daniel turned around to scan the bunks for whatever dull and contemptuous face it would be this time. And he found it—broad and ruddy, with a short crop of orange beard. *Esau,* Daniel thought. *Why, God, did you pick this moment to send me the slow-witted son of Isaac?*

With the forced tone of patience and exasperation typical of a parent who has given a child the same instruction ten times, Daniel said, "If you want to know what I'm doing, I'll tell you. But you're going to have to find a better way to ask."

"Esau" pushed himself to his feet and scratched his chest through an olive t-shirt. A strip of light from the curtained window illuminated the layer of orange fuzz that coated his arms and shoulders. "Wouldya get a load o' this fucker?"

Daniel's fingers trembled as he coiled the leather straps— either residue from his morning bout of terror or the reflex of

23

impending confrontation—or both. He stored his phylacteries and tried to relax his mind. How could "Esau" bear the cold so well? Maybe you needed a hot head to have a hot body. Or maybe it was all that hair. He smiled.

"What's so funny, ass-wipe?"

Daniel clenched a quivering fist. Why now? After all that had happened, what sense could be made of a fight like this? He was much too weary—both in body and in spirit. But Daniel had acquired a certain amount of physical power in the army—a power he had never owned or had ever even wanted to own before he'd enlisted. He relished this power and kept it in reserve, amassed for those times when it was most needed—to dig or to hike or to run—or to fight. But not now. Not now.

"Pipe down, willya? I'm tryin' ta get some shut-eye." The command came from Sergeant Ramos, propped up on an elbow on a cot by the entrance.

Most of his roommates remained still, buried under blankets, but a few faces were drawn to the conflict, including the beardless, baby-face of Kopeki.

This most current assailant pointed a finger at Daniel, screwed up his face, and then glanced at the sergeant. "Aw, fuckit." He sat down.

Daniel let his shoulders relax. He grabbed his helmet and shaving kit and, with a quick glance at Kopeki, left the room.

He hoped the redhead would pull a different guard shift and they'd never have to see each other. But part of him wished for a chance to cast his might upon Esau—in the form of a fist upon that bristly jaw.

Daniel saluted. "Private Rabinowitz, sir."

The captain set his coffee on the desk. Daniel noted the design on the mug—the open-winged eagle perched on a swastika. The mug and the office had probably belonged, not long ago, to a German officer who was now either dead, captured or on the run. But the tenant at hand was the round-faced Captain Burkhardt, Daniel's new Company Commander.

Burkhardt returned the salute and retrieved a paper from the pile on his desk. He pushed the silver spectacles higher on his nose and studied Daniel's orders. "Relax, Rabinowitz."

Daniel stood at ease.

"Says here you requested to stay behind at this hellhole."

"Yes sir."

"Had enough of fighting?"

"Yes sir. No sir. I mean I thought I could help. If I stayed."

"Says here you speak Yiddish."

"Yes sir. A bit. Enough."

"You speak Polish?"

"No sir."

"German?"

"I can manage with German. It's not too far from Yiddish."

"Aren't many Jews in the camp, Rabinowitz. Two, three thousand, tops. You seen 'em?"

Daniel nodded.

"They're the worst off—unbelievable." He scratched his blond head. "Volunteered for this duty, huh? Personally, I'd risk a hundred potshots by the goddamn Hitler Youth rather than spend two seconds in that place."

"Yes sir."

"I need you to go in there to them—to the Jewish ones—and tell them there's food and medical supplies on the way. Any problem with that?"

"No sir."

"And Rabinowitz—"

"Yes sir?"

"Don't spend too much of your spare time in that cesspool."

"Yes sir." Daniel saluted, performed an inelegant about-face and left the captain to his coffee. He pulled on his gloves, flipped up the collar of his field jacket and headed toward the prisoners' compound.

Staying behind had been the same kind of spur-of-the-moment decision his enlistment had been. His mother had packed him off to the draft board to confirm the deferment that was due to him as a seminary student. "Rabbis don't shoot guns," she'd reminded him again and again. But when he sat in front of the men of the board, and the fat one asked him, as a matter of routine, if he desired the deferment, Daniel had shocked himself with his reply. He said, "No." He didn't know what had possessed him. Later on, he'd told himself he thought of all the Jews in Europe—relatives of his and his schoolmates—that no one had heard from in years. He'd told himself he thought of Pearl Harbor. He wanted to help. Help free the Jews—help free the world. But that bucketful of ideology offered little comfort a few weeks later as he sat trapped within a packed train that mile after agonizing mile, had extracted him from his Brooklyn cocoon.

Now it felt like that again, like he put himself on the wrong train and there was no way to get off. Only this time it was worse. This time he was all too aware of the nightmare that waited for him at the end of the line.

If I could speak I would tell them he is not what he seems. If I could speak I would shout that his boots are too new and his fingernails too clean. He weaves in and out of a crowd wearing some mottled version of the same striped uniform—the uniform of the starved men trapped within these gates. The uniform I wear myself.

But I cannot speak. Although my tongue and throat do not trouble me, words have never passed my lips. I do not know why. I imagine it is the way I was born, although I have no memory of a childhood. No memory outside these prison walls. If there is another world beyond these gates, as some men speak of, I do not know it. It is better this way because I do not miss it. I do not wail at loss or curse the keepers of this jail. This is my life.

My only life.

Death is all around me but I do not weep. The piles of bodies wither and decay. They join the porous earth. Many men, raw and unsettled, have been born into my world through those gates, and most return to the soil. It is the path here. Birth to death. Flesh to dust.

I sometimes wonder that if I did not have my mission here, if I would rather lie on the ground and let my body join the earth. But I remain among the talking, walking, breathing for one reason. The Boy.

He is the only one with colors and they mesmerize me. The names of the colors I only know from the comments of others. "Are you sure you're a Jew, Boy? With those blue eyes and blond hair, you look like a Nazi." They laugh but I do not understand the humor. The other prisoners, the other haftlings, have no colors—only shades of dullness. Like the earth, like the barracks, like the trees and the guns. I sometimes peer at the others to see if they see it too. None are as dazzled or as amazed as I am. To them he is just another maggot in our kettle of vile soup.

Why is the Boy, and only the Boy, so brilliant to me? Why are his stripes a faded version of the color of his eyes? Why do the tones of his skin own a hue I see on no other? I have no answer. Nor do I care to put the question to myself very often. He is what he is. I am what I am.

His protector.

Now that I know his colors I cannot let them go. I must not allow him to fade away and return to the earth. So I keep him safe. From the guards. From the Kapos. From himself.

Before the new soldiers came I watched most of the Nazi guards disperse and leave. I observed the apprehension in those that remained. When gunshots cracked the air I became a shadow. I hid near the hospital barrack and peered through the barbed wire and the wooden slats that separated the prison from the SS compound.

New soldiers with round helmets pointed guns at a cluster of Nazis with their hands on their heads. There they were, perhaps a hundred, huddled and shifting nervously in the empty coal yard. The new soldiers pointed rifles at them. Behind a machine gun propped on three skinny legs, a gunner squatted. Rifles pop-popped all around in the distance. Then the pop-pop exploded into thra-tat-tat, thra-tat-tat, thra-tat-tat. With grunts and screams, the Nazis dropped where they stood. It continued until one of the new soldiers pushed the gunner away. I wanted to leap over the fence and feel the steel of that machine gun in my own hands—to eradicate every being that had been a threat to the Boy. What kind of soldiers were these, who could not finish a job?

Americans. That's what they're called. They carry rifles but have not used them often since they took the camp, and never against the haftlings. They keep the gates locked and this helps keep me calm because I am unsure of what exists outside the gates, unsure of how I would protect the Boy out *there*.

Still, I am disturbed by the new order. The new soldiers, these Americans, have shed tears for the haftlings but I fear that they could turn. I trust no one.

The Americans have not washed all the vermin from the camp—the Nazi vermin who ate their fill when the Boy had none. Who killed for sport. They were the greatest danger to the Boy. They left me cold with frustration and fear because of the random and limited power I had over them.

My enemies then. My enemy now. In front of me. Unarmed. Disguised.

A Nazi in the rags of a haftling. Clean boots. Clean fingernails. I can feel the brightness he is trying to hide. The brightness of health, of a washed body. If I could speak, I would shout out that he is an imposter. I would shout that he could still be a danger to the Boy. But I cannot speak and so I quicken my pace and follow the bright spot through the dull and dying masses until my clogs step into his boot prints. Until I can smell the soap underneath his rank clothing.

I grab the back of his collar and throw him to the ground. He shouts some angry words and the crowd parts. I squat and rip his jacket open. Buttons fly. The washed scent of his hairless chest stings my eyes. He flails, tries to right himself. I fix my heavy foot on his neck and catch his sleeve. One swift tug bares his right arm.

There it is. The others see it too. The painted mark on the inside of his upper arm. The tattoo of the SS.

There is fear in his eyes now. He sputters words. The crowd tightens, forming a circle of compressed rage. Trapped beneath my wooden clog, the Nazi's voice becomes shrill.

A tattered boot plummets into his side. The glob of haftling spittle dribbles down the Nazi's cheek. I see a shovel raised and I release the pressure of my foot. The shovel falls in an angry arc and, with the sound of a shovel penetrating river muck, the steel edge splits the Nazi's face. I back away through the growing throng as the men of the camp tear my enemy limb from limb.

I sigh and unclench my fists. One less danger to the Boy.

The smell woke Avrum. At first he thought it was a dream. He often dreamed in his sleep but preferred the half-dreams he conjured during the long waking hours—during the interminable roll calls—the relentless marches. He had learned to keep his daydreams from drifting toward his family. That left only fantasies of freedom—an allusive idea, almost out of his experience.

But this smell was not a dream. The clanking of spoons was not a dream. Herman, who looked about ninety but claimed to be thirty, slipped Avrum one of two opened tins of meat. A child-like grin transformed Herman's withered face. "From our Yiddishe Amerikaner." He walked away, scooping the reddish mush into his mouth.

The aroma brought tears to Avrum's eyes and saliva pooled in his dry mouth. He dipped a dirt-caked finger into the tin and opened his mouth.

Vladik swatted Avrum's raised hand and bits of Herman's precious gift splattered on the wall. Vladik scooped away the can.

Avrum choked on the lingering aroma. "Back," he croaked. "Give it back."

Vladik had already pocketed the prize. Only his head and shoulders visible, he stared at Avrum from under a shelf of bushy eyebrows.

One tear trickled along the edge of Avrum's nose and the other plopped on his sleeve. "Why, Vladik? Why?"

The line of Vladik's mouth looked like it had been chiseled there.

"I hate you." Avrum had meant his croak to be a scream. "I hate you." He rolled his body over and faced the wall. The effort drained the last of his energy and he fell into an angry stupor.

Moans and howls filled the barrack. It smelled more like a latrine than ever. In the bunk across the aisle Herman groaned in pain. "Mama. Mama." his raspy voice pleaded. "Mama, help me!"

Herman, Avrum knew, had last seen his mother, long ago, in a selection process that separated the strong from the weak.

Herman would soon be dead.

Vladik stirred beside Avrum. He slipped a piece of rolled cloth beneath Avrum's head and put a spoon to Avrum's mouth. The broth was not hot but it slid down Avrum's throat and soothed the unrelenting ache in Avrum's belly. Vladik had saved Avrum from indulging in Herman's fatal error—cramming a shriveled belly with food.

1 May

Daniel stepped aside for a procession of three jeeps that crossed the cement bridge in a noisy cloud of dust and gasoline. More bigwigs, it seemed, who had come to see the show. The jeeps pulled into the arched tunnel that cut through the two-story brick gatehouse and stopped at the iron gates. Papers and passes were presented to the American guards.

Daniel hitched the rifle strap higher on his shoulder, rubbed his collarbone through the layers of his uniform, and followed the jeeps through the gate. The two guards reminded Daniel of Abbott and Costello.

The plump one had a scarf wound around his neck like a bulky bandage. "You're the new guy, right?"

"Danny Rabinowitz. Transferred from I-Company yesterday."

"James Leigh." He rolled his eyes. "But they call me Slim. This here is Truman."

"No relation to the president," said Corporal Truman.

They shook hands.

Truman slid a cigarette between his lips and held the pack out to Daniel.

"No, thanks. I don't smoke."

"Might be a good time to start," said Truman. He cupped a hand over his mouth and snapped the lighter. "Helps with the smell."

Slim shifted his bulk from one foot to the other. "Fuck that. Nothing helps with the smell."

"I'm your relief at noon," said Daniel. "I'll see you later."

Slim crossed his arms and shoved his hands in his armpits. "Don't be late, mac. I'm fuckin' freezing my balls off here."

A stream of gripes faded into the air behind Daniel. "First day of May and it's fuckin' freezing. Don't the fuckin' Krauts know when to end the fuckin' winter?"

The three jeeps that had been idling near the gatehouse knocked into gear and growled across the gravel. The sluggish masses parted for them and then closed in again behind. Doll-size at 150 yards, a uniformed cameraman popped up in the middle of the sparse sea of blue stripes and stood on the hood of a jeep with his movie camera. He took a sweeping shot of the administration building, which extended almost the entire length of the square and faced it in a squat U.

The main square had become the heartbeat of the camp. For a prisoner strong enough to stray from his over-crowded barrack it must have represented fresher air and improved freedom—a place to gather information, renew social contacts, barter for black market items—or perhaps simply to bask in the collective life-force, such as it was, of the healthiest survivors.

"Hello, Joe. Zigaretten?"

Daniel lifted his gloved hands to the hollow-cheeked inmate shuffling beside him. "I'm all out." Which was a lie, but Daniel knew better than to make food or cigarettes visible in a crowd of the impoverished. Besides, he had plans for the government-issued cigarettes he never smoked.

The Lagerstrasse, a wide street that ran north from the square, divided two rows of identical one-story barrack buildings, numbered A, B, C, D and then 1 through 30; even numbers on the left and odd on the right. Very orderly. Against each of the short barrack walls that faced the street, a pair of feather-shaped trees stood at attention and, all together, decorated the avenue with two rows of swaying green that converged on a distant vanishing point.

Between Blocks Three and Five, a half dozen internees rummaged through a double pile of half-clad corpses, pulling out useful items. One of them, in a black coat with a white prisoner's X sewn across the back, pointed and gave instructions in some Slavic language. At the edge of the pile, a toothless teenager squatted at the edge of the scene. He smiled and waved at Daniel.

The smile irritated Daniel, although he couldn't fathom why. Daniel walked on.

As the Block numbers turned to double digits, Daniel sensed a shift in the neighborhood. With the bustle of the roll-call square far behind, the population began to consist, for the most part, of a spattering of those too weak to move or too crazy to care.

"Hey, Buddy!"

A couple of GIs stood by the line of cadavers between Blocks Eleven and Thirteen. Roaming soldiers were not unusual. Eisenhower was encouraging units in the area to stop by and get a dose of *Why We Fight*.

"Take a picture for us, willya?" One produced a camera.

"Sure. How do I...?"

"The button on the top. It's all ready to go."

The pair stepped around the mottled corpses and Daniel framed them in the rectangle of the camera's eye: two grim-faced American soldiers towering behind a line of ill-shaven, open-mouthed, stick-like dead people.

Carts propelled by six or eight of the stronger inmates made regular stops along the road to remove this type of waste. More than once Daniel had passed a loaded death cart, heavy with layers of a sinuous cargo that heaved and shook with the forward motion. The jostling intensified the purge of fetid gases from the bodies which generated, above the creaking of the wheels, an unearthly prattle of squeaks and moans.

The camera put a distance between Daniel and this ghoulish portrait of life and death—a distance he wished he could continue.

Click.

"Thanks, Buddy."

"No problem." Daniel handed the camera back.

"What outfit you with?"

"45th Infantry. You?"

"92nd Signal Battalion."

The other remained silent, working his jaws around a hidden wad of chewing gum.

The photographer looped the camera's strap around his neck. "You think anybody at home is gonna believe this shit?"

"I'm not sure I believe it myself."

He snorted. "Yeah, no shit. I heard there's a gas chamber and ovens and stuff like that. You know where it is?"

The shoulder that bore the weight of Daniel's rifle twitched. He scraped taut fingers against the material gathered near the canvas strap. He cleared his throat and pointed north, down the tree-lined Lagerstrasse. "Go to the end and make a left. There's a gate with a guard, but he'll let you through."

Wide-eyed and gaping, the pair of Signal Corpsmen sauntered away.

The touch of his hand on the handle of the wooden door triggered a reflex in Daniel's gut, and a charge of acid bile bubbled up his throat. Knowing what lay ahead, he swallowed, took a final breath of resolve and pulled open the door of Block Fifteen.

For a moment, as he crossed the threshold, he was the little boy at the zoo who'd been forced, despite fevered protestations, to wade through the thick pool of rancid air trapped inside the monkey house. He grabbed the closest post as if it, like his father's unyielding hand, would prevent him from running away.

Heads and feet poked out from the shadows at every level. Here and there a slack-skinned figure sat at the edge of the lowest platform, his shoulders hunched beneath the shelf above. Others leaned against the girders.

With a spurt of determination, Daniel released the post. He pocketed his gloves and tucked his helmet under his arm. Conscious of a slight totter, he moved along the center aisle, greeted by hoarse hellos, hollow hand claps, nods or stares. Some touched him. Some—those more robust—spoke to him. Daniel, as he juggled the assault to his senses, added his second-generation Brooklyn Yiddish to the varying accents and inflections boxed within this bizarre tenement.

"Stop here a moment so I can thank you again for the blanket. Look. You see how it keeps me warm?"

"I'm happy, very happy, that it keeps you warm..."

"I have a cousin in New York. Maybe you know him. Meyer Katzman. No, no. Mickey. In America he's called Mickey. Mickey Katzman. Maybe you know him. "

"New York is a big place."

"I think he would take me in, my cousin."

"Where does he live?"

"I told you. He lives in New York."

"Pardon me. But maybe you know the name of the street."

"Street? How should I know what street? He packed his things and he went to New York. He said he was getting out while he still could. A crazy person, we called him, my cousin Meyer, who left a good business and took his wife and his baby on a boat to America. My wife said maybe we should go too. Do you know what I said? I said this Nazi foolishness, it would all blow over. That's what I said to my wife. My wife, oh my Sophie. Oy veh is me, my Sophie, never again my little bird..."

"Has anyone seen my button?"

"Amerikaner. Amerikaner. A bite to eat. A tin of something. Some chocolate."

"I can't. It would hurt you to eat that."

"Hurt me to eat? It hurts me *not* to eat! Something. Something. Please."

"Believe me, it would make you sick or—or worse. Water and broth. Wait for the broth."

"You gave yesterday. I saw you give yesterday."

"Not yesterday. The day before. But—but I didn't know then. It was a mistake..."

"A white button. I lost it, you see. A white one."

"Rabinowitz, we need paper. Did you bring paper? And

pencils. Did you bring them?"

"No, I'm sorry. I don't have paper. Here's a pencil, though. Here."

"What good is a pencil without the paper? A list of the dead and a list of the living. We should start it right away."

"I'll bring paper tomorrow, I promise. I have to find some, but I'll bring it tomorrow..."

"Have you seen my button?"

"Hey, Max! Here's another one for your lists. Yonkel Horovitz or Horvitz or something like that. Put him on your list of the dead. Which is fine by me. For two days he's been shitting all over the place."

"Has anyone seen my button?"

"Tell me again, young man. Tell me again what I want to hear. Once more and then I won't bother you."

"Yes, I know. It's all right—Hitler is dead."

"From the book of life, may his name be erased forever."

"May his name be erased."

"He's really dead? You're sure?"

"My sergeant told me."

"So this war, it's over."

"Not yet. Almost..."

"A white button. I had it here and now it's gone."

"And one more thing, Mister. How about you go over there and tell that meshugenah putz that nobody has his stupid button."

Daniel pushed open the door and the vacuum of his lungs sucked in the blast of cold air. He tried to blink away the white speckled veil that coated his vision. It muffled the green of the trees. Floated from heaven to the earth. It tickled his eyelashes and dotted his palm with pinpoints of moisture. He set the helmet on his head but couldn't feel its weight and as he continued along the Lagerstrasse he watched snowflakes dissolve into the creases of his palm. He'd forgotten something. What was it? He paused in front of the double line of corpses laid out between the two Jewish barracks. White powder coated clay lips and pooled in hollow sockets. He'd forgotten something—Captain Burkhardt's orders—to tell them something. Food and medicine. That was it. Food and medicine were on the way.

And Daniel was suddenly very sad that the food and the medicine were far away—that the food and the medicine weren't there to help—and he was there to help, but he could only help a little, sometimes, and sometimes not at all, and sometimes what he did was even worse—and he was sad also that his home was far away, that he couldn't hop on a trolley and just be there, count the squares of the sidewalk and just be there, or at least, please God, wake up, wake up from this nightmare of red blossoms and blue stripes...

The canvas strap slipped from his wilted shoulder. The rifle clattered on the ground. Daniel squatted. Sat on a heel. Leaned his knuckles into the icy carpet. Dropped his forehead to the back of a damp hand. A great sob strained his esophagus and exploded into the air. The spray from his mouth and nose inked warm stains on his olive-drab thigh. Daniel's chest heaved in waves of remorse. He tightened his eyes against the pain.

Avrum reclined on the lawn among other blue-striped skeletons healthy enough to trade the stink of the barracks for green grass and sunshine. A rise in the temperature and a break in the clouds had dissolved the morning snow. Those strong enough to walk further congregated on the appelplatz for the May Day celebration. The music of a band, full of spirit and promise, breezed by at varying volumes. Nearby, five men squatted around a makeshift fire, studying the tin can dangling above it and Avrum caught a whiff of coffee.

When the Germans had ruled the camp, any inmate who set foot on this lawn—a perfect stretch of green between the western row of barracks and the electrified fence—would have been shot on sight. Instinctively, Avrum squinted up at the nearest guard tower. Empty. Of course, empty.

Avrum glanced at Vladik, crouched against the whitewashed barrack wall with his cap pulled low on his forehead. After the incident at the riverbank and the disappearance of the gray-eyed rabbi, Vladik had joined their motley group and attached himself to Avrum. At first Avrum hadn't trusted him but after a short time, as weary and full of despair as the rest of the slowly dying, Avrum simply accepted Vladik as another means of prolonging his life. As time went on and Vladik's attention continued, Avrum couldn't help but embrace the fantasy that Vladik was actually a mystical creature conjured from river mud.

But he didn't want to think about Vladik. He didn't want to think at all. He just wanted to feel—the sun on his face, the grass on his fingertips. He turned his attention to the blue and purple sky and took deep breaths of the crisp air.

"Contemplating the heavens?"

With the sun behind the man addressing him in Polish, Avrum couldn't make out his features.

"I have a question for you, if you're up to it," said the man.

He squatted and Avrum could see the black beret and the wire-rimmed glasses. The diagonal crack in the left lens made it look like there were two half-eyes behind it. Avrum couldn't tell their color.

"I'm looking for someone and thought you might know him."

Avrum rested the back of his hand on his forehead.

"His name is Herman Ginzberg."

He couldn't keep his eyes from the broken lens.

"Ah well, that's quite all right. I can see you are a man of few words." He prepared to stand.

"An engineer?" said Avrum.

"Yes," said the man.

"About thirty?"

"Why, yes!"

"Dead," said Avrum.

"Pardon me?"

"He died."

"Ah." said the man. "I see." He touched his finger to his forehead, his chest, his right shoulder and his left, linked his fingers and mumbled some words. He stood in the shadow of the fence for a few minutes and said, "I think I'll just sit here for a moment, if you don't mind."

The badge on the man's coat was hidden beneath his short wool jacket. He rested his forearms on his knees and let his hands dangle. His profile revealed a hawkish nose, white stubble flecked with red and a fan of dirt-stained creases emanating from the corner of his eye. "A good man, Herman," he said. "Did you know him well?"

"Not really."

"I thought I caught a glimpse of him a week or so ago. Funny how exciting it can be to see a familiar face. Of course it's hard to tell and one's eyes play tricks. But I felt certain it was my old friend Herman."

"He died yesterday."

"Yesterday. Oh, my Herman, to have come so far for only a small taste of freedom." He removed his glasses and ran a sleeve across his eyes. "God is a mysterious fellow."

Avrum knew at least a half dozen names for God, and "mysterious fellow" wasn't among them. Avrum recalled a playmate. He must have been very young, when they were still living in their home in Warsaw. He overheard Papa asking Mama if it was a good idea for Avrum to be playing with a goy. *Mama, why can't I play with a gentile?*

"But maybe a small taste of freedom is better than none at all. What do you think, my young friend?"

"He ate too much. That's why he died."

"Ah."

"He's probably still on the pile by the street if you want to see him."

"I think not." The man hooked his glasses around his ears.

Avrum leaned sideways and pushed himself into a sitting position. He plucked a blade of grass for each of his friends. Mendel in the ghetto, and Ari who snuck books from his father's secret library, and the fiery Lena. Shlomo from the first camp—no the second—and Tobi who did not make it to the third and Eliezer who had perished on the last march. The green shoots that criss-crossed his palm pulled at Avrum's heart. "Herman was happy when the Americans came," he said. "Three days of happy is not so bad."

"Quite right!" said the man. "May God bless Herman and his three days of happiness." He swept the beret from his head and bowed. His oily twists of his hair, backlit by the setting sun, flickered red and gold. "Rudolf Prochazka, at your service. But please call me Rudy."

You can't trust the goyim, Avrum's father had said. With a twist of his wrist, the broken stalks floated to the ground.

"Perhaps you'd like to give me your name." Rudy winked. "I promise to be very careful with it."

How long had it been since he had said his name, his whole name? "My name is Avrum," he said. Complete names were reserved for complete people, not haftlings like him. "My name is Avrum Loewenstein. My father's name was Yitzak Loewenstein. He's dead."

"It's a pleasure to meet you Avrum Lowenstein. And I'm sorry to hear about your father. I'm sure he's in a better place."

"I don't see how it could be worse."

Rudy slid the beret over his sparkling curls. "Quite true."

The effort of declaring his name had tired Avrum. He inched himself back down and lay the great weight of his head on the bristly lawn. The colors of the sky had deepened and he saw Herman's grin in the wisp of the clouds. "How did you know him?"

"Herman, do you mean? He and I were in school together." Rudy straightened his legs and leaned back on his hands. "Ah, the debates we used to have! Philosophy. Religion. Politics. Then we went our separate ways. He stayed in Poland and I returned to my family in Prague and became a man of the cloth."

"What cloth?"

Rudy laughed heartily. "Avrum, you are a priceless human being."

Avrum felt his face flush with anger and wariness. Why was this man laughing and did "priceless" mean he was worth nothing or everything?

"Don't make such a frown," said Rudy. "The expression simply means that I'm a priest. Of course you wouldn't know that and I apologize if I offended you."

Avrum fought the heaviness of his eyelids. "If you're a priest, then why are you here?"

"My dear Avrum, this pretty little complex has been a home away from home for many a priest and for many a year. I, myself, was quite accurately accused of anti-German activities soon after my country handed itself over to the Nazis." Rudy tilted his head, apparently to get a better view through the good lens. Who is that man sitting over there, staring at us?"

"That's just Vladik."

"Is he all there?"

Avrum yawned. "All there?"

"He brings to mind—it doesn't matter. My silly head is full of folktales and I've spent many hours imposing them on my colleagues."

Avrum's mind became alert but he kept his body still.

"Some consider this habit somewhat un-Christian," continued Rudy, "but the tales of my childhood remind me of another life and I suppose they've kept me sane in an odd sort of way. That, and my faith of course."

Avrum closed his eyes. His heart pounded. Could this priest have heard stories of the golem? Avrum had kept his conflicted feelings about Vladik's supernatural origins entirely secret. But this priest may have just made the same association. It was as if someone had opened a hidden window and peeked into the deepest recesses of his mind. It frightened him.

"There I go again," said Rudy. "I see I've been talking entirely too much."

Avrum felt a gentle pat on his shoulder.

"Rest well, my friend."

Avrum's level of energy surprised him. He wasn't ready to run but after a few satisfying meals and a relatively sound sleep in the barrack he was steady enough to give in to his curiosity—a sensation at once new and familiar—and explore more of Dachau's miraculous transformation.

At the end of the grassy lane, Avrum approached the massive square with caution. Crowds and noise filled a plaza previously reserved for roll calls, marching columns of weary inmates, and public executions.

Near Avrum, the crowd grew around a smiling soldier passing out cigarettes. Two Americans tried to communicate with a smaller group of prisoners, using hand gestures to fill in the gaps of understanding. Their shouldered rifles still made Avrum nervous.

Stronger inmates pulled big-wheeled wooden carts, carrying soup canisters from the kitchen to the barracks, or corpses from the barracks to the gate. Others strolled among the sunlit chaos, alone or in pairs.

More soldiers darted this way and that on some official business or other. How strange that it wasn't the business of brutality.

It hit him like a punch in the stomach.

He wished his father could be here to see this.

Maybe he could have done more to keep his Papa from that work detail. Hauling cement sacks all day long. Covered in gray dust. Unable to move. Unable to eat. A lifetime before that, his father's joyful face as Avrum, a little boy lifting his arms in the air, sang, "HaShem is here!"—touching his toes—"HaShem is there!"— spinning around and around—"HaShem, HaShem is everywhere!"

Avrum's head dropped back and he let the sun sting his eyes, hoping one pain would drown out the other. His knees let go. He fell into strong arms, supporting him under his armpits. He knew who it must be. He found his feet and pushed away.

Vladik.

"You've been following me." Avrum straightened his shirt. "I don't need your help." He turned and tripped, regained his balance and staggered away. He bumped into a broad man with the red-triangle badge of a political prisoner who shouted, "Watch it, Kike."

Vladik had always been there—with an extra bowl of soup or coveted spoonful of jam—holding him up during eternal roll calls or helping him when he thought he couldn't lift another stone or lay another brick. Hadn't Vladik saved him from eating himself to death just three days ago? But Vladik was part of the haze and shadows of camp life—a nightmarish voyage through the barbed and unpredictable course of mortal fear. Where did Vladik fit into this new world? Was he a mystical protector formed from clay, or a fellow inmate with a constricting fixation?

"Leave me alone," said Avrum. Whatever Vladik was, this small, bittersweet taste of independence was Avrum's, and he wanted it all to himself.

Avrum followed a noisy open car with a square can bouncing on a rear shelf and a spare tire bolted to its back, transporting four bubble-topped soldiers. He had never seen a vehicle like that before. It snaked its way toward the brick gatehouse and pushed through a thicker swarm of inmates, grumbling in an odd conglomeration of languages. Hunched shoulders and scowls infused an atmosphere of frustration and impatience into this corner of the appelplatz. The incarcerated, teased by their liberators with crumbs of freedom, remained caged.

Caught in a frame between the bent profile of a man on his left and the raised arm of another to his right, Avrum glimpsed the soldier from the barrack—Daniel Rabinowitz—who had declared, "Ich bin a Yid."

Avrum maneuvered himself toward the gate and found a cart rammed against the brick wall of the gatehouse, its wooden carcass leaning with the burden of a missing rear wheel. Two boys sat with their legs dangling from the back, sharing a cigarette. Avrum climbed past them, to the tilted bench in front, where he might have a clear view. He closed his eyes until his lungs and heart recovered from the exertion.

A plump soldier swung open the gate, bringing its iron inscription to within a meter of Avrum's face. Avrum looked through the German announcement, Arbeit Mach Frei, *Work Makes One Free*, to the Yiddisher Amerikaner posted on the other side of the gate.

A Jew with a gun. Avrum had seen his friend Ari's gun, smuggled into the ghetto and unwrapped for a clandestine viewing in a corner of Ari's squalid apartment. Avrum had also seen Ari and his entire family, including his five-year-old sister and infant brother, hanging by their necks in the public square as a warning to others who might have been contemplating resistance.

Here was a Jew wearing a weapon, and maybe—probably—concealing others. He had surely pulled the trigger of that rifle. Avrum pictured it—saw Daniel standing tall before his enemies and routing the evil force just as Yehudah HaMakabi, Yehudah the Hammer, had driven the idol worshipers from the Second Temple.

Except he didn't look much like the broad, muscular figure that was the Yehudah HaMakabi of Avrum's imagination. In fact, nothing he had seen of the American army lived up to Avrum's childhood image of the triumphant Makabees. The Americans looked like... ordinary men.

The Nazis were men too, Avrum supposed, but it had never been possible for him to picture them at home with a family. Each of them had been an unpredictable source of terror. Never to be trusted. Always to be feared.

Avrum was sure the army of Yehudah HaMakabi could have smashed the Nazis. God would have championed Yehudah, as He had at the Temple with the miracle of the oil, and the Jewish people would have been saved.

But the Makabees were long dead and the time of miracles long gone.

It was, instead, the time of the Americans; the time of this modern Yehudah.

The dignity of the ancient warrior was present in Daniel's narrow face and in the straight line of his nose, but his eyes, which drooped slightly above his cheeks, wore a film of sorrow. It was the sorrow; yes the sorrow that drew Avrum to Daniel.

The other American, the fat one, clanged the gate shut and Avrum watched the vehicle with the bubble-headed soldiers spew smoke as it accelerated through the gatehouse and across the bridge.

As Avrum's gaze retreated from the Outside to the Inside, he found the eyes of Yehudah upon him. The soldier named Daniel approached. Had he done something wrong? Was it against the rules to sit on this cart? He pinched the yellow star on his shirt. Was this area forbidden to Jews? There didn't seem to be anger in the face that loomed closer, but that had never meant much. An SS recruit with apple cheeks had practically skipped past Avrum at an evening roll call, raised his pistol to the forehead of the man swaying beside Avrum and pulled the trigger.

"Gut morgn," said the somber Yehudah. He had stepped back and lifted his head in order to have a direct view of Avrum.

Avrum wanted to return his greeting but could do nothing but stare.

"My name," he continued in Yiddish, "is Daniel."

It took a great amount of strength for Avrum not to turn away from Daniel's direct gaze. "I know."

"You're in Block Seventeen, yes?"

Avrum sucked in a breath of surprise. Daniel had seen him—more than seen him—remembered him.

"What's your name?"

Avrum caught himself on the verge of rattling off his prisoner number, but exhaled his name instead. "Avrum Loewenstein."

"Avrum, I was wondering if you would do me a favor, if you're up to it."

Avrum would have jumped into a den of lions if Daniel had asked him to.

"I have something for Max Yoskovitz. Do you know who he is?"

Avrum nodded.

"When you go to the barrack, could you bring it to him? It's not too heavy."

"Yes," said Avrum. "Yes, I'll bring it."

Daniel retrieved a rectangular package tied in brown paper and handed it up to Avrum. "It's the only blank paper I could find." Daniel extended his hand. "Thanks, Avrum. I owe you."

Avrum hugged the thin package to his chest, leaned forward, and offered his own hand. Daniel's grip was warm and strong. In all his years on Earth, Avrum had never felt more like a man.

An ambulance pulled up to the gate and waited to enter. Daniel swung open the black grid until the truck had passed, and closed it again against the groan of the crowd.

It was time to escape the confines of the camp. Lying in a bed that had recently been occupied by an SS guard and staring at the photos of smiling German wives and girlfriends tacked to the walls kept Daniel from relaxing into a much-needed nap. He reached into his musette bag and pulled out the pouch that contained his prayer book and tefillin. He had given up on davening. He just couldn't conjure the prayers he had repeated time and time again since he was a little boy.

Daniel noticed it scribbled in among other dates in the last pages of his prayer book. May *1: Lag BaOmer.* The 33rd day of 50 days counted from Passover to Shavuos—from the exodus of the Jews from Egypt to the gift of the Torah at Mount Sinai— celebrated the end of a second-century plague that took the lives of thousands of rabbinic students. Daniel closed the siddur. What did it mean to celebrate the end of a plague? He didn't feel like throwing a party.

"Not gonna play with your strings today?" The orange-haired gorilla who had interrupted Daniel's morning prayer on his first dawn in this new Hell was called, as Daniel should have guessed, Red. There was always some loudmouth like Red who felt the need to reaffirm the popular assumption that Jewish soldiers were cowards and shirkers.

Daniel had crossed the Atlantic in an airless, sweat-soaked hold of a troop ship, jammed into one of the hundreds of steel-framed bunks, stacked five high. Through waves of nausea, Daniel had overheard a GI reading a so-called joke from one of the popular variety of pub flyers: "First man to sink an enemy battleship—Colin Kelly. First man to set foot on enemy territory—Robert O'Hara. First woman to lose four sons—Mrs. Sullivan. First son of a bitch to get four new tires—Nathan Goldstein." All the listeners had hooted with laughter. Daniel couldn't stand up to them—he could hardly stand up at all. There was nothing to do but prove them wrong.

Daniel shot Red a hot glance. "Why don't you give it a rest?"

Red grunted and turned away.

Daniel packed his tefillin away and walked out the door.

At the main entrance to the SS compound, under the white arch dominated by a carved eagle, Daniel stepped aside for the first canvas-covered truck bearing a bright red cross. One after another rumbled past, filling the space with dust and noise. Handwritten on a cardboard sign, tucked between a dashboard and a windshield, Daniel read "127th EVAC." *May the Lord bless General Dwight David Eisenhower... and Captain Burkhardt too.* Food and medicine were not merely on the way, an entire front-line evacuation hospital had arrived.

In the dusty wake of the caravan, with his collar up against the cold, Daniel walked the short distance into the town of Dachau feeling somewhat the conqueror. He hitched the strap of his rifle and reminded himself not to get too cocky. Near Nurnberg, during a routine march in the wake of the retreating German army, Teddy Morgan, their newest replacement, had collapsed with a bullet hole in his heart.

Turk shook the sniper from his perch with a grenade toss—like an overhand football pass—right into the branches of the tree. The sniper, his fallen body twisted among the tree roots, turned out to be a boy, not more than eleven or twelve, with a one-shot pistol, vintage 1914. Hitler's youth.

He passed a tavern filled with the boisterous sounds of a group of GIs disregarding Eisenhower's order not to fraternize with the Germans.

Turning left and then right, he came upon a picturesque town with clean sidewalks, manicured trees and a white steepled church, all nestled within rolling green hills. The single suggestion of war in this town of polished windows and sunny store signs was that the only young men it contained were in American uniform.

A bell tinkled as Daniel stepped into the bakery. He unfastened the top button of his jacket to let the warmth soak his neck.

The teenage girl behind the counter looked up at Daniel, her only customer, and tucked some stray blond hairs back into place among the tidy flips and curls.

She looked just like Reuven Pearlman's younger sister, Rachel. In his senior year, Daniel had found himself visiting Reuven more and more often. One Thursday evening, when the scent of fresh challah filled the Pearlman house, Reuven had asked him, "So are you here to see me or my sister?" Daniel, embarrassed that his feelings were so transparent, couldn't respond. Reuven had laughed. "Let me warn you, she's a pain in the tuchas."

The smell of the bakery. The flush of her cheeks. It was as if Daniel had suddenly stepped out of the war.

"Can I help you?" she said. Her voice was not Rachel's, but it was sweet. "Some bread?" She cocked her head. "Maybe cake?" Her blue eyes twinkled.

"I—um— You speak English."

"A little bit."

"Bread then. Yes, bread."

"Dark bread or vite?"

"White. White bread please."

Her yellow dress shifted over her hips as she reached for the bread on the top shelf behind her. "Is good to have za Americans."

"Pardon me?"

She turned around with the loaf in her hands. "I am very glad the Nazis are—how you say?—kaput."

"Finished."

"Ya, finished." The girl swaddled the bread in white paper. "Something else you vould like?"

Daniel would have liked to sit under a tree and hold her hand. "No, that's all. How much?"

She threw a look at the door that led to the back of the shop. "This time, no charging." She bit her lip. "But maybe you come back again."

Daniel cleared his throat. "No, I insist." He handed her two bills. The army doled out spending money in the local currency. After crossing the Rhine, everyone had turned in their francs for reichsmarks.

"You are a nice boy. This I can see." The girl pushed a button on the register and the tray sprang open. She sighed and slid the coins from it, one at a time. "This var. So terrible. People like you. Like me." She held Daniel's hand and dropped the change into his palm. "Not so different, Ya?"

Daniel felt his face flush. He dropped the money in his pocket. "Maybe not."

She lowered her eyes. "You think I am a bad person to speak this vay."

"No. No, of course not. I'm sure you're a—a very nice girl."

She exposed her prominent teeth in a bright smile. "Yes. A nice girl. A good girl. Never vith za Nazis. I only pray for za peace."

Daniel tucked the loaf under his arm. "Thank you for the bread."

"My name is Brigitta."

"Thank you, Brigitta."

A hefty man with white hair and a walrus mustache stepped in from the room behind the counter.

Daniel took a few steps backward and banged into the door. The jolted bell clanged and jingled. Daniel opened the door and closed it behind him.

He blinked in the sunlight, buttoned his jacket and called himself a bonehead. Here he was, a soldier in the United States Army, behaving like a shy, sheltered, tongue-tied Yeshiva boy. He had put up with a lot of teasing about being a virgin, but only his buddy Tony had known he'd never even kissed a girl.

"Hey, Danny!" Kopeki, with his arms around a box, paused for a horse-drawn cart to clip-clop between them and crossed the street toward Daniel.

Kopeki reminded Daniel of the Jack Russell terrier that their upstairs neighbor on 53rd Street owned—a wiry little dog that yapped incessantly and pranced around the sidewalk, making twisting leaps to nip at the tzis-tzis, the corner fringes of Daniel's undergarment, if they happened to have come un-tucked. Daniel hated that dog.

"Look what I got." Kopeki shifted the suitcase-like box and unlatched the lid. "A Victrola. For only six cigarettes." His grin spread ear to ear.

"Very nice," said Daniel. "Did you get any records?"

Kopeki's face fell. "Well no. All I had was the six cigarettes."

"The crap game?" Daniel had watched the game in the barracks as he fell into a fitful sleep the night before. He saw the pile of reichsmarks on the floor and knew Kopeki would take a beating.

"Guess I'm not much good at craps."

Daniel pulled out a pack of army-issued Lucky Strikes. "Here, go get some music."

"Come on with me, Danny. That store, it has everything."

Daniel followed Kopeki across the street and down an alley, out of sight of Brigitta and the bakery window.

The door to the shop had a rusty latch and no bell. The interior was crowded and dim and smelled like his Aunt Esther's basement. Kopeki rested the portable phonograph on a glass cabinet filled with tarnished jewelry. He used a finger to make a spinning motion over the case and shouted, "Rec-cords," as if the crusty old man sitting behind the cabinet was the village idiot, as well as deaf.

The man pointed to the opposite corner.

Daniel, with the loaf of bread still tucked under his arm, followed Kopeki, stepping over and around a jumbled assortment of junk. "This place is a dump."

"I know but it has some really swell stuff." He moved a pile of rags and unearthed a milk crate full of dusty phonograph disks. "See! Look at these." Kopeki leaned his rifle against a rack of old coats and squatted by the crate.

"Just take the whole thing and let's get out of here."

"The whole thing?"

"Yes, Kopeki, the whole thing. Come on. Let's go."

Kopeki shouldered his rifle and heaved up the crate.

From behind the glass cabinet, the old man held up eight fingers. "Acht Zigaretten."

"Zwei." Daniel dropped two cigarettes on the counter.

The man scooped up the payment and turned his milky eyes to the wall.

In the alley, with a loaf of bread under one arm and the phonograph under the other, Daniel paused in front of the shop's grimy window.

A brass lamp, a china tea set with five cups, and a carved wooden elephant were displayed across a narrow table. A yellowed cloth barely covered the table's depth, but fell to the floor on either end. Horizontal stripes and fringes adorned each end.

"What is it?" said Kopeki. "You see something good?"

Daniel's head pounded. He set the bread and the box on the sidewalk, never taking his eyes from the fringes. He rose slowly. The shopkeeper, with his lower lip protruding and his eyes narrowed, glared at Daniel through the glass.

"Could you make up your mind?" said Kopeki. "This is heavy."

Daniel squeezed the door latch and threw his shoulder against the door. Piles of loose merchandize rattled. Daniel walked around the glass counter, lifted the shop keeper by the arm and threw him aside. He reached into the display area and sent the contents on the table crashing to the ground.

"Schweinhund!" shouted the shopkeeper.

Daniel scooped up the length of cloth and clutched it in both hands.

Kopeki was back in the shop. "Cripes, Danny, what is it?"

Daniel could barely push the words through his rage. "A tallis."

"A what?"

Daniel turned around to the shopkeeper who was leaning against a credenza and holding his injured arm. Daniel shouted into the man's face. "A tallis!"

The shopkeeper scowled.

Daniel stared at the holy article in his hands. A ritual prayer shawl. That must once have been treasured by a man of faith. That must once have been stripped from him. Because why would he need a tallis in a concentration camp? And why would he need it if he were dead? And why not use this man's holy treasure to decorate a dirty table. In this dirty shop. In this dirty town. In this goddamn dirty war.

Daniel controlled each motion as he folded the tallis. Just as his father folded his tallis every Saturday after the Sabbath service. Just as Daniel would fold his when he attended shul as a married man.

An old woman appeared. She matched the old man wrinkle for wrinkle and scowl for scowl. She cowered next to her mate and shooed Danny in German. "Go. Go away."

Daniel opened a button and slipped the folded cloth inside his field jacket. The Yiddish words shot from his mouth like lava from a volcano. "You filthy Nazi bastards. Living next door to a death factory. Smelling that stink every day."

No doubt the couple recognized the Jewish derivative of their own language. The woman covered her mouth and her eyes opened wide with fright.

"And making money." Daniel's stomach turned. "And selling— selling—" Daniel looked around the shop. Coats. Candlesticks. Picture frames. Jewelry. "Dear God. Dear God. Selling the remnants of men and women sentenced to death for—for—for *nothing*."

"No. No," begged the man in German. "I am an honest merchant."

"You," said Daniel, "are a Nazi pig."

"I am not a Nazi," said the man.

The woman shook her head. "Never with the Nazis."

Daniel had heard those words before. In Scheinheim. In Aschaffenburg. In Nurnberg. He swung his rifle around, released the safety and loaded the chamber. Tick. Snap. Click. He squared the sight on the man's wrinkled brow. "No one is a Nazi. Not one Nazi lives in this entire fucked up country. Tell me, you pig. You bastard. Where have all the Nazi's gone?"

The wife pleaded in a high pitched whine. "No. No. Please."

A dark stain seeped down one leg of the man's trousers.

Daniel's hands trembled. His vision blurred.

Tony, lifeless on the snow.

The dead man in the box car.

Green eyes.

Red blossoms.

Daniel pulled the bolt, popped the shell from the chamber and clicked on the safety. He stomped past the cowering couple, pushed Kopeki out of the way and flung open the door. Daniel booted the bakery package he had dropped on the sidewalk. The white paper split and the package rained crumbs.

A single word boiled in Daniel's throat and erupted from his mouth.

"Murderers!"

He raised his weapon above his head and drove the butt of his rifle through the plate glass.

3 May

It wasn't a noise that woke Avrum, it was the quiet. Even the sleeping sounds of Dov, the one-eyed man who had shoved himself in beside Avrum in order to escape the coughs and sobs of Moshe in the bunk below, seemed muffled. The silence made Avrum uncomfortable and he climbed down from the wooden shelf, careful not to crush a hand or a foot as he balanced a boot on the edge of the bunk below.

Avrum pushed open the door and exchanged the dark closeness of the sleeping block for the damp, hazy chill of first light. He shoved his hands in his pockets and wandered, half-asleep, along shadowed alleyways tucked between ghostly barracks.

To the right, across the roll-call square, the flagpole at the top of the gatehouse threw a long shadow across the gravel. The red and white folds of the American flag swelled and wilted as if with human breath. No other movement broke the stillness. Where were the cooks and the garbage collectors? Where were the guards?

Avrum shuffled across the square. He rubbed his eyes and sniffled. There must be someone around who knew what was going on. Tired and disoriented, Avrum halted at the iron gate. It was open. Cigarette butts littered the hard-packed dirt but there were no dusty boots, no smoking sentries—no one.

They were gone? The Americans were gone? A hard pit of fear settled in Avrum's gut. Panic, like a bristling vine, swelled and stretched and filled him with a paralysis born of dread. His mind whirled around a single thought: The Nazis had returned.

At any moment German fiends would rise in the watchtowers and he would be caught. The dull crack of a gunshot would puncture the silence. Why had he exposed himself like this? What was he thinking? Avrum clutched his head and dashed through the gate. He turned left, threw his body against the brick building that flanked the entryway and froze.

The only sound was Avrum's rasping breath. The only

movement was Avrum's heaving chest. He was alone. All alone.

Alone and stupid. Of course the Nazis had not returned. No one was around—not the Americans, not the Germans, not anyone. Dawn had barely broken and the American guard must have snuck away to relieve himself. Avrum forced himself to dismiss, by degrees, his self-inflicted terror.

A flash of pink caught Avrum's eye as he wiped a sleeve across his sweaty forehead. Avrum hardly ever saw pink—only the smudged pink badges of the homosexual prisoners now and then. But this was a soft pink—a flower pink—and it called to him from the woods across the bridge. He pulled the weight of his body from the brick wall. He drifted toward it.

In the woods, through light and shadow, Avrum made his way between thick-trunked trees and spidery shrubs. Once, because he had to watch for high roots and low branches, he lost sight of the color that had lured him. But it signaled him again, just ahead through the forest—a wave of pink, like the corner of a curtain in a warm breeze. He thought he smelled lilac. Avrum hurried.

The closer he got, the further away the patch of pink seemed. He saw it to the left. Then to the right. Then higher. Then lower. Bright in the sunlight, then dull in the shadows. It was only when he stopped to catch his breath that the elusive wisp of pink began to take shape.

A shoulder. The hem of a skirt.

Partially concealed behind a tree, not five meters away, was a woman.

"Hello," said Avrum. "Hello, there. I want to talk to you. Please."

A hand appeared, white against the bark of the broad elm. A head tilted from behind, exposing an eye and eyebrow. Long hair slipped across a pink-patterned sleeve. The eyebrow lifted in surprise. And then the woman stepped out.

Avrum gasped. It couldn't be. It was his stupid imagination again. He closed his eyes and opened them. But she was still there.

"A-Avrum, don't you know me?"

The voice—he knew the voice. And there she was—more real than he could imagine. How lovely she looked in her pink dress. A tiny, croaked whisper was all that Avrum could manage. "Mama?"

"Avrum. Oh, my Avrumel. I've been looking for you. Searching and searching."

Avrum's eyes burned. His heart pounded.

Mama wiped a tear from her cheek. "God must have been listening." She held out her arms. "I prayed that you would find me... and here you are."

Avrum ran to her.

After two steps, a root caught his toe, and he stumbled into a bare, squat tree. Avrum pushed against it, trying to right himself, but the barbed branches snagged his jacket. He twisted around and back. He tore at his coat and pushed at the limbs. "Mama!" He wanted to be free—needed to be free. There was his mother, his mama—right there—and he was stuck in a goddamn tree. Avrum beat at the branches. Clutched them. Shook them.

The branches held him. They scratched him, whipped him.

"Mama! Mama!"

Avrum perceived another voice—a man's voice—harsh and close, but he ignored it.

"Mama! Mama!"

Sour breath penetrated Avrum's frenzy. With a tight, desperate grip on the branches, Avrum paused. Panting, his vision blurred by tears, he focused on the hard angles of the face that cut his vision.

It was Dov—one-eyed Dov with the broken nose... on the wooden shelf... in the sleeping block.

"I'm not your mother, you fucking lunatic. Let go."

The half dozen drains in the floor sucked soapy brown streams, twirling into the depths beneath the tile floor. Jets of water shot from the shower heads and rained on half-soaped bodies. The laughter of men and the hiss of water hung heavy in the steamy air.

Daniel had shed his clothing with a mixture of excitement and apprehension. He hadn't taken them off (all the way off) in such a long time that, as foul and rank as they were, they had almost become a part of him. It had been like peeling off layers of a protective crust, exposing a raw and tender epidermis.

For the past two days, in order to ward off the typhus-infected lice, anyone going into or out of the prisoner's compound was subjected to a dousing of DDT powder—pumped up sleeves, down pants and under shirts. As a result, patches of white dust coated the layers of dirt caked on Daniel's thin frame.

Daniel trod across the slippery tile, unsteady on his bare feet, mesmerized by the water seeping between his toes.

Truman stepped away from a steaming jet, his tanned face stark against his white body. "Heaven," he said to Daniel as he smoothed his dripping hair back with both hands. "Fuckin' Heaven."

Daniel took Truman's place and plunged his body into the prickling heat. He sighed a heavy sigh and surrendered his face, head, shoulders, chest and back to the tender sting. The warm water caressed his genitals and stung the rash between his buttocks. It swirled around his legs and coated his feet.

Daniel was in Brooklyn on a Friday afternoon, standing in the claw-foot tub, showering before Shabbos. His father knocked on the door. "Hurry up, Daniel. We don't want to be late for shul." But Daniel wanted to spend just a few more moments in this curtained sanctuary before he put on his suit and tie and black dress shoes and walked the five blocks to their synagogue.

All week, Daniel's father stooped over the stocking feet of ladies and children and men, fitting them for shoes—cheap shoes during the depression and no-nonsense shoes during the war—in his little shop on Thirteenth Avenue. But for Shabbos, Samuel (born Schmuel) Rabinowitz shaved his face, knotted his tie, squared the black fedora on his head and walked to shul straight and tall. Daniel enjoyed those walks with his father, relaxing into the dusk, meeting friends and neighbors along the way.

Sunday through Thursday, Daniel's father trudged through the door of their apartment, ate his supper and retired to his arm chair with a copy of *The Forward* (The New York Times of Yiddish-speaking Jews) and *The Brooklyn Eagle*. But on Friday night and Saturday, between Shabbos services, Sam entertained Daniel with stories of his childhood in Russia and discussed the week's Torah portion. Daniel always had more questions than his father could answer and Sam would eventually say, "Your brain, I can't keep up with it. Your mama will plotz if you don't go have a nosh. Run along and let me rest."

Daniel soaped and scrubbed and rinsed and soaped and scrubbed and rinsed again. A mechiah. An intense pleasure. It made him feel human again. With his palms pressed against the wall and the water pelting his back, Daniel spontaneously recited the prayer reserved for special occasions, large and small. "Baruch Atah Adonai Eloheinu Melech ha'olam sheh'hecheyanu v'kiy'manu v'higyanu lazman hazeh." Blessed are You our God, King of the universe, who has kept us in life, sustained us and brought us to this moment.

Water trickled down the tiles and around Daniel's fingers. Brausbad. Showers. That was the sign on the door inside the brick building he had entered with I-Company just days ago. The empty room had drains just like this one, and shower heads. Since then, Daniel had learned the actual function of that windowless chamber. His mind had rejected the idea at first. Human beings just didn't do that to each other. Even the Germans weren't barbaric enough to develop a scientific method of mass murder. But the piles of bodies and the ovens and the old German political prisoner who showed him the slot where the pellets were dumped—all these forced him to imagine the unimaginable.

In boot camp Daniel had learned to use a gas mask. The thought of poison gases had shortened his breath and strapping the rubber mask over his face had all but stopped it. The instructor had to smack him on the back and tell him to take a deep breath. But there was no such rescue for the naked victims of the "Brausbad."

Daniel pushed himself upright. After all these months fearing for his life, now that he could finally ease himself into the notion that he would most certainly live, he realized in a flash of grief and terror that he was hereby sentenced to a lifetime of horrific visions.

Damn You God. Damn You to hell!

Daniel left the shower on for the next dirt-caked body.

In the locker room, Daniel wiped the chill from his skin with a government-issued towel and headed for the line of tables set up with new uniforms, pressed and folded. He took one of everything in his size and one of everything in a size smaller, plus extra socks and skivvies.

"One per customer, dogface," said the supply sergeant, moving his wet lips around the soggy stub of an unlit cigar.

Daniel swallowed hard in order to contain his anger. In this new world of inverted, nonsensical realities, why were people still bothering him with rules and regulations? "It's for a buddy of mine," he said. "They quarantined him—think he may have typhus." He was finding it easier and easier to lie.

"Fine," said the sergeant, "but I happen to know you're full of shit."

Daniel turned away with his bundle and found a spot to dress.

Olive green undershirt and shorts (to remain camouflaged even when undressed). Fresh socks. Trousers and a shirt that smelled of detergent and crinkled stiffly against his knees and elbows. He pulled his helmet, boots and field jacket from the cubby where he'd stashed them.

Outside, he plopped down on a bench that faced a park-like patch of Nazi lawn and settled his helmet and the extra clothes on his lap. The breeze stung the inside of his ears, not yet dry. He dropped his head back and let the sun warm his face and neck.

"Feels good, huh?"

The soldier sitting beside him held a cigarette between fingers black with grease.

"I'll say," said Daniel.

"Compliments of the 40th Combat Engineers."

"Is that your outfit?"

"Yup. Got the generators up and running last night. Sid Feldman." He held out his hand.

"Danny Rabinowitz." After they shook hands, Daniel resisted the urge to wipe his hand on his trousers.

"Where you from?" asked Sid.

"Brooklyn. You?"

"Philadelphia, P.A., U. S. of A."

"Well, Sid Feldman from Philadelphia, P.A., U. S. of A. — for bringing hot water back into our lives, may you live until a hundred and twenty."

Sid released a good-natured snort. "Jeez, you sound like a rabbi." He took a long, contemplative drag on his cigarette. "Let me tell ya, fixin' that generator is a hell of lot better than what they started me doin'—bulldozin' bodies into trenches up on a hill." He forced a long stream of smoke into the air. "Some Holy Joes up there too. Wouldn't want their job either."

Daniel's thoughts ran ahead before he could catch them. "Any of them Jewish?"

"Hell of a lot of 'em, probably."

"I mean the chaplains."

"The Holy Joes? Na. All three of them were doin' that up-and-down hand thing all over the place." Sid raised an eyebrow. "You're not thinkin'...?"

What was he thinking? Hadn't he just cursed God? "Do you think we can get a minyan?" Imagining the scene on the hill triggered another wave of nausea.

Sid looked to the sky. "Jeez. Jesus. First guy I meet here and he's a damn rabbi or somethin'."

Daniel swallowed and gathered his feelings. "It just doesn't seem right."

"Jesus. I guess." Sid scrunched his face into a grimace. "You want to say a prayer?"

Daniel nodded.

"And you need ten guys." The grimace tightened. "Ten Jewish guys?"

"Preferably. But let's take what we can get." Daniel's stomach pushed bile up his throat.

"I guess you're right." Sid shook his head. "Those poor sons of bitches." He let out a long breath. "I'll see what I can do. You know where it is?"

"I'll find it."

"Meet me there in an hour. Better make it two."

"Thanks, Sid."

Sid ground his cigarette into the grass. "Jesus!"

Daniel waited at the bottom of Leitenberg Hill beside the tracks of earth torn by the bulldozers. He would enter this lion's den unarmed, with a kippah instead of a helmet. But unlike his biblical counterpart, Daniel knew he could not possibly return unscathed. The roar and screech of American machinery echoed from above like the anger of God in heaven. Or maybe it wasn't God's anger, Daniel thought, but his own.

Kopeki stood beside Daniel with his head down and his hands in his pockets, clicking one heel against the other. He had replaced his helmet with a garrison cap when Daniel had told him they were going to a funeral.

Daniel had mixed feelings about asking Kopeki to come along—not anxious to expose him to this, but determined that ten men should be present when he recited the Mourner's Kaddish. The prayer was usually recited graveside by close relations. But there was no one left to pray for these anonymous victims and Daniel felt a deep and pressing need to honor these souls—to acknowledge their existence.

"Did ya hear, Danny?" Kopeki squeaked. "The Russkies took Berlin."

Daniel scanned the expanse of grass up to the tree line. "I

know. You told me three times."

"Oh. Sorry."

Sid Feldman and four others came into view, approaching them with heavy steps.

"This is Woody," said Sid, pointing. "Steiny, Tex and Lieutenant Green."

Daniel didn't salute and Lieutenant Green didn't seem to expect him to.

"Let's get this over with," said Sid. He tied a white cotton surgical mask around his mouth and nose and trudged up the hill. Daniel and the others followed in silence.

The soldiers operating each of two bulldozers bounced in their saddles, yanking the levers back and forth. Both wore helmets and surgical masks. The machine at the far end of the level hilltop sunk its shovel into the grass and with a screech of gears, backed up to dump the load of earth. The bulldozer closest to them dug its shovel into a surreal mountain of bare bodies. It reversed gears, rotated its contents into full view of the group and dumped the flaccid tangle of human remains into a trench.

Sid waved both arms over his head until he had the attention of both drivers and signaled them with a cutting motion across his neck. The engines popped and whined and left the hill in silence.

The Angel of Death has no form. The Angel of Death is an odor.

Kopeki hunched on the ground with his face buried in a handkerchief. Daniel pulled him up by the arm and Kopeki stood motionless, hands and handkerchief still pressed to his face. Tex turned away and retched.

I have met the Angel of Death.

Their group was seven plus the two drivers hunched on their seats and waiting. Three local farmers who had "volunteered" to help with the clean-up, broke from their task of throwing spilled bodies into the trench. One wiped his brow with his cap. Daniel shouted at him in Yiddish to put his hat on and he obeyed.

Tex got the message too and returned his helmet to his head.

Daniel reached into his jacket and touched the tallis from the Dachau shop.

This is for you too.

He tried to fill his lungs, but the stink choked him. What had possessed him to do this? For all these years, God had been ignoring the prayers of thousands of thousands. Why would God listen now to Private Daniel Rabinowitz of the 45th Infantry Division, who used to live in a little Brooklyn neighborhood on the other side of the universe?

He recalled that first day inside the camp—a capped head on the ground, kissing his boot.

Don't do that. Don't do that. I am nothing.

He fumbled inside his front pocket, pulled out the prayer book he always carried and opened it. His thumbs pressed white against the edges and he gripped the thin volume as if it were the life buoy that would keep him from drowning.

Daniel's mind ached. He struggled to evoke the familiar rhythm, to hear it, to feel it, but pressing his tongue into a word would be like relinquishing one finger's hold on his lifeline. So he began with a sound (Yis) that became the first word (Yis-ga-dal), and he continued the Mourner's Kaddish (ve-yis-kadash), one phrase at a time (she-mei ra-ba), until he sensed that he wouldn't drown (be-al-ma di-ve-ra)...

"Let the glory of God be extolled, let His great name be hallowed in the world whose creation He willed. May His kingdom soon prevail in our own day, our own lives, and the life of all Israel, and let us say:" *Master of the Universe, You let this happen.* "Ahmain. Let His great name be blessed forever and ever. Let the name of the Holy One, blessed be He, be glorified, exalted, and honored, though He is beyond all the praises, songs, and adorations that we can utter, and let us say:" *How could You let it happen?* "Ahmain. For us and for all Israel, may the blessing of peace and the promise of life come true, and let us say:" *What did they do to deserve this?* "Ahmain. May He who causes peace to reign in the high heavens, let peace descend on us, on all Israel, and on all the world, and let us say:" *It could have been me.* "Ahmain."

Captain Burkhardt leaned over his desk and shuffled through a mass of papers. He ran a hand through his short blond hair. "At ease Private."

Daniel was pretty sure why he'd been summoned to his commanding officer and wondered who had pointed the finger.

"I have a complaint that an unknown member of the occupying force drew his weapon on a good citizen of Dachau and smashed the window of his shop."

Daniel took some comfort in the sarcastic edge in Burkhardt's tone.

Burkhardt straightened himself. "You know anything about that, Rabinowitz?"

With Kopeki as a witness Daniel was sure he couldn't remain anonymous. "Yes sir."

"The MP"s aren't here yet and I don't like to have to do this kind of police work.

"Yes sir."

"Who did it?

"I did, sir."

"You did." Burkhardt exhaled through his teeth. "Okay, just to satisfy my curiosity, why?"

Daniel thought about explaining the desecrated tallis in the shop window but he didn't know how to convey the concept and he wasn't sure if Captain Burkhardt would be sympathetic in any case. "He said he wasn't a Nazi."

Captain Burkhardt plopped himself down in the leather chair that had once belonged to a German camp official. "He said he wasn't a Nazi? Rabinowitz, how long have you been in Germany?"

"Seven weeks, sir."

"And in that time, have you ever come across a citizen who said he was a Nazi?"

"No sir."

Burkhardt slid his glasses up to his forehead and massaged the ridge of his nose. "Look, this place can eat at you like a disease." He squared the glasses on his face. "The thing is, reports have been coming down. Reports about what the Russians are doing in Berlin. They're leveling the place. Raping anything in a skirt and butchering anything that breathes. And the Russian high command doesn't give a damn—they say the Berliners deserve it. But we're not the Russians, Rabinowitz, you understand?"

Daniel's soul was torn between wishing an instant end to all the suffering of the world and being allowed, like the Russians, to release an unfettered rage. "Yes sir."

"We need to keep some order here, to put an end to the fighting. You understand?"

It was Captain Burkhardt who didn't understand. The real fighting wouldn't be over for a long time. The official war would end soon but what about the next war, the personal one, the one where everyone had to put their lives back together again? Food and medicine were the tip of a drowning iceberg that could only be resurfaced by replacing layer upon layer of its foundation— clothing... shelter... community... family... love—each sliver broader than the last, with a massive upheaval required for every upward push. "I understand sir."

"Good, Rabinowitz, good. I'm assigning you extra duty. The 127th opened for business yesterday and they need help."

"But sir—"

"And I don't want to hear word one about you shaking things up with our Jerry neighbors. You got it?"

"Yes sir."

"That's all, Private." Captain Burkhardt picked up his coffee mug and looked in disgust at its contents. "And stay away from the Frauleins."

Daniel clenched his teeth and saluted. "Yes sir."

"What's this?" Max held a type-written form under

Daniel's nose.

"It's a questionnaire."

"I know it's a questionnaire. Do you think I'm an idiot?"

Daniel had befriended Max the day before on a visit to the Jewish barracks. Caught in his own fury, Max had taken over the administration of the two thousand or so Jewish inmates. Daniel had admired Max's energy and determination and arranged to meet him again on the corner where the lagerstrasse, the prison street that divided the camp, met the roll call square.

"What's the problem?" asked Daniel.

"Problem?" He slapped the page for each item he called off. "Name. Date of Birth. Nationality. Religion. What could be easier?" He shoved the page under Daniel's nose and pointed. "Except for this part: 'Intended Destination Upon Release.' Do you know who was living in my house in Lodz last time I heard? The stinking milkman. He's probably shitting in my toilet right now. If I ask him, "Excuse me Mr. Milkman, I'd like my house back please,' do you think he'll get his good-for-nothing ass off my bowl?"

Daniel rubbed the ache in his forehead. "No, Max."

"Oy gevalt, Daniel." He scratched the black stubble on a jaw that had obviously been broken and badly repaired. "You're not the one I should be yelling at."

"It's okay, Max. I don't know what to tell you." They started walking toward the gatehouse. "My boss isn't very happy with me now, but I'll see if I can get more information. How's it going with the list?"

"There are a few of us working on it. It takes a while to get all the information down. Thanks for the paper. Any chance you can get us a Yiddish typewriter?"

Daniel offered Max a look of tired disbelief.

"Never mind. Just thought I'd ask. The list of the living is the hardest to keep because every time someone croaks he gets crossed off and added to the list of the dead. And now they're starting to take the really sick ones over to the hospital. We try to get them on the list first, but who knows what happens to them over there."

"I'll be working in the hospital. I'll try to see what kind of records they keep."

"The Nazis were very good in the record-keeping department. But for some reason they felt the need to burn all their precious documents." Max snorted. "You don't think they were feeling bad about anything, do you?"

"Very funny, Max."

"When are you coming back? We need help with the questionnaires."

"I'm not sure. I'm pulling double shifts now."

Max halted and raised his palms. "Where can I go?" His voice cracked. "Where can any of us go?"

Max's grief brought tears of anger and frustration to Daniel's eyes. He rested a hand on Max's shoulder. The inadequacy of this gesture pained him. And who was he to offer comfort to this tortured man? All he could think to say was "Go work on the list."

Max shook Daniel's hand with both of his, then turned and limped back toward the lagerstrasse.

After another undignified dousing of DDT outside the gate, Daniel double-timed it through the SS compound. The glow cast by the street lamps made him feel dangerously vulnerable. For months, he had spent his nights hidden in the darkness, afraid even to light a Shabbos candle for fear of exposing himself to the enemy.

He arrived at a large army tent with red crosses painted on the roof. Two litter bearers clomped on the wooden planks as they exited the tent with a blanketed skeleton stretched between them. Before entering the one-story building nearby, they directed Daniel to a corporal in a building across the street, who directed him to a lieutenant barking orders up the road.

"Get your typhus shot," he said, pointing his thumb over his shoulder. "Then find Sergeant Mackey."

Under a sign that said Pro Station, Daniel passed a line of GIs. With their hands in their pockets and stomping their feet against the cold, they waited for a shot of penicillin to cure the syphilis which they would still claim to be the result of contact with Mademoiselles, because venereal diseases contracted from Frauleins would imply unauthorized fraternization with the recently conquered citizens of Germany.

He caught the eye of Red, in the middle of the line, and might or might not have heard a mumbled insult as he passed.

Daniel made inquiries of medics and orderlies scooting here and there until he found the small room of a converted building where typhus inoculations were administered.

In her wool pants and mannish blouse, the only thing that seemed womanly about the nurse was the blue and yellow kerchief knotted at the top of her head.

"Roll up your sleeve," she said.

He couldn't remember the last time he'd spoken to an American girl and those few words evoked waves of nostalgia and homesickness. His ruminations were silenced by a jab in his arm that he thought should earn him a purple heart. He slunk away, pressing a square of gauze to the wound.

Daniel found Sergeant Mackey directing a clean-up of an abandoned building. "The last convoy of the one-twenty-seventh is rolling in tomorrow and this needs to be a supply room by o-nine-hundred," said the sweat-soaked sergeant. "Clear everything out and dump it in the back. Dead Krauts get piled on the side." He turned away and barked at four GIs maneuvering a wide desk through a narrow doorway. "Take an axe to that fucker and get it the hell out of here."

It crossed Daniel's mind that he had intended to light a candle this Shabbos. He pictured his father's slippered feet resting on the floral ottoman in their Borough Park apartment. He hadn't had a real Shabbos in more than a year and had become accustomed to its absence. What irked him then? Probably the fact that on this Friday night, God's commandment had been superseded by Captain Burkhardt's infuriating command.

Avrum sat with Max on a bottom bunk, their shoulders

hunched against the shelf above. Max had taken over the sleeping slot after Binyamin had been carried away on a stretcher by soldiers with red-cross armbands.

Avrum concentrated on his name as he wrote it on the questionnaire, dimly illuminated by a bare bulb hanging from the ceiling. How long had it been since he'd put pencil to paper? When the Nazis decreed that Jewish children could no longer attend Poland's public schools, Avrum's father had taught him arithmetic and spelling at home. Avrum could sense an undercurrent of impatience in his father but he had still reveled in the warmth of his presence.

His father had been a studious man, a professor of history. Although he came from a religious family, Avrum had never known him to be a strictly observant Jew. After their family had been deported to the ghetto, his father began to change. He let his beard grow and always kept his head covered. Their lessons turned more and more to God and Torah and continued even after there was no more paper to be found, and still after all their precious volumes had been confiscated. It was Avrum's turn to bottle his impatience then. There were more immediate tasks more relevant to their survival. But he reluctantly coveted that time of intimacy with his father, as if there were none other he could share. And it seemed to make his mother a little brighter. Since their move to the ghetto she had begun, like a flower propped in a waterless vase, to wilt and then wither at an alarming rate.

Avrum added his Date of Birth and Nationality, but hesitated on Religion.

"Put a J," said Max.

Avrum's pencil floated above the page.

"Go ahead," said Max. "It's suddenly not a death sentence to be a Jew."

"Tell that to Horowitz," said Yossi, reclining under his new blanket in the next bunk.

"What about this one?" asked Avrum. "Positions Held During Confinement."

"Scum of the Earth" said Dov from the bunk above.

"Slave to Pharaoh," said Moshe as he inched himself down the aisle, holding his pants up with one skeletal arm and supporting himself with the other.

"Never mind that one," said Max. "Leave the rest blank."

Avrum held Vladik's questionnaire too, but all he could fill in was the first name. Because Vladik had a prisoner number, his name must have been written somewhere, but Avrum had no idea what that was. Piotrek, the block elder in the camp at Maidenek, had said the new man, speechless and lumbering, reminded him of a village simpleton he knew in Minsk named Vladik, and the name stuck.

The atmosphere in the barrack changed with the click of the latch. Avrum knew it was Daniel before he saw him. Bodies rustled, turning to catch a glimpse or say a few words to the young symbol of hope. Good evening. How are you? Is the war over yet? Daniel's boot steps clunked slowly down the aisle as he returned greetings and answered questions in his soothing voice.

He halted in front of Max, shifted a bundle of clothes to his left arm and shook his hand. "Good evening, Max." He turned to Avrum. "Nice to see you, Avrum."

Avrum nodded, excited by the familiarity of their communication.

Daniel eased himself down on the other side of Max, his long body rounded to fit the closed space. He rested the bundle on his lap and let his helmet rock upside down on the floor. "Shabbat Shalom."

"You look like hell," said Max.

Daniel ran a hand through his black hair. "Thanks."

"Did you find out anything about where they're going to send us?"

"I'm afraid not. But I have more paper." He dropped a pile in Max's lap.

The letterhead on the blank pages made Avrum shiver:

Waffen- *ϟϟ*
ϟϟ-**Standortkommandantur**
Dachau

"And this." Daniel handed Max the pile of clothing.

Avrum recognized the American army uniform, neatly folded. He tightened his grip on the questionnaires in order to resist the urge to touch the olive wool.

"It's the best I can do for now," said Daniel. "I thought you'd like it."

Max ran knobby fingers across the buttons. "What's not to like?"

Yossi propped himself up with a groan and eyed the gift with hunger. "Why can't we all get new clothes?"

Daniel massaged his left shoulder. "They opened a warehouse full of clean prisoner uniforms but I was working in the hospital and got there too late. I'm sorry."

"Don't listen to him," said Max. "Where's he going to go with a new suit? Shul?" He sorted through the treasure. Buttoned shirt, undershirt, underwear, socks, belt and trousers.

Avrum stared at the questionnaire. All he owned was his name. That, and the lice-ridden rags on his body.

The date of his birth haunted him. Born into this world on October 6th, 1928. Nurtured long enough to understand what it was to be loved, only to be left completely alone. Was this God's idea of a joke? Who was this God to whom his father had become more and more attached? Not a loving God. Avrum had witnessed too much of His handiwork to believe that. Even in the Torah, God was often vengeful. He smote every soul on Earth before sending Noah off in his ark. The patriarch Abraham tried to save the city of Sodom by giving a long argument to God. What if there were just ten righteous people in the city? But God obliterated Sodom anyway. Avrum wondered about the children. What about the infants, God? Did one have to be righteous at birth in order to escape Your wrath?

Max and Daniel's conversation floated in the distance as Avrum turned his attention from his name to Max's new clothes. He wanted to own more than just his name. He wanted something more. He longed for—he didn't know what he longed for. New clothes? More than that. A book. A father. A song. A touch. A mother. The thoughts became a jumble in his head, crashing into each other and exploding before they could be fully formed. His stomach turned and his head swam. He crossed the aisle without standing upright and climbed to the second tier, crumpling the pages as he did.

"What's the matter, boychick?" asked Max.

Avrum ignored him. He slipped in beside Vladik, who lay on his back staring at the bunk above, as still as stone. At least with Vladik beside him he could retreat into the sorrow of his soul and know his body would be protected. Avrum brought his knees to his chin, covered his head with his hands, and attempted to muffle the fiery bursts that filled his head.

"You want to what?" Sid Feldman sat across from Daniel in the mess hall, a metal bowl of apples between them.

"Keep your voice down," said Daniel.

Sid ground his cigarette into the goo of the eggs that remained on his dish. "What are you trying to do, Danny?"

"Help."

"They're being helped. The hospital is full of 'em."

"Not the ones in the hospital. The ones still stuck in the barracks. They're not getting a fair shake. The International Committee distributes the food and clothes."

"The what?"

"It's like the camp government, made up of prisoners. They say everyone gets the same, but by the time it gets to the Jewish barracks, well, nobody in this place has a problem short-changing the Jews."

"There's gotta be channels. You know, officers in charge."

"I tried that," said Daniel. "Everyone says they'll look into it, but meanwhile nothing changes. Not enough food. Not enough clothes. The Poles are proud of being Polish. The French are proud of being French. They're all taking care of their own. And none of them ever gave a crap about the Jews, before or after they all got dumped together in this sewer."

"And you want to be some kind of knight in shinin' armor?"

Daniel leaned his forehead in his hand. "Come on, Sid. I just can't leave them like that."

"Look, Danny. I'm not like you. I'm a kid from south Philly. Being Jewish just meant a couple more schmucks pickin' fights with me. Meant I got to crack a few more heads, is all. I don't know shit about prayin' for the dead. Christ, my mom wouldn't think twice about cookin' us up some bacon and eggs."

Daniel stabbed a chunk of rehydrated powdered eggs. "Better eggs than this, I bet."

In Daniel's yeshiva, a boy like Sid would have been scorned. Many believed quite ardently that non-observant Jews were personally responsible for the delay of the Messiah and the everlasting peace that would accompany him. But Daniel could feel nothing but admiration for Sid. He was a good person, tough and simple, who knew how to take care of himself. Saving the world was a luxury Sid was never able to afford.

Daniel felt that if he didn't act, it would consume him. His anger was a faceless monster, too murky to distinguish. He wished it was as easy as "crakin' heads," but God didn't have a head to crack. The Nazis were defeated. He was powerless to change the attitude of the American army or the camp politicians. As a soldier, he was still bound by orders and regulations, which included uniforms, guard duty and non-kosher food. And into the mix swirled the nightmarish memories of combat, chronic homesickness, and the pounding weight of the sins committed since crossing the Atlantic. His mind leapt to the unarmed soldier he'd killed behind the crematorium.

"What a puss," said Sid. "What are you, in charge of guilt or something?" He lit another cigarette. "All right. All right. I'll do it."

Daniel sighed. "Thanks Sid."

"It'll take a couple of days though. Maybe Tuesday. Yeah, Tuesday night."

"Tuesday? But that's... three days. Why do we have to wait that long?"

"Cause word is my unit ships out Wednesday and I don't want to be here when the shit hits the fan. And besides, you wanna steal a truck."

"Borrow."

"Excuse me, borrow. Well, it'll take a couple days to borrow a truck."

Daniel shoved his plate aside. He wanted to do this tomorrow. Today.

"Do me a favor, Danny."

"What is it?"

"Take a break. Get out of here. I don't know. Go for a walk. Get laid."

Daniel thought of Brigitta, the girl in the bakery, and felt the heat rise in his face. Anger—embarrassment—he didn't know which.

"Okay, skip the Fraulein idea."

Daniel scanned Sid's face for signs of amusement but found none.

"All I'm sayin' is you need a break. Who the hell doesn't?"

"Look, Sid, if you don't want to do this..."

"That ain't it and you know it. I'm talkin' pal to pal about you, ya know, keepin' all your marbles."

"I guess you're right." Daniel leaned back in his chair. "Sometimes I feel like this place is eating me alive."

Sid stared into the distance. "You and me both."

"What will you tell them?"

"Who?"

"Your family." Daniel swept the air with his arms. "About this."

"Nothing," said Sid. "Not a goddamn thing." He lit another cigarette. "So in a couple of days we requisition a truckload of clothes from some Kraut bastard in town." Sid pointed at Daniel with the two fingers that clamped his cigarette. "In the meantime, you leave the rabbi-in' to the rabbi."

"What?"

"The real rabbi."

"What are you talking about?"

"New Holy Joe's been pokin' around and he's Jewish. Holy Hymie." Sid laughed at his own joke. "He's probably savin' souls right now. Heard they're settin' him up for a shindig in the kitchen or the laundry room or somethin'."

"Right now?" Daniel shoved his chair back.

Sid laughed and shook his head. "I probably shouldn't have told you about it, you friggin' fanatic."

Daniel picked up his helmet and paused. "Thanks, Sid. I mean it—"

"Yeah, yeah. I'll catch up with ya later. Just don't forget what I said about takin' a break."

Daniel followed a large group of residents of the village of Dachau being escorted into the prisoner's compound. He'd seen this once before. Someone higher up in the ranks had the good idea to parade these people through the house of horrors right at the edge of their town. Look here, folks. Fascism at its finest. They seemed jittery and anxious. Good.

After a furtive and unsuccessful scan for Brigitta, he broke off from the group and headed to the far end of the administration building. He paused at a movie camera aimed at an empty podium in the center of the roll call square. Its operator, a corporal with his hands in his pockets, stared at the ground and pushed his feet into the gravel.

"What's going on?" Daniel asked the corporal.

"Supposed to be shooting a Jewish service out here," said the corporal, "but a bunch of thugs threatened to do some major harm if they did it in public. Jews took it serious and told the chaplain they'd better take it inside." The corporal pointed to a man headed in the direction of the five-deep crowd of Jewish inmates straining for a glimpse inside the laundry-room-turned-synagogue. The hood of the man's parka bounced against his back with each determined step. "Colonel's pretty steamed about it. Says he didn't give up a good job in the movie business and risk his life in combat to watch the Fascists at it again."

Daniel called back "Thanks!" as he hurried to follow the colonel. He clipped the shoulder of an inmate wearing cracked glasses.

"Sorry," said Daniel.

The man touched his beret and bowed his head. "Quite all right," he said in English.

Daniel was intrigued by the man, but more intrigued by what was going on with the colonel, who had eased his way into the overflow of Jews leaning into the doorway of the laundry room.

A field jacket enclosing a broad chest blocked the scene. "Where do ya think you're goin' hymie?" Red extracted a soggy cigar from the corner of his mouth.

"Get out of my way."

"Who's gonna make me?"

Daniel wasn't afraid of Red. At least he'd experienced fear much worse than this. Or maybe it wasn't fear at all. "Gayn kachen offen yam."

"Ooooo, scary Yid words. You're a candy ass, just like that candy ass chappy in there."

Not fear. Anger.

"Supposed to be doin' the heeb thing out here in the open." Red stuck a thumb over his shoulder. "Skedaddled his kike ass right inside with all the other lily liver Christ killers. Hey, maybe they can wash my shorts while they're holed up in there."

Daniel bottled his rage. It was Shabbos and a service was in progress just yards away. He couldn't bring himself to pray on his own but maybe he could find some comfort in davening with others. He forced a civil tone. "Give it a rest."

Red returned the cigar to his mouth and chuckled. "Nah, I wouldn't even trust them with my underwear."

The punch Daniel delivered to Red's gut sent the cigar flying. Red's face turned crimson. Already bent over, he charged, sending Daniel flying back against the gravel.

Daniel felt his body rattle and his head bounce against the ground. He scurried to his feet and ran towards Red, but strong arms grabbed him from behind.

Truman, the member of the guard detail who reminded Daniel of Bud Abbot, stepped between Daniel and Red. "Knock it off."

Red scooped up his cigar stub from the ground by Truman's feet. "You're dead meat, kike."

Truman hitched his rifle higher on his shoulder. "Take it easy tough guy."

Red turned his venom to Truman. "Who put you in charge, dipshit?"

"How about you take a walk?"

Red glanced at Truman's double stripes and threw his

cigar in the dirt. He pointed at Daniel. "I ain't done with you." He turned and walked away.

The grip on Daniel's arms released and Slim, the larger of the Abbot and Costello pair, came into view. "You okay, sport?"

Daniel kept his eyes on Red's diminishing frame as he retrieved the helmet. "Gayn kachen offen yam. Go shit in a lake."

I have seen these kinds of people before. When the Nazis marched us Outside to work in the fields or in the factory, women and old men just like these meandered through their comfortable lives and when they saw us, turned away. New soldiers direct the women and old men up the street—perhaps fifty of them. Haftlings stop to stare. They eye the women with their long hair and the men with their warm coats. The women and old men are frightened and walk with their heads down. Some hold a cloth over their noses. Some cry or retch.

As the Outsiders walk toward the appelplatz, the American soldiers point all around them and shout accusations I do not understand. Eager to learn what the Americans will do with their anger, I follow. Will they torture them? Hang them? I follow the sobbing, somber line across the square, where the soldiers leave them to shuffle, unharmed and unattended, out through the gate.

Dissatisfied, I turn away.

A man stands, watching me through the sluggish river of haftlings in the square. I recognize the circle hat, eyeglasses and tattered jacket. Days ago, I saw him speak to the Boy. I ignore him and stomp along the front of the long Administration building.

The purpose of the Americans is not clear to me. Like the Nazis, they are here to keep us inside the gates. They cart out the dead and feed the living, but they make only some of us work—without threats, and not for very long. What do they want? Will they turn on us? I bury these uncertainties and focus on my own purpose—to sustain the Boy.

The Boy has enough to eat and at least this is one less concern for me. But he is free to wander. It is harder to keep him in sight—more difficult to control him. I must do more.

I sense a threat and glance over my shoulder but I do not recognize anyone around me.

At the end of the building, the smell of damp stone lures me and I turn the corner. A row of abandoned cell blocks and the windowless back of the enemy's building form a narrow alleyway. The dankness comforts me.

A haftling lounges on a wooden chair, his head upturned and his eyes closed beneath a sliver of sunlight. He wears a long wool coat, stiff and new, cut in the lines of a German garment but without the emblems. I see his warmth and contentment and I imagine the Boy in the same attitude of repose.

I watched the Boy's eyes brighten when he gazed at the soldier with the Yiddish words. And I saw them darken when the same soldier laid a meager pile of clothes in the lap of Max, the loud one. If the Boy had that coat his colors would blaze. I would bask in the yellow of his hair and the pink of his cheeks.

I approach the haftling in silence. I cover his mouth with my hand and pinch his nose. His eyes open wide with fright and he pulls at my arm but his meager strength is no match for my purpose. I release his limp body and it thumps on the ground. The rattle of the toppled chair echoes between the walls. His body rolls as I slip the coat from his arms.

"No! No!"

I spin around. The man with the glasses approaches at a pace that obviously strains him.

"Stop," he says, panting. "What have you done?"

I wait for him to come closer. When he is within arm's reach I grab his collar with my free hand and shove his back against the bricks. A bead of sweat rolls down the side of his face.

"Please," he says. "Let me go."

I press him hard against the wall.

"I won't tell," he says. "Take the coat and I won't tell. I just want to help him." His eyes dart toward the haftling lying limp on the ground.

I pause to consider his hat, wondering if I should take it for the Boy.

His body loosens.

I watch his eyes narrow behind the cracked shield of his glasses.

"If you let me go I'll tell you something important."

He may possess useful knowledge of the Americans. I loosen my grip on his collar.

He swallows. "I know what you are."

This is of no use to me. I know what I am. No. I know why I am. Although different from the rest, I have never thought of what I am. Could this weakling know more about me than I know myself? Could he use what he knows? Could I?

Questions. Mysteries. I detest both. If I silence the man, it would end the confusion.

My hand relaxes. I have the coat. It is all I want for now. I release him and he falls to his knees with a huff. If he calls out I will kill him.

I walk away with the coat in my hand but at the end of the alley I stop and turn.

The man with the glasses leans over the fallen haftling who has brought a hand to his head. I have left both alive.

It does not matter. I have the coat for the Boy and the Boy is all that matters.

6 May

"He's here," said Yossi, peering out the window behind his bunk.

Max drew his belt to the extra hole he had punched to accommodate his undersized waist and, for once, was quiet. Most of Avrum's barrack-mates who were healthy enough to walk had already made their way to the roll-call square. But Max hadn't made up his mind if he was going and had asked Daniel to fetch him when it was time.

"What's the date?" said Avrum.

Max, the self-appointed keeper of records, buttoned his shirt to the top. "The sixth of May."

Avrum shoved his arms into the wool coat Vladik had given him. His coveted shower had only made his skin more sensitive and the weight of the coat made his shoulders prickle. "It is nine thirty in the morning on Sunday, the sixth of May."

"What are you," said Max, "some kind of clock?"

"A cuckoo clock," said Yossi.

Avrum didn't care what they said. His camp life had been ruled by whistles and sirens. The seasons changed in a hazy cycle of cold and heat. Only the Nazis owned watches and calendars. Knowing the date and time—the time Daniel had promised to arrive—made him feel more human. It was the hunger, he supposed, that kept him from feeling this way before. More than hunger—a beast that had inhabited his mind and body, existing only to feed itself. He wondered if that was what it really was to be human—a primal body reduced to its barest need. Or was it his humanity that spurred this urge to affirm his existence?

Avrum had accepted, without question, Vladik's gift of a long woolen coat. Grateful for its warmth, Avrum shifted the coat over his shoulders and followed Max outside where the bright light and icy wind stung his eyes.

Daniel, who Avrum had only seen as a pillar of strength,

looked weary. The three walked in silence along the busy lagerstrasse, toward the appelplatz. Avrum glanced over his shoulder at Vladik, trailing close behind.

They made their way around a podium that had been constructed in the center of the square and joined a small crowd surrounded by flapping flags representing a variety of nations. American soldiers, spaced at regular intervals, made a discrete circle around the gathering.

Avrum spotted two different movie cameras on tripods with their olive-drab operators at the ready. The attention, the crowd of Jews, the armed guards—all these made Avrum uneasy. And the promise of a Jewish service? He had learned many times over that promises were lies and lies ended in death. But the closeness of Daniel and Vladik eased his fear. The guards were there to protect them from the non-Jewish inmates who had opposed this gathering—whose vicious threats had already precluded a public service on Shabbos. And so far, the Americans had kept their promises.

The podium supported a few American soldiers and some camp dignitaries. On either side, a flag strained against the wind—the red stripes and white stars of the Americans on the right and the blue on white on the left—an almost-forgotten representation of the Zionist cause.

The ceremony began with some words by the chairman of the International Committee of Prisoners, who was sympathetic to the suffering of the Jews and was glad they could now practice their religion without hindrance.

Avrum glanced at the closest of the American guards, but returned his attention to the podium when the chairman stood aside for Rabbi Eichhorn.

Except for the black kippah on his head and his white tallis (as narrow as a scarf), the trim, balding rabbi, in his gray-green jacket, looked more like an over-aged soldier than a religious leader. He opened the doors of a wooden box propped on the table behind him to reveal a small and unexceptional Torah scroll.

Avrum remembered an impromptu play he and his young friends had performed for their parents during Purim. Mendel, playing the evil Haman, had shouted, "Bow down to me!" Avrum, playing the righteous Mordecai, shouted "Never!" and burst into giggles. Now a macabre stage supported a rabbi who didn't look like a rabbi and a Torah that didn't look like a Torah. It seemed almost as farcical as the Purim production of his youth and it transformed Avrum's wonder and anticipation into anger and resentment.

The microphone carried the nasal voice of the American rabbi across the roll call square. "Baruch Atah Adonai Eloheinu Melech ha'olam sheh'hecheyanu v'kiy'manu v'higyanu lazman hazeh."

Like rain on cobblestone, the Hebrew words filled the gaps between the men who stood together before the makeshift podium. Max's elbow brushed Avrum's arm.

The rabbi continued in the ancient language. Blessed are You O Lord our God, Ruler of the universe, Who bestows favors on the undeserving, for having shown every goodness on me.

The congregation responded in unison to the prayer for those who have survived mortal danger. The response came to Avrum's lips without thought. *May the One who has bestowed every goodness on you, continue to bestow every goodness on you forever.*

The vibrations of the voices around him jarred his soul and hot tears blurred his vision. This togetherness, this quiet bond, filled him with a longing and loneliness too vast to endure. He wept silently, the tears streaming down his cheeks and accumulating on his jaw before they plopped onto the wool of his collar.

Rabbi Eichhorn chanted from the Torah, which seemed to have grown into a document of substance. Moses, in the second year of the exodus from Egypt, counted the number of men in each tribe of Israelites. Instructions were given to the descendants of Aaron to protect the Holy Law. So many numbers. Rules and complications. God's voice to Moses. Avrum strained to hear God's voice, and thought he might, if it weren't for the whistle of the wind and the snapping of the flags and the metallic pitch of the amplifier.

The rabbi spoke in English. The passionate intonations of a teacher and scholar immersed in a war squashed any connections to his giggling friends. In Avrum's eyes, the rabbi became Samson, who had lifted the gates of a city on his shoulders and carried them to the top of a mountain.

Exhausted from the struggle to find meaning in the English words, Avrum's eyes fell from the podium. He spotted Rudy in the crowd and was surprised to see the priest among the Jews. Rudy nodded and smiled. Avrum lifted a hand to return the greeting but Vladik stepped between them, blocking his view.

An inmate stepped to the microphone and repeated the rabbi's speech in German. First was a quote from the Torah portion chanted the day before in the laundry room. "Proclaim freedom through the world to all inhabitants thereof; a day of celebration shall this be for you, a day when every man shall return to his family and to his rightful place in society." This, apparently, was written on a marker in Philadelphia. Not only did the Americans have this marker, they had families to return to. And a rightful place. It chilled Avrum that he had neither.

The translator continued in German: "Today I come to you in a dual capacity—as a soldier in the American Army and as a representative of the Jewish community of America ... As an American soldier, I say to you that we are proud, very proud, to be with you as comrades-in-arms, to greet you and salute you as the bravest of the brave ... What message of comfort and strength can I bring to you from your fellow Jews? ... Full well do I know and humbly confess the emptiness of mere words in this hour of mingled sadness and joy..."

A horse pulling a cart of corpses to the gate clip-clopped behind the podium

"... You are not and you will not be forgotten men, my brothers ... Jews and non-Jews alike will expend as much time and energy and money as is needful to make good the pledge which is written in our Holy Torah and inscribed on that marker in Philadelphia, the city of Brotherly Love."

Hearing Rabbi Eichhorn's assurances strengthened Avrum. He

brushed a sleeve across each damp cheek. He wished only that he hadn't heard them in the language of empty promises.

The translation of the speech ended with a verse Avrum, in the worst of their time together, often heard his father repeat: "You shall go out with joy, and be led forth in peace; the mountains and the hills shall break forth before you into singing; and all the trees of the field shall clap their hands. Instead of the thorn shall come up the cypress, and instead of brambles myrtles shall spring forth; and God's name will be glorified; this will be remembered forever, this will never be forgotten. Amen."

The assembly of Jewish men, all of whom had been relentlessly subjected to the systematic depravity of the Nazi philosophy, erupted into a roar of pride and optimism. Avrum felt his own voice join the others as he punched his fists into the air.

Avrum had heard about the small amount of women in the camp and how they had been used. They had their own barrack and Avrum had never seen any of them—hadn't even noticed the group of fifteen near the podium until they began to sing about America. Their small voices poured out a sweetness that touched Avrum deep in a place of his long-ago memories. He hugged his arms across his body and let the tears stream again.

Avrum felt the weight of Daniel's arm across his shoulders and the whisper in his ear. "It's called God Bless America," said Daniel. "Rabbi Eichhorn must have taught them how to sing it." Daniel looked into Avrum's face. "A Jewish man wrote that song."

Avrum turned to him. Daniel's eyes were rimmed with red. Avrum wanted to say just the right thing, to keep Daniel in this warm and intimate pose, but all he could think was, "This Jewish man, he lives in America?"

Daniel laughed and shook his head.

Embarrassed, Avrum turned away.

Daniel caught his shoulder. "I'm sorry, Avrum. I wasn't laughing at you."

"I can be stupid sometimes."

"You're not stupid. I'm the stupid one. Listen." Daniel scratched his chin. "I was going to take off for an hour or two tomorrow. You know, get out of here. If you want, I'll get you a pass and you can come with me."

Although he wanted to shout out his answer, all Avrum could manage was a smile and a nod. Applause for the female chorus broke the thread of their intimacy and Avrum, through his excitement, turned his attention to the next speaker.

After a speech by the only Jewish representative on the International Committee, Avrum and the men around him, surrounded by wind-blown flags and armed American protection, under a bright blue German sky, in the center of a compound from which they had not yet escaped, sang *HaTikva*, the Hebrew song of Hope. And the seed of Avrum's Hope, buried deep and long-forgotten, sprouted the smallest of buds.

7 May

Avrum had walked through this dim passageway—the arched tunnel cut through the two-story brick gatehouse—twice before. The first time had been to enter this camp at the end of a grueling march and he had little memory of it. The other had been in a dream more vivid than reality. Now, although the echo of his footsteps mingled with Daniel's as they strode through the short tunnel, the eeriness and trepidation of that dream returned.

They stepped out into the heat and blaring sunlight and a tall soldier with gloves and a surgical mask pumped white powder up Avrum's sleeves, underneath his shirt and down his pants.

Daniel shrugged. "Sorry about that, Avrum. I hate it too."

Avrum hitched up his pants and smoothed his shirt.

"Listen," said Daniel as they crossed the bridge. "I just got a package from home. Instead of eating the drek from the enlisted mess, I thought you might like to share what my mother sent."

The meaning of "enlisted mess" became clear to Avrum then, but it was also clear that whatever they were feeding these big Americans, it wasn't "shit." But what did that matter? Avrum heartily agreed to share the lunch sent by Daniel's mother, all the way from America.

Avrum turned around, anxious for a glimpse of his prison from the side of the gate that signified freedom, but instead of the thrill he'd expected, the glance left him sobered. Vladik, stooped and motionless, stared from behind the black grid fence. In one hand Vladik held the coat that Avrum hadn't needed on this warm afternoon.

Daniel and Avrum walked through the SS complex beneath a hot, bright sun. Avrum's muscles tightened as they strolled the avenues previously forbidden to him—where, in these cheerful buildings, his mortal enemies had worked and played and slept. They passed through the massive white arch topped by an imposing eagle and swastika, and emerged onto the Bavarian road.

Daniel flagged down one of the open cars that approached from behind and after a friendly exchange between Daniel and the driver, Avrum found himself bumping and shaking in the back seat. The last time he'd felt that kind of motorized speed he'd been crammed inside an airless boxcar. He couldn't keep himself from laughing out loud.

"What's this thing called?" he shouted.

Daniel held tight to the canvas bag bouncing in his lap. "A jeep."

They rode north, following the longest line of the prisoners' compound, hidden from the road by a high cement wall. Avrum counted the ghostly guard towers as they flew past in an orderly cadence. One... two... three... Five of them until the prison wall passed out of sight, replaced by green fields with waves of yellow flowers.

The driver stopped just before a bridge and Daniel and Avrum hopped out.

Avrum followed Daniel into a wooded area beside the road. Engulfed almost at once in the coolness of the forest, Avrum shivered. He shuffled down the narrow path to the river and held out his arms in order to catch hold of one of the slim trees in case he stumbled.

Sunlight sparkled on the green water. A swan floated near the opposite bank.

Avrum remembered a river like this one, where he'd wasted his precious break time creating a mud sculpture. The trees along the riverbank had blazed with reds and yellows that day, and the German guard had stood at the top of the embankment. Avrum's chest tightened around the memory but he managed to breathe away most of the old fear. These trees were green. The air was fresh. And the Nazis were gone.

Daniel propped his rifle against a tree, sat on the ground and swung the helmet from his head. Sweat pasted wisps of his dark hair to his forehead. "Here, look at this." Daniel opened his shoulder bag and pulled out a tight, shiny package in the shape of a bullet, almost as long as Avrum's forearm. "I remember the sign in Adelman's butcher shop: 'Send a salami to your boy in the army.' What do you think?"

"I think I'm hungry."

Daniel extracted the rest of the contents of his canvas bag. "There's canned tuna. And mandel bread. It's a little dry but it stays good forever. And wine. She hides it in medicine bottles because you're not supposed to send alcohol. I'll save the wine for Shabbos."

With quick strokes of his field knife, Daniel sliced the bullet right through its red plastic wrapping, and Avrum soon had a circle of soft salami resting on his tongue. He closed his eyes and breathed in the taste. There had never been anything like it. Or was there? Far-away images breezed past. Sunlight on a tiled floor. A ruffled apron—pink and green. Scrambled eggs.

"More?" said Daniel.

Avrum chewed and nodded. He munched one slice after another until his jaw hurt.

Daniel grinned. "You'd better slow down." He pulled a jangling necklace from beneath his shirt and, with a can-opener hanging from the chain, cut away the lid of the tuna.

Avrum pointed to the silver tags. "What's that?" he said, spraying a mist of salami.

Daniel pinched the narrow black canister, just three centimeters long that dangled between his identification tags. His thoughts seemed far away. "A mezuzah. My father gave it to me before I left home. For luck." Daniel cleared his throat. "Tuna?"

Avrum had no idea what tuna was but he attacked it anyway with the fork from Daniel's mess kit. Just in time, he realized he should save half for Daniel. This was his lunch too, after all.

But Daniel didn't seem to mind. He leaned back against the tree, chewed his salami slices, and gazed at the river.

They shared water from Daniel's canteen. They watched sunlight sparkle on green-brown water and talked. Daniel was from a place called Brooklyn. He'd been studying at a yeshiva and had considered the rabbinate. Daniel didn't have a car. He rode the trolley. Avrum told Daniel about the trolleys in Warsaw—he hadn't thought about them in a long time. He thought about his mother but couldn't bring himself to talk about her. Instead he told Daniel about his father, about the books that he had loved and the students who used to visit the house.

They were silent for a time. Daniel gazed over the water as Avrum gathered the courage to speak. Avrum cleared his throat. "I'd like to go to America."

Nothing in Daniel's relaxed demeanor changed. "Maybe someday you will."

Daniel didn't understand. How could Avrum explain his desire? He wanted Daniel to take him there—to Brooklyn, to the yeshiva, to the trolleys. It seemed to Avrum that Daniel could do anything. Why wouldn't he be able to do that? Avrum took a breath to speak.

"I have something for you," said Daniel. He pulled the canvas bag onto his lap and studied the contents.

Avrum swallowed his words. He couldn't imagine what kind of treasure could be left inside that bag.

"I don't know what to do with it," said Daniel. "Maybe you'd like to have it—could use it—I don't know." He extracted a folded cloth with blue stripes and fringe.

Avrum tucked his lower lip between his teeth. Daniel placed the tallis on his outstretched hands and Avrum felt the weight of it—the softness.

With a systematic zeal, over the course of so many years, everything Avrum had owned in his life, from the toys of his childhood to the last tattered photograph of his parents, had been either abandoned or taken from him. Now—now something—something tangible—was his. And unlike boots or a coat or a bowl, this tangible something had nothing to do with keeping his body alive. Avrum clutched the tallis tight to his chest. Dropped his chin into it. He lifted his face, and spoke to Daniel with a new sense of authority. "Thank you."

Daniel let out a long breath, as if relieved of a burden. He swung the flap of his bag closed, sat on his heels and pushed himself to his feet. "Time to go."

Avrum sighed. He didn't want this to end. But he was tired. And his belly hurt.

For the return trip, Avrum was treated to a ride in the cab of a rumbling army truck, sandwiched between Daniel and the pimply-faced driver. The driver had a high, thin voice and as the steering wheel jiggled his hands, he let loose a stream of excited words. Daniel asked a few questions and when the last one was answered, he lowered his head and murmured, "Baruch HaShem."

Another cramp in Avrum's gut swelled and receded. He wondered what reason there was to declare a blessing from God.

Daniel addressed him in Yiddish. "Germany surrendered, Avrum. The war's over. At least the war over here."

Avrum struggled to understand what Daniel meant by the war over here. There was another war someplace else? Where? He hoped it was far away, and wanted to ask, but couldn't because the stomach spasms had started to come in more painful waves. He took a sharp breath every time the truck lurched or bumped over a rut in the road.

Daniel pushed the helmet back on his head. "Are you okay?"

"I'm fine," said Avrum. "I guess it's just that—it's pretty bumpy."

"Maybe I shouldn't have—maybe I let you eat too much."

"No, no. I'm not used to riding, that's all."

"Do you want to walk?"

Avrum shook his head.

Daniel leaned back and rested his elbow on the window opening. "Okay then. But if you're going to throw up, give us some warning."

Avrum forced a smile and concentrated on keeping his breath steady through the pain.

The lumbering vehicle passed under the white arch, thundered through the streets of the SS complex, and jerked to a stop at the bridge leading up to the iron gates of the prisoners' compound. Daniel jumped down to the dirt. He offered Avrum a hand, but Avrum declined it, and climbed to the ground, careful not to drop the white cloth clutched to his chest.

Avrum straightened his body. The movement stretched the pain from his hips to his chest. He swallowed. "I just wanted to say—you really—well, I liked this very much—thank you—so much."

Daniel's eyebrows came together as he scrutinized Avrum's face. "You know, I have some time. I think I'll walk you to the barrack."

It was becoming more difficult for Avrum to maintain his posture. "You don't have to, really..."

Daniel took Avrum by the elbow. After a few words with the sentry Daniel led Avrum through the gate and into the compound. They crossed the roll-call square and walked down the lagerstrasse. By the time they reached Block Fifteen, Avrum was bent and sweating and leaning on Daniel's arm.

"I think I made a mistake," said Daniel. "I should bring you to the—"

They stopped just outside the door. One of the prisoners stood in their way. All Avrum saw was wooden clogs and striped pants. He would have shouted, "Move it!" if he could find the strength. The best he could do was to lift his head and throw an angry stare. But Avrum's anger dissolved before he had a chance to convey it. The eyes that met his were Vladik's.

"Excuse us," said Daniel in Yiddish.

Vladik pushed his striped cap lower on his head so that his fleshy ears, like mottled wings, stuck out beneath it.

Daniel waved his hand. "Would you please step aside?"

Like a mound of wet cement, Vladik settled himself into the doorway.

The muscles in Daniel's arm tightened.

Avrum tapped Daniel's wrist. "It's okay. He's a friend of mine."

"This is your friend? Then maybe you can ask your friend to get out of the way."

Vladik's murky eyes scanned Avrum's stooped body. They

paused on Avrum's hand, gripping the tallis tight against his stomach.

Avrum prepared a breath sturdy enough to speak over the pains that stabbed his gut. He spoke in Polish. "I have a bellyache, Vladik, that's all. Daniel was just walking me back to the barrack."

Vladik's hand, fingers spread, darted out to grab Avrum. Daniel moved quickly and pulled Avrum back, just out of reach, so that Vladik swiped the air.

Vladik's eyes widened. He glared at Daniel from under the forest of his eyebrows. A single blast of pure hatred shot from his eyes.

Avrum's mind reeled in the aftershock of Vladik's explosive glance. Vladik had only a small repertoire of expressions, and this one could not be mistaken. In the half year or so since he'd known Vladik, Avrum had experienced it only once before, in a different camp, when he and Vladik had been assigned to the same work detail on a nearby farm.

The sting of the Kapo's whip had woken Avrum from a stolen slumber in the potato field that day. Bruno Komenski, selected as Kapo because of his natural penchant for cruelty, rained punishment across Avrum's neck and back. Komenski struck Avrum again and again, one slice of horror after another. Avrum, shocked into a bizarre, other-worldly consciousness, heard whimpering and realized that the sound must be his. "This will teach you," shouted the Kapo. "If everybody digs potatoes, then you—dig—potatoes—too." The nightmare ended as abruptly as it had started. Avrum forced his eyelids apart and winced in the sun. Komenski removed his cap and used it to mop the back of his neck. Sweat darkened the armpits of his striped uniform. Behind the Kapo stood Vladik, his rigid body radiating the fierce power of a locked furnace. Komenski, oblivious to Vladik's blistering stare, swung the whip over his shoulder and stomped away. The following morning, everyone had been surprised to find that Kapo Komenski had expired during the night.

Vladik pressed his lips together and tightened his stubby

fingers into a fist.

"No, no," Avrum told Vladik in Polish. "He didn't hurt me. I just have a belly ache. All right, Vladik? All right?"

Daniel spread his feet in a pose of military alertness and shrugged the rifle from his shoulder.

It seemed to Avrum that there was a chasm between Daniel and Vladik almost too wide to breech. He closed his eyes and stepped over this dark pit, feeling that his foot might never find solid ground. But after the small, heart-stopping leap, Avrum landed safely in the doorway beside Vladik.

Avrum blinked sweat from his eyes and grasped Vladik's arm. "I had a good time, Daniel. But now I don't feel well, so I'd better go. Vladik will help me now." Still clinging to Vladik's blue-striped forearm, Avrum rotated his protector's taut body, and, hobbling under the weight of his pain, pulled Vladik into the barrack.

Hot tears welled in Avrum's eyes. Frustration choked him. This wasn't how it was supposed to be. A jostling jeep ride, a sparkling river and salami slices—that's what he wanted. Not a barrack permeated with the smell of human sweat and excrement. Not dry coughs and dark shadows. Not pain that—

Avrum's knees softened and he felt himself crumble to the floor.

The strong arms of Avrum's protector scooped him up. Over Vladik's shoulder, Avrum glanced through the open doorway. Daniel stood in the sunlight, his fingers curled around the wooden stock of his rifle. The soldier's lips were parted, as if words were waiting there—a question trapped behind his straight, white teeth.

A dark heaviness filled Avrum's skull. He closed his eyes and let his head drop into Vladik's neck.

The barrack latrine housed eight porcelain seats. With his arms around Vladik's neck, and his forehead limp against Vladik's gnarled shoulder, Avrum balanced on the edge, his bare bottom suspended over the bowl of brown swill.

"Why do you do this for me, Vladik? I want to know what you are."

Avrum flushed his bowels with a final spasm. He sobbed and pressed his face into the neck of the man who supported him, grateful for Vladik's strong scent—earth and grass tinged with the sourness of dormant water—because it kept at bay the toxic stench of the open toilet.

"Why can't you talk to me?"

The effort of speaking drained Avrum's limited energy. His body protested with quivering muscles and perspiring skin and his voice was nothing more than a hoarse whisper. But Avrum talked on without stopping, as if speech had become another involuntary reflex, as relentless as his heart or lungs.

"You can't be mean to him, Vladik. He brought me to the river and he told me about America. He might become a rabbi, Vladik. You must be kind to him—absolutely kind."

Vladik lifted Avrum from the trough and cradling the boy in his arms, carried him into the sleeping area of the long barrack. Avrum's bare legs dangled against Vladik's blue-striped uniform.

"Just because he has a gun doesn't mean he's the enemy. He's not. Our enemies are gone. There was never an enemy like the Nazis. They were strong—too strong even for you, and you're a—you're the strongest man I know. But the Americans, the Americans are even stronger. Stronger than the Nazis."

Vladik squatted and turned Avrum onto a straw mattress on the floor. Avrum let his head roll across the rigid pillow, and slid his hand along the coarse towel beneath him. Mattresses, sheets and towels—luxuries known only since the liberation.

"And good. Daniel is good. I can tell. He's my friend. You shouldn't look at him like you did. You shouldn't scare him or make him worry. And don't pretend that you don't understand. Do you promise to be good to Daniel? Like you're good to me."

With warm water and a gentle touch, Vladik washed Avrum's body, from his sweat-stained forehead to his grimy feet, and even the dirtiest crevices in between. Avrum supposed he should be embarrassed, but he was too tired to care. Vladik kept him covered at least, but—oh, who cared?

"I don't even know your name. Tell me what it is. Your real name. What is it?"

Vladik slid the towel away and covered Avrum with a sheet and two blankets. He sat on the floor beside his charge, circled his knees with his arms, and gazed blankly across Avrum at the bare-planked wall.

"Maybe you're not what I sometimes think you are. Maybe you had a son like me. Maybe you sang to him when he was scared. My papa used to sing to me. In the ghetto and then in the camps. I mean, before the camps, he sang Shabbos songs, but that's different. I told him I was too old for lullabies. He said be quiet, he was singing to himself. But he wasn't. I knew he wasn't. He was singing to me. Would you like to hear one? Would you like to hear one of Papa's songs?"

Avrum stared at the ceiling beams, as if he'd find the melody there.

"Under baby's little crib... Stands a little golden kid... The little kid has gone off selling... 'Raisins, almonds,' yelling... 'Raisins, figs, who's buying?'... The child will sleep without crying."

Avrum's throat clogged with the sweet nonsense of the song. "There's more," he said. "I'm a little tired now but I want you to hear the rest." He swallowed once and then relaxed again into the mournful tune.

"Go to sleep in sweet repose... Soon your lovely eyes will close... Close them tight, then open wide... Now your Papa's by your side... Papa, papa, softly creep... The boy is going to fall asleep."

Avrum's body melted into a weightless inertia. The only sound was the delicate rush of his own breath. In through his nose and down his throat. Exhale. In through his nose and down his throat. Exhale. In through his nose and down his throat. How many times had he heard that sound? The last sound that came before death. The spontaneous echo of life uttered by a corpse. Exhale.

Avrum filled his lungs.

"You never knew him. He died before I met you. "

Vladik draped a wet cloth across Avrum's forehead. It felt cold, like a splash from the river.

Through Avrum's hazy eyes, Vladik, round-backed beneath his low-seated cap, seemed collapsed and stagnant—a clay model melted by the heat. Avrum swallowed and looked away. "Gray eyes. Did you ever know anyone with gray eyes? At the river. A rabbi. You never met him. He disappeared just before you arrived. I need to tell you about him. I need to understand. But not right now. My belly still hurts a little. Gray eyes are strange, don't you think? I'll sleep for a while now."

But sleep did not come easily. Memories trickled into half-wakefulness—memories of color and light that had been pushed aside in order to make room for the gray, droning pattern of survival. He didn't want those memories—struggled to remain conscious enough to push them aside. They were too painful—they taunted—feelings and images from a world that could never be his again. But sleep was the victor and the dream-memory came, unbidden...

The curtains billow white around him. Sunlight tickles his fingers. He takes his soldiers from the battered cookie tin and lines them up, one by one, along the window sill. The painted bodies of his metal army stand with their backs against the wind. He tells them they were strong, and commands them to stand in the way of everything that is wicked and frightening.

Mama bursts through the living room trailing the sweet scent of spring. "Avrumel. Avrumel. Look what I've brought." She rushes past and before removing her jacket, tears the brown paper from her package. She places the shiny black disk on the phonograph and cranks the handle. "The Blue Danube, my little Avrum. A waltz!"

Mama's cheeks are flushed and laughter dances in her eyes. She loves her music. Papa says it takes too much of her time, but he smiles, just the same, when he watches her play it.

She lowers the bulging arm of the phonograph, and after its faint scratch-scratching, Mama's music fills the room. Daa da-da-da-dum. Da-dum. Da-dum. It bounces from the blue walls and the flower vases and the crystal lamps. It swirls across the reds and browns of the carpet, and around the brass legs of the coffee table.

Mama throws her jacket across the sofa. She takes his hands in hers (so soft, so warm) and they dance. The room blurs behind the field of pink blossoms that is Mama's dress. He wishes he was as tall as Papa. He wishes he could hold his mama in his arms and twirl her across the carpet and hear her laugh forever and ever.

She must know his thoughts because she grabs him up and holds him close and spins him around and around. Her arms are strong and her hair is soft against his cheek.

The last notes of their waltz, powerful and triumphant, wilt into the scritch-scritch-scritch that is the sad farewell to Mama's music.

She releases him and lets him slide to the ground. Too soon! Too soon, he thinks, and he wants to cry out, but Mama kisses his forehead. The breeze from the billowing window tingles the damp imprint of her love. It calms him and he catches his breath.

"I like your smell, Mama."

"It's lilac, Avrumel. Do you remember lilac?" She strokes his hair with gentle fingers. "No? Then I will bring you some tomorrow."

Mama is a garden of soft petals and sweet smells.

The air is still. One by one, he returns his soldiers to their cookie-tin barracks. "Tomorrow," he tells his army, "Mama will bring lilac."

The fury of a storm churns inside me. I have known this feeling before—when a Nazi let a Shepherd loose on the Boy—when a Kapo struck him. I stole medicine to heal the dog bites. I took the life of the Kapo. Each remedy brought relief. But now, as the Boy's colors dim with each passing hour, the crashing waves inside me swell and strike with greater force.

I kneel by the Boy, cradle his head in my hand and touch a spoonful of broth to his cracked lips. Some of the soup slides down his throat, some down his chin. I dab the mess on his ashen skin. He blinks and a hint of pallid blue helps to keep the storm at bay.

I allowed him to leave the confines of our world and he returned with sickness. The confusion of the new order overwhelmed me, tricked me, and I let him stray too far. Now I pay the price, perhaps the final price, for this failure. I will not let it happen again.

Americans enter the barrack. Cowards with faces covered by masks and hands encased in rubber. They approach the bunks one by one. The foolish haftlings smile toothless smiles and wave bony hands. They want to touch the Americans, to make sure they are real. I know they are real. Because of one of them, the Boy is ill.

The sickest haftlings are carried away on lengths of canvas stretched between poles. Not the dead. The dead we dispose of ourselves. Drag them out and heap them on the ground or into carts. The Americans burn the corpses or bury them. I do not care which. I do not care where they take the sweating, shitting haftlings. I only know they will not take the Boy.

One of the masked soldiers approaches. I stand before him, a stone in his path. He speaks to me with words that have no meaning. I answer him with silence. He steps as if to pass me. I block him. He steps again. I block. Softer words. Step and block. My fists clench and I am ready to act. He glances over my shoulder and retreats.

Cowards.

Four Americans arrive.

The one who brought the Boy to me is not among them.

Two of the soldiers approach. They do not hide behind masks. They are armed.

I set myself, like a mound of earth, between them and the Boy.

They speak in a soft cadence of unknown words but they do not fool me. I am ready to fight. Their speech becomes louder, more demanding. The smaller one steps back and swings the rifle from his shoulder.

If I let them take the Boy, what will be left for me? Gray. Only Gray. The empty, hollow grayness of the non-living. The waves of the storm pound inside my head.

I lunge.

The larger soldier slams my body and rocks my balance. My shoulder strikes the floor. A rifle anchors my chest. The smaller American hovers over me, hands tight on his weapon. The shadow of his helmet hides his face. His darkness penetrates me. If he did not have this weapon I would snap his neck. Hear the crack. The gasp.

The Boy! They slide the Boy onto the slim carrier. Two sets of boots thump on the wooden floor. The stretched canvas bounces between them—bounces with the weight of his bones and his flesh and his light. Through the door—and he is gone.

The larger American's rifle points at my eye. I stare into its endless funnel. The black hole expands. Fills the room with dread. I am in the murky depths, where the sound is muffled and the pressure constricts.

The soldiers leave me paralyzed beneath the weight of utter darkness.

As if buried beneath a thousand corpses, I heave my body upright. I pause to find my strength and take one heavy step after another.

There is nothing to do but follow.

8 May

Natalie pushed open the pine door, pulled the cotton surgical mask from her face and took a deep breath of evening air. She felt like she could curl up on the stoop right then and there. Not that she hadn't been more tired than this. For months and months, across France and then into Germany, she'd tended to a blurred and relentless stream of mangled men with faces (if they still had them) dirty and unshaven and eyes (if they were open) distracted by the shock of being alive.

Things were different since the close of the war in Europe. The wards of the mobile 127th Evacuation Hospital had been transformed into a ghoulish refuge for the victims of the Third Reich's gruesome idea of incarceration. Natalie spent her twelve-hour shift tending to hoards of diseased beings who looked like aliens and suffered like—like nothing even remotely within her experience.

"Hi-ya, Nat!" Harold Nordstrom, a corporal on the penicillin team, waved as he crossed the street.

Natalie snapped off a rubber glove and lifted her hand to return the greeting. She even pushed the corners of her mouth into a feeble smile. She'd covered for Harold at the dispensary a few days before and found the monotonous job of jabbing the relatively healthy rear ends of syphilitic GIs an absolute relief from the wards.

"Excuse me, ma'am."

Natalie turned to a young, lanky private with his helmet in his hands.

"I'm looking for someone," he said. "A boy."

Did she look like the lost and found? Natalie rubbed her eyes with her fingers and pinched the bridge of her nose. "A boy?"

"Yes, ma'am." He lowered his eyes and slid the edge of his helmet around and around between his fingers. "About sixteen. Blond hair." He cleared his throat. "He was sick and the medics took him. Took him here, I think."

Natalie sighed. Not a bad looking boy. Dark eyes. Long lashes. He wouldn't look at her, though, and her worn emotions reacted with numbed pangs of both compassion and annoyance. "This is a four-hundred-bed hospital crammed with twelve hundred patients. Men and boys—it's hard to tell the difference. And if it's typhus, he'd be at the 116th, on the other side of the compound." She waved a limp hand to the east.

"I think he'd be here," said the soldier.

"Look, Private," said Natalie. "I don't have the time or the energy to take you on a tour and I don't think anyone else does either."

The soldier's eyebrows came together and he blinked. "Yes, ma'am." He flipped his helmet onto his head. "Sorry for the trouble." His right hand twitched, as if he wasn't sure if he should salute. Instead, he hitched the rifle strap higher on his shoulder, turned, and sauntered away.

"Is he a friend of yours, this boy?"

The private halted and turned around. He looked right into her eyes. "Yes, ma'am."

"When did he come in?"

"Last night."

"Wait here a minute." Muttering to herself that she'd give her eye-teeth to be sprawled out on her lumpy, scratchy straw mattress, Natalie pulled open the door. The thick stench reminded her to press the surgical mask back up against her face. In the vestibule, she recognized the carefully tweezed eyebrows of Sally McBride peeking out between the scarf knotted around her hair and the white mask that covered her nose. Sally was tying the string of a cotton surgical gown around her waist.

"Hey, Sal," said Natalie. "Do you know about a kid brought in last night? About sixteen? Blond hair?"

Sally paused. "Ward Ten. Dysentery."

"Thanks."

Outside, Natalie told the soldier, "It might be your lucky day. Try Ward Ten."

"Yes, ma'am. Thank you, ma'am." He gazed dumbly down the

street at the series of one-story buildings that had been commandeered by the evacuation hospital. Bright red crosses had been hastily painted on the outside doors.

Natalie decided she must be nuts. Totally and absolutely nuts. She never had a day off and hours were precious. But the words seemed to form in her mouth on their own. "Follow me."

Natalie led the soldier into the fourth building. In the foyer, she helped him tie a surgical mask behind his head. "Have you had your typhus shot?"

He nodded. In the light of the bare bulb, his eyes glistened—probably a reaction to the stink. As she pushed through the inner door, Natalie thought, *You ain't smelled nothin' yet.*

Three rows of cots filled the open room, two rows along the walls and one down the center. On each cot was a slightly different version of the same being—translucent skin stretched tight across a protruding ribcage, a scalp sprouting recent growth, knobby joints, oversized hands and bug-eyes. The symptoms, more than the features, distinguished them— dysentery, scurvy, TB, bedsores, ulcers, infections dripping pus, or some combination, or all of the above. And through the heavy, putrid stench of rotten flesh and excrement, at odd and unpredictable angles, traveled the spontaneous chorus of suffering—sobs and wails, shouts and groans, coughs and rattles.

Natalie stepped aside for a ward boy, gowned and masked, who was transporting a corpse. With two hands and little effort, he carried the lifeless body in a blanket sling, holding it in front of him as if it were yesterday's trash. Natalie glanced back. The soldier hadn't moved beyond the first few cots, and was watching with wide eyes as the ward boy and his cargo approached. Natalie noticed the slight sway of the soldier's thin frame and rushed back, trailing the ward boy, until she could grab him. She tucked one hand under his upper arm, and with the other, held his wrist. A look of puzzlement filled his eyes, but he held her gaze.

"It takes a little getting used to," she said.

He blinked and whispered, "A little."

"Listen, you don't have to stay. I'll try to find your friend if you want me to."

"I'm okay."

"You're sure?"

He nodded.

She kept her hand on his arm as they continued. He seemed to gather strength as they traversed the room. His steps became more sure. When they reached the center of the room, Natalie, in an embarrassed moment, realized that her hand had been resting contentedly in the crook of his arm for the final portion of their journey and she withdrew it.

The soldier scanned the crowded ward. He moved tentatively, then spotted his objective and walked quickly to the bedside of what was, indeed, a young male. The boy was not as emaciated as most of the rest, although his cheekbones were prominent. A couple of weeks' worth of soft blond growth covered his head. Clutching his gray wool blanket in tight fists, he quivered and cringed in a fitful sleep.

Natalie picked up his chart. Sally had been right, as usual. Symptoms: Fever and bloody diarrhea. Diagnosis: Dysentery. Treatment: Fluids and penicillin. And this one looked relatively healthy. He would probably live. Natalie told as much to the soldier, whose eyes relaxed with relief.

The soldier sat at the edge of the bed. The movement woke the boy who blinked fever-hazed blue eyes and then let loose a tirade of delirious chatter, replete with tones of worry and pleading. The language sounded terse and guttural. German?

The young private laid a gentle hand on the boy's shoulder and spoke. "Avrum. Avrum. Es vet zine gut."

Soft and low and steady, the soldier's voice seemed to enfold the boy and the patient's disease-ridden body eased beneath his blanket. "Daniel," he murmured. "Daniel. Daniel."

Natalie gave in to the weariness of her legs and sank to the corner of the bed. She watched the soldier sweep long, thin fingers across the blond head. The glazed eyes of the boy opened wide with trust and adoration. The makeshift cot supported three but it was just the pair who spoke, face to face, isolated within their own circle of intimacy.

Like mannequins suddenly warmed by a heartbeat, the two came alive for Natalie. Not just another olive uniform—a shy and gentle boy named Daniel. Not just another emaciated victim—a child starved for love. Pain stabbed her throat. Hot tears welled and flowed and accumulated in a moist pool beneath her mask. How stupid. How stupid, she thought. If she cried for two, why not for ten? For a hundred? Or a thousand? Dear God, she thought, she had better hurry up and jam a finger in this dyke—or it would burst.

"He wants his tallis."

Natalie ran a cuff across her eyes and sniffled. "What? His what?"

Daniel had twisted to face her. "Um... a piece of white fabric, with blue stripes and fringes. A religious item. He says he had it last night. He's worried it was stolen. Are you all right?"

Natalie forced herself to focus. White fabric. Fringes. "Tell him—tell him not to worry. I'll find out what happened to it." She pressed her hands to her knees and winced through the effort of standing. "Tell him that he should rest and sleep and that he's going to be fine."

Daniel stood and reassured the boy.

"Zei gezunt, Daniel," whispered Avrum.

Outside the hospital building, dusk had veiled the camp in gray. Natalie shoved the cotton mask in the pocket of her trousers and adjusted her red-cross armband.

Daniel fitted the helmet to his head. "This was a lot of trouble for you. I'm sorry."

"No," said Natalie. "No. It wasn't any trouble. I'm glad you found your friend."

"Thanks. Thanks very much." Daniel bit his lip. "I could walk you." He cleared his throat. "It's getting dark. If you'd like, I could walk you home."

Natalie offered Daniel half a smile. "It's a long walk to

Framingham, Massachusetts."

Daniel grinned and then turned away, as if it were very important for him, at that moment, to study the lilac bushes.

"I wouldn't mind the company, Daniel. That's your name, isn't it?"

"Yes, ma'am."

"I'm Lieutenant Wells, but as long as there aren't any other officers around, I'd rather you call me Natalie."

"Yes ma'am—I mean Natalie."

They walked in silence along the asphalt, their boots clumping in an uneven rhythm. They stepped aside to let a jeep pass.

"The lights," said Daniel.

"Hmmm?"

"I'm still not used to the lights. Since the war ended. Headlights and street lights. Everything all lit up at night."

Natalie chuckled. "You're not kidding. I can't tell you how many times I almost killed myself trying to find my way to the— well, anywhere at night. That's all over and done with, though, isn't it?"

"What's that?"

"You know. Bumping around in the dark. Bullets. Bombs. The war."

"Yes, the war. That's over."

"Don't feel like celebrating?"

"Do you?"

Natalie didn't answer.

She said good-night to Daniel outside the former barrack for SS officers, shuffled into the musty room she shared with three other nurses, and collapsed onto her narrow bed. She hated the way the straw filling moaned and creaked in her ears.

Natalie thought about Daniel. He knew a Hell on Earth too. Perhaps one that was worse than hers. She could see it in his eyes.

His eyes. That's what was strange. In the beginning, in the first stampede of mangled men and boys, she had stared into the mirrors of those suffering souls, and come away shaken. She had to stop, to concentrate on her work. She packed intestines back into bellies, suctioned punctured lungs, dressed burned flesh and prepared ravaged arms and legs for the doctor's saw. She wiped brows, held hands and spoke comforting words. But she had avoided their eyes.

Daniel paused a moment after he left Natalie at her door. It had been easy to talk to her. Even nice. So nice that he'd almost forgotten it was Tuesday night.

He quick-timed it back through the SS compound to his own barracks and arrived there a bit out of breath. This was the first day he hadn't had to work double guard duty. Either Captain Burkhardt had rescinded his punishment or Sgt. Ramos had scheduled him out of it on the sly. In any case, working extra shifts and trying to help Max had left Daniel tired to the bone.

He found Sid flipping through a magazine in the room Daniel's company had converted into a communal area. Five men sat on mismatched chairs around a salvaged table, playing cards. Red had night duty. Probably more of Sgt. Ramos's savvy scheduling.

Kopeki was where he usually was—in the corner playing his Victrola—sometimes annoying oom-pah music, but mostly classical pieces Daniel didn't recognize.

"Hey, pecker," someone yelled, "turn that crap off already."

Kopeki pouted and lifted the needle from the disk as Sid stood and meandered to the doorway.

Daniel joined Sid out the door. On their way to the motor pool, he stopped and turned around. "What's that?"

Kopeki stepped from the shadows.

Daniel thought again of his neighbor's nipping terrier on 58th Street. "What are you doing here?"

"I know something's up," said Kopeki. "I want to help."

Daniel and Sid looked at each other and Sid shrugged.

"Come on then," said Daniel.

Kopeki approached them at a noisy trot. The sheathed knife hanging from his belt flopped against his hip.

"And keep it down."

They walked in the shadows of the trucks lined up in the dimly-lit parking lot of the motor pool.

"Do you have the keys?" whispered Daniel.

Sid threw Daniel a look that was hard to see but easy to translate. *Are you an idiot?*

Daniel kept quiet as Sid led them to a deuce-and-a-half in the far corner. Daniel knew they wouldn't be utilizing the three-ton capacity the truck was named for, but it would serve their purpose just the same. Sid opened the driver-side door and slipped in while Daniel and Kopeki rounded the truck and hopped in from the other side. Both Daniel and Sid waited to shut the doors until Sid had gunned the engine.

Sid rolled out and took a turn-off out of the lot Daniel hadn't even seen.

Daniel made Kopeki curl up by his feet before he showed the first of his forged passes to Slim at the compound exit. Slim raised an eyebrow but waved them on.

Once they'd bumped up onto the road toward the village Kopeki reclaimed his middle seat. Sid flipped on the headlights, eased back into the seat and lit a cigarette.

"Where are we going?" said Kopeki.

"Moonlight requisition," said Sid.

Kopeki started to speak but stopped himself.

"The dicks are here," said Sid.

Daniel leaned forward. "The what?"

"Dicks," said Sid. "MP's."

"I've seen them around," said Daniel.

"No, I mean they have arrived. In force. Actin' real dick-like."

Kopeki squirmed.

"Do you want to call it off?" said Daniel.

"Hell no," said Sid as he maneuvered the truck off the main street of Dachau. "Just wanted ya to know they're probably gonna be takin' over your doorpost duty pretty soon."

Daniel had two thoughts. *Not soon enough* and *I have to stay and do more to help.*

The back streets were quiet. Quaint lamps cast a dim light on the sidewalks. Sid made a tight turn just past the second-hand shop with its boarded-up window. Another turn and they were squeezed into the back alley. The two-story walls tossed the engine's rumble from one side to the other.

Sid cut the engine and they sat in eerie silence.

Daniel took a breath, hopped down and made a bee-line for the back door of the shop. Pad-locked.

Sid came up from behind with a bolt cutter. Kopeki jumped when the lock snapped.

They walked into the musty stench of old things. Daniel and Sid clicked on their flashlights. Clothes on racks. Stacks of furniture. Shelves dotted with housewares and dishes.

"Now what?" whispered Kopeki.

"Start grabbin'," said Sid.

"Clothes," said Daniel. The dark anger this place had inspired returned. "And anything good for trading." He thought of the tallis and wondered if Natalie would find it for Avrum.

Sid slipped back and flipped on the lights, illuminating a haze of dust. Daniel must have looked as concerned as he felt because Sid grinned and shrugged. "What the heck. We might as well see what we're stealing."

They each grabbed an armful of clothes from the racks and headed to the back of the truck. Large empty ammunition containers littered the platform. Daniel hadn't thought of how they were going to carry everything into the barracks. But Sid had.

On his second trip back into the shop Daniel stopped at the sight of Kopeki and Sid staring into the back corner. He heard the old man yell, "Kommen Sie aus meinem Geschäft h'raus!"

"What's he jabbering about?" said Sid.

"He says to get out of his shop."

"Tell him as soon as we're done."

Daniel walked to the alcove and faced the shopkeeper

who stood in bathrobe and slippers at the bottom of a staircase. The old man recoiled at the sight of Daniel. Daniel called the wife down and spoke calmly to them in Yiddish. "Sit on the floor and put your hands on your head. If you move I'll kill you. If you tell anyone we were here I'll come back and kill you. Do you understand?"

Without a word, they did as they were told.

Sid and Kopeki continued to load the truck while Daniel stared at the cowering couple. Daniel studied their wrinkled skin and thinning hair, their darting eyes and trembling fingers. Even without a rifle pointed at them, they were frightened. He knew he wouldn't hurt them.

"That's it," said Sid. "Let's go."

Daniel started for the door but strode up behind the register instead. He found an old tin lock box and pried it open with his field knife. A cache of cigarettes, both hand-rolled and factory-made. Four piles, arranged end to end; each pile stacked neatly to the top. Like the bodies.

Sid called from the back. "You readin' a book?"

Daniel tucked the box under his arm and with a last look at the cowering couple, followed Sid out the door.

They drove back to the camp giddy with relief.

"Milk run," said Sid.

"Yeah, milk run." Kopeki giggled. "Did you see the look on that old guy?"

Daniel cranked open the window and let the cold air sting his sweat-soaked brow. He never wanted to see that old man's face again.

At the prisoner's compound, Daniel showed the guard at the gate the second of his forged passes. It might have been Red at that gate. The thought chilled him. Something else he'd forgotten to plan for. It wasn't the first time in his army career that good fortune had trumped careful planning. He supposed he was as good a criminal as he was a soldier.

They rumbled down the darkened lagerstrasse. The tires crunched gravel and the headlights lit the poplars that lined the street, one ghostly tree after another.

The buildings were clearly numbered. One through thirty. Even numbers on the right, odd on the left. Sid swung left onto the grass between blocks seventeen and nineteen.

After the short rest on the ride back Daniel was almost overcome with weariness. "Kopeki, go keep a lookout."

"Sure, Danny." Kopeki duck-walked to the edge of the building and peered up and down the lagerstrasse.

Daniel fetched Max from Block 17 and Max improvised a silent bucket line of Jewish inmates. Sid, careful not to scrape the bottom of the truck bed, lifted a metal box to Daniel and Daniel handed it off to Max. It went to a pair of hands in the doorway and disappeared inside the barrack. When all the brimming boxes had been deployed, the bucket line reversed and Daniel lifted the empties back to Sid, hidden under the canvas roof.

As Daniel hoisted the last empty ammo container up to Sid, Kopeki came rushing over. "Someone's coming." He pushed Daniel against the tailgate. "Get in. Get in."

Bewildered, Daniel obeyed. Sidestepping between metal boxes, Daniel joined Sid in the darkness. He heard Kopeki's footsteps, controlled and casual. And Kopeki's voice. "Hiya fellas."

"What are you doing here?" An American voice. Young.

"Pulled dawn patrol," said Kopeki.

"Hey, it's the little pecker."

"Yeah, hi, it's me."

"Where's your rifle?"

Pause. "Lost it."

"Lost it! What a meathead."

Kopeki chuckled. "Meathead. Goofball. Yeah, that's me."

"You're gonna get your ass handed to ya for this ya know."

"I was just retracing my steps and—and I remembered I took a nap."

A few footsteps. Daniel couldn't tell how close.

"I took a nap over there."

The footsteps receded.

"How many people did you get killed pullin' shit like this?"

Red's voice. Daniel swallowed hard.

Kopeki's voice cracked. "Just over the bridge."

"You mean by the smokehouse?"

"Yeah, it's nice in the woods. Anyhow I'm going to have a hard time finding it, in the dark and all. Could you help me look for it? Could you?"

"Whadaya say, Red, should we give the little pecker a hand?"

"Shit."

"Aw, that's swell. Thanks fellas. Right back there..."

Kopeki's volume dwindled as the three walked south toward the crematorium.

"Son of a bitch," said Sid as he hopped to the ground. "That's one gen-u-wine hero we got right there."

9 May

When Avrum opened his eyes he found the orange-haired priest sitting by his feet at the edge of the cot.

Father Rudy addressed him in Polish. "Good morning, my friend. How are you feeling?"

Avrum stared up at the light bulb hanging from the ceiling by its cord. He blinked from the light. "Better," said Avrum. "I'm feeling better."

"I'm pleased to hear it," said the priest.

Avrum shifted his head on the pillow so that he could look down the length of cots, each supporting a patient tucked neatly beneath a gray blanket. Just like him. He turned his attention to Rudy. "Are you sick too?"

"Heavens no," said Rudy. "They let me come here to anoint the dying."

"I'm not dying." Avrum tried to remember the meaning of anoint. "Am I?"

"No, no. Certainly not. But you must take your vitamins." Rudy opened his hand and revealed two pills in his palm. "I found them under your mattress."

It was hard for Avrum to explain the paranoia that kept him from trusting those pills.

"Perfectly understandable," said Rudy. "You're not the only one who hides them." Rudy smiled. "It seems there's a veritable pharmacy hidden within the beds of this ward."

Avrum pulled his hands from beneath the blanket and struggled to sit up. Rudy shifted Avrum's pillow and helped him move his body to a more upright position.

"You shouldn't do too much," said Rudy. "You must rest here and they will take good care of you. Would you like some water?"

Arum was tired from the effort of sitting up but proud of the accomplishment. He was certainly feeling better. More aware. Aware enough to be bothered by his surroundings. Grunts, rattles and moans.

"Yes, please. I'd like some water."

"Very well then." Rudy slapped his knees and rose. He winked an eye behind his preposterous glasses. "Don't go anywhere."

Rudy returned and helped Avrum lift a tin cup to his lips. Rudy held out the pill.

It was a decision of trust and Avrum made it. He swallowed the vitamin with a sip of water that quenched his throat and cleared his mind.

"Well done!" said Rudy.

Avrum had to smile. Rudy had reacted as if swallowing the pill had been some miraculous feat of courage and intelligence. Perhaps for Avrum, it had been.

"You're in good spirits and that cheers me," said Rudy. "Although I thank God I'm at last permitted to practice my faith, administering the Viaticum to the multitude of those departing this particular portion of the globe is quite fatiguing."

Avrum needed some time to decipher this.

"Never mind," said Rudy. "If you're too tired I will leave you to rest."

"Oh no," said Avrum. "I'm not too tired."

"Then what shall we discuss?"

Avrum strained for a subject. "Where are you from?"

"I hail from the magnificent city of Prague."

"I've been there," said Avrum. His own answer surprised him. He hadn't thought about it in a long time. "My—my grandparents lived there."

"Ah, so you have experienced the glory of that city. A glory I hope to find restored if I am ever able to return."

Avrum never considered Prague a glorious city. He was very young the last time his parents took him on their yearly visit to his paternal grandparents. It was a world so different from his own. Sabah wore long black coat and a tall yarmulke. Avrum would sit on his lap and touch the roughness of Sabah's white beard. He sensed a tension between Sabah and Papa and guessed that Sabah didn't like that Papa, unlike Avrum's uncles, shaved his face. But none of that stopped Avrum from enjoying the attention of his aunts and uncles and the raucous play of his many cousins.

Savtah's main delight seemed to be watching Avrum consume all of her delicious meals and snacks. Avrum had been puzzled by Savtah's gray hair, which always seemed to be a little askew; until his mother had explained to him privately that his grandmother wore a wig. When they were in Prague Avrum's mother wore long sleeves and kept her hair covered with a scarf. Although Avrum always enjoyed the adventure of that world within a world, he was happy in the evening, in the privacy of the guest room they shared, when his mother let her hair free.

Mama. Papa. Avrum had to erase them from his mind.

"I was wondering," said Avrum. "If you've seen my friend."

Rudy frowned. "Which friend might this be?"

Avrum understood the confusion at once. He'd met Rudolph Prochazka the day after Herman had died from eating too much—the day after Vladik had saved him from the same fate. Rudy had asked about Vladik and hinted of folktales. The intrusion on Avrum's secret fantasy of creating a golem had disturbed him then. And it disturbed him now.

"I have an American friend," said Avrum.

Rudy seemed relieved. "Thank God for the Americans."

"It doesn't matter." said Avrum.

"Oh but it does," said Rudy. "I seem to have disturbed you. I'm so very sorry. Please tell me about your friend. Perhaps I can help you find him."

Avrum's desire to see Daniel outweighed his caution. "His name is Daniel Rabinowitz. He's a private and he's from Brooklyn, New York."

Rudy held his chin. "I saw you with a soldier when the American rabbi spoke."

"Yes, yes," said Avrum. "That's him."

"Very well then, I'll see what I can do. But keep in mind that these soldiers come and go." He smiled at Avrum's favorite nurse, who had brought a tray of bread and broth. "Unlike these tireless angels of mercy."

The nurse greeted Rudy pleasantly and they exchanged a

few words in English. He handed her the remaining vitamin pill and pulled on his beret. "It is time for me to depart," he said. "Eat your broth and take your medication and you will be well in no time at all. I'm sure of it."

"You don't mind looking for him?"

"I do not mind in the least. May God be with you, my son."

The nurse sat by Avrum's side and laid a napkin across his chest. A white cloth masked her nose and mouth and a scarf covered her head—like the scarf Mama wore when they were in Prague.

Natalie showed Avrum the empty bowl of broth and smiled at him. "Good job," she said.

"Good yobe," mimicked Avrum.

Natalie placed her palms together and brought her hands to her cheek. "Sleep," she said.

"Sleep," said Avrum. "Ooh-kay."

Natalie tucked the blanket around him and went outside. She had asked the priest if she could talk to him before he left.

She blinked at the sunlight, untied her mask and joined Father Rudy on a garden bench that faced the building.

"What can I do for you, my dear?"

"I'm a little worried. It's probably nothing."

"A little worried is never nothing."

Natalie stared at the red cross painted on the door to the ward. "There's an orderly I don't like. One of the prisoners. I don't know. He just gives me a bad feeling. Is that crazy?"

Rudy tilted his head and studied her through his damaged glasses. "No. I do not think it's crazy."

"I've been wanting to point him out to you but he's never around when you're here."

"Please tell me more."

"He never looks at anyone and never speaks. He works hard—mops the floor and takes the trash. No one knows anything about him. They don't care as long as he works, but…"

"But?"

"But I've caught him staring. At Avrum. And sometimes at me. Maybe it's my imagination…" Natalie glanced at Father Rudy. He had crossed his arms and lowered his chin. "You know him."

"I believe I do."

"Is he dangerous?"

Rudy sighed. "If this is the man I know, that question will be hard to answer."

"You're scaring me, Father."

"Oh I don't mean to alarm you, my dear. You see, I believe this man, Vladik, considers himself to be Avrum's protector— a guardian angel if you will. Since there have been no incidents in the days that Avrum has been in the hospital, it seems he's merely being watchful. Is Avrum being moved or is he scheduled for any procedure or surgery?"

"No. Avrum is recovering nicely. Actually better than I'd expected. Should I have this—this Vladik removed?"

"Ah, there is the tricky part. In my opinion, no. He will not want to be parted from Avrum and I'm not sure how he would react."

"But how can I allow a person like that in my ward?"

"I understand your concern. Perhaps you'll give me some time, though, to talk to Avrum and to find his friend before you do anything."

"Do you mean Daniel?"

"Why yes. Is he a friend of yours as well?"

"Not at all." Natalie turned away. "He came to visit Avrum yesterday."

Something in Father Rudy's manner softened. "All this must be very hard for you."

Natalie wanted to tell him how hard it was. She wanted to tell him that she was overwhelmed by the amount of pain human beings could inflict on each other. That she was lonely. That she was worried about her father and hadn't had a letter from home in weeks. That she was afraid to cry. But priest or not, how could she burden a man who must have suffered so much more than she had?

"Have you talked to God?" said Father Rudy.

The question jolted Natalie. Her childhood included sporadic trips to church. Hard benches, a droning minister, and her broad-shouldered father in a frayed suit drumming tanned and calloused fingers on his knees. He'd bolt before the last words of the closing hymn while Natalie and her mother waited in line to shake hands with the clergy. By the time they'd catch up to him at their old Ford his tie would be pulled loose and he'd be halfway through his second cigarette.

At home, no one talked about God. Actually, no one talked much at all. Natalie had tried to pray in her room once or twice but she was too conscious of breaking the silence and too nervous that someone would hear. She'd tried to imagine what God would look like but all she could come up with was a somber Santa Claus in a white robe and that wasn't very appealing.

Now she had witnessed a Hell on Earth. Even if there was a God, she couldn't imagine what she would say to Him.

"Father, I don't know how to pray."

"Are you familiar with the Lord's prayer?"

"Yes, of course."

"That might be a good place to start." Father Rudy stood and bowed. "May God be with you."

"And also with you."

Too tired to eat, Natalie headed straight for her new quarters in a pretty house among a row of pretty houses on the northern stretch of the SS compound. It was afternoon but the blackout curtains kept the room dark. She checked on Angela, fast asleep in the top bunk of a former children's bedroom. Angela was an Oklahoma girl who had lost her fiancé in the Ardennes last Christmas—the perennial mother hen who fussed over all the girls, who had a dubious source for a continual supply of lipsticks, and who still sobbed into her pillow at night in the delusional privacy of utter darkness.

Natalie slipped on her nightgown and slid between the soft sheets of the lower bed. She and Angela had pushed aside the tailored children's clothes and colorful toys to make room for their belongings. It was much more clean and comfortable here, but sometimes she almost preferred to be back in the musty barracks.

"Hey, Nat," whispered Angela.

"I thought you were asleep."

"Trying. This room gives me the creeps."

Angela was right. What kind of people could have raised their children here? Natalie shivered. "Me too."

"I'm trying to pretend I'm back home with my folks."

"And we're having a sleep-over?"

"Sure. And we're going to work together tomorrow. I got you a job at Saint Cat's."

"Good thing I brought my whites." Natalie loved her white uniform. Every time she put it on she felt a bit of the exhilaration of the day she graduated nursing school. Nothing else in her life seemed as clean or new.

"Pressed and ready for the morning."

"Extra starch in the caps?"

"I'm going to put some lipstick on you. You're going to turn heads when the doctors see you."

Natalie never considered herself pretty enough to turn heads and besides, there was one doctor in particular she preferred not to think about. "Which ward?"

"Surgery."

"Not a chance," said Natalie. "How about maternity?"

"No, not that."

Natalie could have kicked herself. Angela's dream of a home and a houseful of children had been shattered by the death of her childhood sweetheart. "Geriatrics then. When's the last time we saw an old person?"

"A really old person? My grandmother, just before I left." Angela produced an Italian accent. "Nice-ah girls no go off on-nah boat. Nice-ah girls stay-ah home an-nah help-ah dah mama."

They both laughed.

"Good night, Ange."

"Good night, Nat."

Natalie tried to sleep but her mind kept turning to Daniel and Avrum. Together, they had woken something in her. It was a feeling she couldn't quite place. The kind of connection they made was somewhere between a vague memory and a new experience. Honest. An honest connection. She wondered if she ever really had one, or ever could. Tainted by fear, she had locked her emotions in a secret place. And Daniel had turned the key. If she opened her heart would the prevailing pain of what she'd witnessed in this camp seep out? Would the monsters creep in? Vladik, for instance. He frightened her. She had to keep her guard up. Watch for danger, heal the sick and keep a smile on your face.

What had the priest said? "All this must be very hard for you." He'd been the first person to acknowledge the difficulties she faced. It wasn't until now that she realized the enormity of the strain she lived with day after day. Father Rudy had suggested she talk to God. Natalie was sure God couldn't possibly have time to listen, but she might as well give it a try.

She buried her face in her pillow and whispered. "Our Father, who art in heaven, hallowed be thy name. Thy Kingdom come, Thy will be done, on earth as it is in heaven. Give us this day our daily bread and forgive us our trespasses..." She paused to consider if this was worth her while and decided to continue. "...as we forgive those who trespass against us. And lead us not into temptation, but deliver us from evil. For Thine is the kingdom, the power and the glory, for ever and ever. Amen."

A whisper of solace lulled Natalie to sleep.

Daniel squatted by the crate and flipped through the records. If he heard *Lili Marlene* one more time he was going to scream. Marlene Dietrich's sultry song wasn't bad, but the men reclining in the communal room of the barracks were straining to sing along to the German record in English. Besides, it reminded Daniel of all the times Tony had started up a motley chorus of it when they were trapped in a transport truck or camped out somewhere, waiting.

The 40th combat engineers, their bulldozers no longer needed, were shipping out in the morning—a day later than Sid had expected. Sid had come to say good-bye to Daniel and an impromptu farewell party had formed around a "procured" case of bourbon.

Just as the lounging soldiers, with glasses raised, finished up with a loud "Lili Marlaaaaane!" Daniel spotted a brown paper cover stuck behind a Strauss Waltz. He pulled out the disk. Gold letters across the top of the blue label spelled DECCA. The English words that followed startled him. He said, "I Want to Be Happy."

Sid balanced on the back legs of a wooden chair, his feet up and criss-crossed on the edge of the table. He eyed Danny above a cigarette he was about to light. "Don't we all, buddy. Don't we all."

"No," said Daniel. "That's the name of the song. I Want to Be Happy."

"In English?"

"Yes."

Sid rocked his seat forward. "You serious?"

"Do you think I could make that up?"

Sid swung his feet to the floor. "Which one is it?"

"What do you mean, which one?"

Kopeki leaned over Daniel's shoulder. "Chick Webb and his Orchestra."

Sid sprang to his feet and flung his arms in the air. "Ella!"

It was Danny's turn to eye Sid. "What?"

"Ella Fitzgerald, you schmo." Sid lowered his hands to his hips. "Don't tell me you don't know who Ella Fitzgerald is."

"Of course I do." Daniel scanned the label and read, "Vocal chorus by Ella Fitzgerald."

"Well then, what are you waiting for?"

Daniel handed the disc up to Kopeki who placed it gingerly on the turntable.

"How do you like that?" said Sgt. Ramos, refreshing his tin

cup. "A Kraut smuggling some good ol' Negro music into the Fatherland."

Truman made a mustache with two fingers. "Right oonter der Fuhrer's nose."

"Naughty, naughty kraut." Slim laughed so hard the liquor shot from his nostrils.

Kopeki lowered the needle and turned up the volume. After a couple of seconds of scratching, the perky music of the jazz band filled the room. Sid bounced up into a sloppy Charleston, kicking his legs to the upbeat rhythm. He grabbed Kopeki and swung him to the sugary wails of the woodwinds rolling over the cheery blasts of the horns and the snappy beat of the drums. The sergeant and Slim and couple of other GI's paired up for some drunken swing dancing.

Ella's voice rang with sweetness and authority. *I want to beee happy. But I won't beee happy.* Sid sang along. "Till I make yooou happy tooooo." More voices joined in as Sid jumped up on a chair. "Life's really wooorth livin'" He rocked his hips and clapped his hands. "When we are miiirth-givin'!" He leaned over and wagged his finger at Daniel. "Why can't I giiive some to yooou?"

Laughing, Daniel stood up to get a better view of Sid's arm-flailing performance on the chair. "When skies are graaay and you say you are bluuue, I'll send the sun smi-hi-hi-ling throoough."

Daniel clapped his hands and joined in at the top of his lungs. "I want to beee happy, but I won't beee happy" ...The dancers were slowing down... "till I make yooou happy" ...Why was Sid standing at attention?... "Tooooo." As Daniel finished the last note on his own, he spotted Captain Burkhardt in the doorway. Daniel joined the rest of the room in the well-known pose—feet together, chin up, arms at sides. He noticed some swaying, especially from Sid, still on the chair.

"At ease," shouted Burkhardt over the piano highlight of Chick Webb's mirth-giving music.

"Private Kopeki!"

"Yes sir!"

"Turn off that music."

"Yes sir!" Kopeki twisted the knob and the merry tune faded

away.

"That's better. Is Private Sidney Feldman in this room?"

"Yes sir!"

"Get down off that chair before you break your neck."

Sid stumbled down and struck a swaggering pose of attention on the floor.

"At ease, all of you."

Everyone spread their feet to shoulder width and held their hands behind their backs. But no one was at ease.

"It has come to my attention," said Captain Burkhardt, "that a robbery has been committed in the town of Dachau. It seems the perpetrators were three men in American military uniform." He paused. "Rabinowitz!"

"Yes, sir!"

"I want to ask you a question."

Daniel braced himself for the launch of his dishonorable discharge. "Yes sir."

"Do you think that it would be possible for three German civilians to commit a crime while disguised as American soldiers?"

Daniel thought it would be more likely to catch his Talmud teacher eating a ham sandwich. But he wasn't stupid. "Yes sir!"

"What about you, Kopeki?"

"Possible, sir? Why I'd call that more of a probability. Sir."

"Sgt. Ramos!"

"Yes sir!"

"What's that you're drinking?"

"Bourbon, sir."

Burkhardt sighed. "Bourbon. I could use a shot of that right about now."

Heads turned. Eyes peered in confusion.

"Well, sir," said Sgt. Ramos, "it happens that we have some to spare. Maybe the captain would like to join us?"

Burkhardt adjusted his silver-rimmed glasses. "The captain sure would." Sgt. Ramos filled an empty glass and handed it to Burkhardt who eased himself onto the sofa.

Daniel was surprised to realize how young the captain appeared.

"Ella Fitzgerald," said Burkhardt. "I haven't heard that voice in a dog's age. How about if we have another listen?"

"Yes, sir," said Kopeki. He positioned the needle at the outer edge of the magical black disc and turned up the volume.

Burkhardt sipped his bourbon and Sid was quick to start up the dancing again.

Daniel sat on the floor and leaned his head back against the wall, feeling he was living in the midst of the just and the righteous.

10 May

Kopeki ran up to Daniel on duty at the SS compound entrance. "Sgt. Ramos said that Captain Burkhardt said that he wants to see you right away. Captain Burkhardt, that is wants to see you. Right away. And I'm supposed to relieve you."

Daniel would be very relieved to step away from the stone arch topped by a massive sculpture of an eagle clutching a swastika.

"Do you think we're in trouble?" said Kopeki.

"I have no idea."

Daniel found Captain Burkhardt at his desk sipping coffee from a cup decorated with the same eagle and swastika that hovered over the SS gate. Daniel saluted.

"At ease, private."

Daniel rested the butt of his rifle on the floor.

"There's trouble."

"Yes, I know sir, I—"

"Not that trouble, Rabinowitz. Although I must say you've been nothing but trouble since I agreed to your transfer here." Captain Burkhardt pushed up his glasses and rubbed his eyes. "The MP's are knocking themselves out trying to break up black market trading—in town and in the camp." He replaced his glasses. "That's why it was easier to get them off your tail, and mine, for your shenanigans in that shop."

"Thank you sir."

"Don't thank me Rabinowitz. No good deed goes unpunished. I'm pretty sure you know a prisoner named Max Yoskovitz."

"Yes sir." Daniel swallowed. "Is he all right?"

"Except for being under arrest, he's fine."

"Under arrest?"

"You heard me. He's been a bit of a rabble rouser, complaining to the International Committee and insisting the Jews get moved as a group to their own DP camp. This is probably not news to you."

"No sir." Daniel knew plans were being made to move the tens of thousands of prisoners out, either with a stopover in a Displaced Persons camp in Germany or straight home. The first problem was that the International Committee was made up of representatives from each country—Germany, Czechoslovakia, Poland, Russia, Hungary, Belgium for starters. They were each fighting for their own and naturally each representative wanted their compatriots to stay together through the process of getting back home. It made sense for everyone but the Jews, who didn't have a representative, who no longer had homes to return to, and who, in the DP camps, would probably be subjected to the same kind of prejudice and mistreatment that had been standard practice long before Hitler made it a crime to be a Jew.

How could he explain all this to Burkhardt? "Sir, it would be better if they could stay together."

"The US policy is to do this by nationality and not by religion. If we kept the Jews separate, wouldn't it look like we were doing the same thing the Nazis did?"

Appearances. Now it was all about making the victorious freedom-fighters look like the golden children of democracy. Or maybe the big shot in charge of this absurd burlesque really believed that everyone in America was treated equally.

"Don't give me that look, Rabinowitz. I'm certainly not the one calling the shots around here." Burkhardt massaged his temples. "And neither are you."

"I'm sorry, sir." Daniel realized Burkhardt must have been pretty hung over.

"The point is, Yoskovitz is under arrest for marketeering."

"Marketeering?"

"Just listen. The MP's found a gold mine of cigarettes under his bunk. The way it comes down to me is they're acting like they've nabbed John Dillinger." Burkhardt squinted and took a sip of coffee. "Which is pretty funny considering we know who the real bank robber is around here."

Daniel hung his head. "Yes sir."

"The MP's need a translator for the interrogation. The PFC who spoke Polish got his jaw broken by an irate baker with a pretty granddaughter. Do you think you could translate for Mr. Yoskovitz?"

"Translate? Yes. Yes sir."

"And just in case you're thinking about getting all noble, think again. I stuck my neck out for you and I don't want my head handed back to me. You understand?"

"Yes sir, I understand, and I'd like to say—"

"If you thank me one more time I'll have you back on extra duty. Now get out."

"Private Rabinowitz, sir." Daniel saluted Lieutenant Chase in the basement hallway of the large gymnasium which had been converted to the headquarters of the Military Police.

The Lieutenant returned the salute and studied his clipboard. "Have you ever acted as an interpreter before?

"No sir."

"I want it fast and I want it accurate."

"Yes sir."

Daniel followed Lt. Chase into a windowless room with a table and four chairs. On one chair sat Max, back in prison stripes. A goliath MP with a holstered pistol and Billy club came to attention.

"Relax Finn," said Chase.

Finn closed the door behind them and leaned his massive frame against it.

Daniel clenched his jaw and kept his gaze on the cinderblock wall behind Max. He hoped Max would get the hint.

Chase, with the band of the Military Police positioned perfectly around his left forearm, sat opposite Max and motioned for Daniel to sit as well. "What is your name?"

Daniel looked at Max for the first time. Clean-shaven, his lopsided jaw seemed even more prominent. "Vi heistu?"

"Ich heys Max Yoskovitz. Tsvey-nayn-zibn-finf-zeks."

"His name is Max Yoskovitz. Two-nine-seven-five-six."

Chase brought his eyebrows together and addressed Daniel. "Sounds more like German than Polish."

"It's Yiddish sir."

"It's what?"

"Yiddish. A language common to European Jews. A derivative of German, sir."

This was obviously news to Lt. Chase, who was either pondering the historical significance of the language, or wondering what "derivative" meant.

"You can translate precisely in—Yiddish?"

"Yes sir."

"Fine then. Let's get on with it." Chase turned to Max. "Yesterday afternoon a large quantity of cigarettes was found hidden under your mattress. This is considered black market contraband and we want to know how they came into your possession."

Daniel repeated the statement in Yiddish.

"Tell him to go shit in a lake," said Max.

Daniel's hesitated. Chase had been expecting a Polish interpreter. What if he knew enough German to catch Daniel in the instinctive lie he was about to tell? "He says he doesn't know what you're talking about."

Chase leaned forward. "A box of cigarettes was found under your bed."

Daniel never considered himself much of an actor, but he gave it a try. He stared at Max with what he hoped was an expression of reproach. "You never had a box of cigarettes under your bed."

Max's eyes registered a flicker of agreement. "A box of cigarettes?" he said. "Never saw such a thing."

"He doesn't know anything about a box of cigarettes," said Daniel

Chase leaned back and crossed his arms in front of him. "If you come clean now we'll be lenient."

Max leaned back and crossed his arms, mimicking the Lieutenant. "I will tell you the truth."

Daniel protecting Burkhardt. Max protecting him. The chain of loyalties would come undone if Max told Chase the truth. Daniel almost wished he would.

Daniel forced a neutral tone. "He'll tell the truth."

Chase leaned forward and overlapped his hands on the table.

Max struck the same pose. Chase flinched as Max narrowed the distance between them. Max lowered his voice. "If I had a big pile of cigarettes it would be because God had answered my prayers." He leaned back, spread his arms open and raised his voice. "Do I look like a man whose prayers have been answered?"

It was difficult for Daniel to keep from smiling as he translated.

Lt. Chase jumped from his chair and pointed at Max. "What kind of a confession is that? Look, you little kike, a man who has risked his life for your freedom discovered the illegal contraband under your bed. That's all the evidence we need to keep you locked up for a long time."

Daniel recognized the inflated tone of a soldier who had never advanced across an open field under enemy fire. Who'd never watched a friend die. The false bravado that some men used in defense of their relative safety.

Max wasn't impressed either. "Listen schmuck, locked up is something I'm not afraid of."

"He says he—he's been a prisoner for a long time."

"This is one cocky son-of-a-bitch," said Lt. Chase.

Max faced Daniel "And one more thing," he said in Yiddish. "Only a schlemiel would leave something like that under his bunk, for anyone to come along and take, right from under his nose."

Lt. Chase paced back and forth behind Daniel. "What did he say?"

"Only an idiot would leave that under his bunk where anyone could come along and take it."

Lt. Chase squinted at Max. "You mean you should have hidden them better?"

"Of course I should have hidden them better," said Max

"Of course he would have hidden them better," said Daniel.

"So you're hiding more?"

Max threw up his hands. "Oy gevault."

"What does that mean?"

"It doesn't mean anything really. He's, umm, exasperated."

"Good." Chase banged his hand on the table. "Let's start from the beginning."

And so they did. Max maintained he had no knowledge of illegal contraband. He could never be in a position to possess such a large quantity of the most valuable trading commodity in the black market. Far from a black market mogul, Max was just a poor Jew, trying to get by in a crazy world.

"Now it's my turn to have a question," said Max.

Daniel took a faltering breath. "He has a question."

"All right. What is it?"

Daniel nodded to Max.

"Who is this American dreykop who says he found this golden treasure under my miserable bed?"

Literally, dreykop was twisted head and meant liar. Not only was Max protecting Daniel, he was fishing for ways to twist the situation to their advantage. "He wants to know who found the— the supposed cigarettes under his bed."

"Supposed? Supposed? These cigarettes aren't 'supposed.' It's a stash worthy of Fort Knox." Chase's face reddened. "Tell this money-grubbing maggot that Private First Class Russell Whitmore Jr., a decorated combat veteran, found his excessive hoard. And Whitmore could have kept it all to himself, couldn't he? But he didn't. He turned it in. The guy's a goddamn hero."

Startled by the name, Daniel cleared his throat in an attempt to keep his tone with Max as stern as Chase's had been. "You have the heart of a lion and the balls of a bull. Private Russell Whitmore found the cigarettes that weren't under your bed. The Lieutenant says he's a decorated hero but I happen to know he's a first class putz. I'll find a way to deal with him."

"What's the bastard smiling about?" said Chase.

Daniel was almost beginning to enjoy this. "Far vos shmeychl du?"

Max held up both hands. "Even in my innocence, I was admiring the Lieutenant's intelligence and cunning."

Lt. Chase flipped a hand palm-up to check his watch. "Tell him he can admire it some more tomorrow. Finn, lock him up. We'll see if he'll soften up after another night in the brig."

Finn saluted. "Yes sir."

Daniel followed Lt. Chase out the door.

"About the kike remark, Rabinowitz. It's nothing personal."

"Of course not, sir."

"He knows more than he's telling."

"I'm sure of it, sir."

Daniel headed straight for the prisoner's compound. Squirming from another unpleasant dousing of DDT, Daniel approached Slim and Truman at the gate.

"I don't have a pass," said Daniel. The MP's hadn't taken over the guard duties yet, but since the GI tourism had slowed down, they'd been ordered to become more cautious about who entered and exited the compound. Containing the typhus epidemic was still a concern, and so was the illegal black market trading that had become rampant.

"Your pass looks fine to me," said Truman.

Slim winked.

Block seventeen wasn't as crowded as the first and last time Daniel had been there. It didn't smell as bad, or maybe Daniel was becoming immune to the eau de camp. He leaned his rifle on a bunk post, sat on Max's straw bed and wedged his helmet between his boots. Yossi and Moshe slid their skinny bottoms on either side of Daniel and filled him in. Yesterday evening a big soldier with freckles had ordered them all out of the barrack. Max hadn't been there. The soldier pulled Yossi back into the barrack and stood him by Max's bunk.

"I was so scared," said Yossi. "I couldn't think. I told him Max's name."

"When we came back in," said Moshe, "the place was inside out. A mess."

"And the cigarettes," said Yossi. "Gone."

"They arrested Max last night," said Moshe. "Pulled him right out of bed. What do you think they're going to do with him?"

"He's all right," said Daniel. "I saw him this morning."

"Baruch HaShem!"

"Did the big man with freckles do this to any other barrack?"

"No."

"Have there been any other soldiers here?"

"Not except for the two that took Max away."

"Good. If anyone asks, you don't know anything about a box of cigarettes. And you'll pass the word along about this, okay?"

"Whatever you say," said Moshe.

"Is there anything else missing?"

"No."

"When can you make another delivery?" said Dov, tilting his one good eye as he weaved a cord trough the loops of his new woolen pants.

Requests came from every corner of the barrack. "Meat... Chocolate... Bread."

"Yes, fresh bread," said Yossi.

Moshe closed his eyes and took a deep breath. "Steaming from the oven."

Could Daniel blame them for their self-interest? "There won't be another delivery."

A voice from the top bunk across the aisle broke the pouting silence. "The baker will give you bread." The intonation was more German than Yiddish.

"Who's that?" said Daniel.

"Yonatan Klaus," said Yossi. "He's been at this camp longer than any of us. Years. Pretended to be a goy, but got arrested anyway." Yossi leaned closer and whispered. "He's a faigeleh. That's why he got arrested. Came to our barrack three days ago, wanting to be with his own kind. Not my kind. But Max said a Jew is a Jew and let him stay."

The electric bulb illuminated Yonatan's sallow face and sunken eyes.

Daniel looked away. According to every interpretation of Jewish Law, homosexuality was an abomination. But his perception of abominations had changed. Daniel met Yonatan's gaze. "Tell me more about the bakery."

"Every day they marched us out to labor in the factories or quarries or if nothing else, just to have us move rocks or sacks from one side of a road to another. But the bakery, that was the best detail of all. We worked hard but sometimes the baker's granddaughter would distract the guards and the baker would give us bites of bread or dough." Yonatan sighed. "We always swallowed quickly and opened our mouths so he could check for crumbs. If they ever caught the baker he would have been shot."

"Do you mean the bakery in town?"

"Not two kilometers away. The baker's name was Schmidt."

"Thank you," said Daniel. He shook Yonatan's hand, scooped up his rifle and helmet and stepped out into an over-bright afternoon.

A freckled soldier who knew where to look for smuggled goods and a baker who had broken the interpreter's jaw on behalf of his pretty granddaughter. Herr Schmidt had risked his life to help the prisoners working for him—even Yonatan who must have been wearing the telltale pink triangle. At the moment, Brigitta's grandfather was probably under arrest for slugging a GI.

Captain Burkhardt had been right. No good deed goes unpunished.

The sky had cleared and the sun cast a stripe of light across the corner of the child-sized desk. Natalie sat with her pen floating over a blank piece of lined paper from a notebook the German children had left behind.

May 10, 1945

Dear Mom and Dad,

I haven't gotten any letters from you recently. As you know, the mail service isn't very steady, but I'm sure they'll catch up to me eventually. We've moved to a concentration camp in Dachau, Germany. I'm sure the censors won't mind me telling you this, now that the war is over. It's hard to describe this place. We're not caring for wounded soldiers here, except for the occasional broken arm or leg. You'd think now that the war is over, they'd be more careful about coming home in one piece. Mostly they're worried about getting shipped over to the Pacific. I guess I am too. I don't have enough points for a discharge. Nurses with more than four years will get to go home, but that's not me!

Anyway, this place is pretty gruesome. The Nazis used it as a prison for political prisoners and let me tell you, the prisoners were treated awfully. They were starved and beaten and there's a terrible typhus epidemic among them—30,000, I'm told, from all over Europe. The wards are over-full with men who are just skin and bones. When we first got here there wasn't much we could do and we were losing about 200 a day, poor souls. Don't worry, I've had a typhus shot and always wear gloves and a mask. We get sprayed with DDT pretty often to avoid the lice!

The quarters for the German officers are very nice and you'll be glad to hear that's where I'm staying. My roommate is Angela, who I told you about already, who's a great kid.

How are you doing? In the last letter I received (March 11) you said Dad had a cough. I hope it's better by now. I don't mean to be a nag, but cutting down on those cigarettes would help. I don't have the energy to write another letter so will you please tell Aunt Alice thank you very much for the package she sent. I shared the chocolates with the other nurses and I was very popular that day! She said Ricky got drafted, but hopefully this will all be over before he gets shipped anywhere. How are the Larkins doing? If you haven't already, please give them my regards and sympathy. Johnny was such a nice boy.

There seems to be a party here every night but I'm never in the mood to go. It's warmed up and at the moment it's still bright and sunny but I think I'll catch some sleep if I can.

Love,

Natalie

P.S. I don't know how long I'll be here but it would be nice if you could gather together some old clothes and send them here for the prisoners c/o US Occupation Forces, Dachau, Germany. Especially socks and underwear.

Natalie sealed and addressed the envelope and leaned back in the chair with a sigh. Her window faced the backyard. Across the lawn loomed a portion of the tall concrete wall that marked the northern border of the SS compound. Their own yard was partitioned from the others by a row of hedges. It gave Natalie some satisfaction that where the children of the German officers once played, American bras, panties and socks dangled from a clothesline. Their long shadows pranced on the handsome green lawn. The bigger satisfaction, though, was the privacy of that particular clothesline. Before coming here they usually made do with a tent brace—a practical solution but entirely exposed to the grinning men who passed by. And it was heavenly to use a sink instead of a helmet full of water that was only hot if it could be pilfered from the mess tent.

An odd item swaying on the line caught her eye. A rectangle too small to be a sheet, it had blue stripes near the ends, and fringes. Something about it jarred her memory. It took a few moments to capture the image. Daniel had described something like that. She forgot what he called it, but Avrum had been worried about losing it. That was two days ago. She felt terrible about forgetting her promise to find it. If the cloth on the clothesline wasn't what he'd been looking for, at least it was a reminder.

Natalie grabbed the envelope and ran down the carpeted stairs in her socks. She stopped by the library-turned-office and knocked on the open door. The head nurse looked up from a pile of paperwork. The radio behind her radiated the melancholy strains of a violin. "Excuse me, Dolores; do you happen to know who hung the—the—the shawl on the line out back?"

"Shawl? Nope. Not a clue."

Natalie dropped her envelope in the crate for out-going mail. "Thanks."

In the living room, Natalie found Sally unlacing her boots and Angela releasing her hair from the scarf knotted at the top of her head. They must have been kept late in the surgery. Evelyn lounged on the couch in a satin dressing gown she insisted on lugging wherever they went. For the first time, it didn't look out of place.

"Does anyone know anything about that shawl hanging on the line?"

Sally looked up. "That's mine."

Angela shook her black waves loose. "Is that what you were hogging the sink for this morning?"

Sally shrugged. "It's a wool wrap. I thought it was pretty."

"Could you tell me where you got it?" asked Natalie.

"Why the big interest?" Sally was smart and efficient and sometimes she knew it too well.

Natalie took a breath. "I was looking for something like that."

"Finders keepers." Sally returned to her laces.

"No, you don't understand," said Natalie

"If you want to trade for it," said Sally, "no dice. It cost me two Hershey bars and three pairs of rubber gloves."

Why did Sally always have to think there was an angle? "I'm not talking about trading for it. It might belong to one of my patients."

Sally pulled off a boot. "That's a good one Natalie."

"Now listen, Sally, you know me well enough—"

Angela winked at Natalie behind Sally's back. "I'll give you a lipstick for it, Sal." "Patriot Red or Pink Queen."

"Do you have Fatal Apple?"

Natalie's impatience grew. "Stop it. Please. I'm serious."

Sally put her hands on her hips. "Why I do believe you are." She raised those perfect eyebrows. "So who does this thing supposedly belong to and how could you possibly know?"

"It's some kind of prayer shawl. Jewish, I think. Trellis. Trallis. No, tallis. A GI was translating for me and the patient was upset he'd lost it. It probably got taken away when they washed him down."

Sally stood up, boots in hand. "I bought it from an industrious corporal and it was clean when I got it. I gave it a fresh wash, though, just in case."

"Do you think the corporal could have found it by the wash-down tent the day before yesterday?"

"Who would pull anything out of the delousing pile?" said Angela. "Yuck."

"I guess he could have." Sally cringed. "If that's the case, I don't want it anymore. It's all yours."

"Thanks Sal." Natalie thought it would have been nicer if Sally's generosity stemmed from respect for a religious article rather than disdain for its former home in the pile of lice-ridden clothing removed from their emaciated patients.

"Get it in the morning," said Angela. "Some night air will do it good."

"And maybe later," said Sally as she walked past Natalie, "we'll get to hear more about this GI translator."

They were headed up the stairs before they could catch the blush Natalie felt rising in her cheeks.

From the bottom of the staircase, Natalie heard Sally say, "Now, let's talk about that Fatal Apple."

Daniel sat at the edge of his cot surrounded by the snorts and hiccups of the day shift, already asleep for hours. He wound the leather straps of his tefillin tight around his left arm and let it loose. Frustrated, he began to coil it for storage but stopped and let it unroll. With greater determination, he repeated the process of wrapping his hand and arm.

His shirtless "bird bath" at the barrack sink hadn't been enough to eliminate all traces of DDT powder. His skin itched.

Daniel pulled the leather tight. Released it. What was the use of thanking God for a soul corrupted by anger and a heart splintered by fear?

He couldn't stop thinking about Red, scheduled for the night shift at the bridge that spanned the moat between the prisoner's compound and the ovens. Daniel dressed quietly and buttoned his field jacket against the pre-dawn chill.

Daniel approached the soldiers by the bridge. The light mounted high on the chain link fence cast two long shadows.

"Who's there?"

"Danny Rabinowitz."

"Aren't you a little early for your shift?" Daniel couldn't see their faces but he knew Red's voice.

"We need to talk."

"Oh, do we?"

"Right now," said Daniel.

"Listen to that, Charlie. The little kike's givin' me orders."

"Cut it out Red," said Charlie.

"We need to talk," said Daniel. "Alone."

"Danny," said Charlie. "Why don't you go back and get some shut-eye."

"Don't worry," said Red. "This is my little buddy and if he says we gotta talk, well then, we gotta talk."

Red followed Daniel along the brick wall of the crematorium. A single floodlight lit the rear courtyard, empty except for the shadows of the trees.

Red lit a cigarette. "You got a problem?"

"Only one."

"And what's that?"

"You." Daniel didn't have a plan. He hardly knew what he was saying. "You framed Max."

"Who?"

"Max Yoskovitz."

"The hymie with the illegal stash?" Red blew out a long stream of smoke. "Serves him right."

"You knew where to look and you know how he got it."

"Oh my Lord." Red brought his hand to his chest in false astonishment. "You mean I got the wrong hymie?"

Daniel had stolen those cigarettes and Red knew it. He lunged. But not quick enough. Red shoved him. Daniel flew back. His shoulders hit the wall. His head bounced against the brick. His bones rattled. He couldn't get the air into his lungs. Leaning back against the brick, he choked. Tried to breathe. Choked again. Took another breath and caught a bit of air. Daniel's vision cleared. Red stooped for the point of light on the ground. The cigarette. With his palms pressed back against the cold block, Daniel let his back slide down the wall. The rough brick tugged at his jacket. With his bottom on the ground and his knees up, Daniel caught a glimpse of a railing. The cement stairwell that led to the basement of the crematorium.

Here he was, in the exact spot where the green-eyed soldier with the SS insignia and camouflage uniform had died. When Daniel had shot him. Killed the Nazi. For smiling. Daniel dropped his chin to examine his chest. No red blossoms this time. No guns. Just him. Daniel ben Schmuel assuming the position of the boy he'd murdered. And it struck him as funny. Red hadn't killed the killer. What a funny trick God had played, leaving him alive. His chest heaved with laughter. He couldn't stop. Tears streamed down his face.

Red took a step closer. "What's so funny, ass-wipe?"

Daniel sniffed the mucus into his nose and wiped tears from his eyes. "You don't think this is funny?" Daniel released a final sigh and examined the face of the man he'd called Esau.

Jacob had stolen his brother Esau's paternal blessing and fled. Esau had a chance to kill Jacob, but didn't. Yet God had called Jacob Yis-ra-el, *He strives with God*. His twelve children became the leaders of the twelve tribes and the Jews became the children of Israel.

Daniel struggled to stand. "Why didn't you kill him?"

"What the fuck?"

"Why didn't you kill Jacob?" If Esau had killed Jacob, Judaism might have been killed along with him.

"You're off your rocker, kike."

Daniel paused through a moment of dizziness. "I want to know why you didn't kill Jacob."

"I didn't kill anyone who didn't deserve it."

"That's why you didn't kill Jacob?" said Daniel. "Because he didn't deserve it?"

"What are you doin'? Pushin' for a Section Eight?"

"One simple question and your pea brain can't get a hold of it."

"Listen, smart-ass, I didn't kill no Jacob. Why should I?"

The anger in Daniel's veins paused briefly in his cheeks before accumulating in a hot pool in his right shoulder. His biceps contracted. His fingers tightened. Daniel's flying fist caught Red in the eye.

Red dropped to the ground.

Daniel stood over Red's inert body, satisfied. "That's why."

Natalie pushed open the curtains and rubbed her eyes. A silly old tune popped into her head and she took some liberty with the lyrics for the benefit of Angela, stirring on the top bunk. "Mama's little baby loves sleep-ing, sleep-ing. Mama's little baby's gonna sleep too late."

Angela growled from under her blanket. "Mama needs singing lessons."

Natalie squinted out the window and yawned. The concrete

wall held back gray clouds and a layer of mist covered the lawn. "Lovely day."

"Rrrr."

"Hey Ange, did you take the tallis in for me?"

"Speak English please."

"The shawl Sally bought. It's not on the line."

"Not me." Angela sat up and banged her head on the ceiling.

"You okay?"

Angela plopped back down on her pillow. "Skull fracture. Limited mobilization and bed rest. Wake me up in a week."

"Ha. Ha."

In the hallway, Evelyn and Sally were switching places in the bathroom. "You can stay, Sally," said Evelyn. "I'm not used to peeing by myself anyway."

"No thanks," said Sally around the toothbrush in her mouth. "Mornin' Wells."

"Hey, Sal. Do you have the shawl?"

Sally popped the toothbrush out of her mouth. "You're still on that subject? No, I didn't touch the shawl. I told you, it's yours."

"Sorry."

Natalie wanted to show Avrum the tallis today. Somebody must have brought it in.

"You know what?" said Sally.

"What?"

"You're going to a concert with me tonight."

"No, I—"

"Don't give me an argument, Wells. You need to relax."

"Okay, but—"

Sally disappeared into her room.

The last thing Natalie wanted to do was go to a concert. She dressed quickly and went in search of the prayer shawl.

Avrum was sleepy and suffering only from a slight headache, but memories of Prague kept him awake. He was a little boy then. Innocent and happy. He remembered looking forward to the trip on the train with Mama and Papa. It took two days, with a stopover in Crakow for the night, to reach Prague on the eve of Passover.

It was a Friday evening and he was sitting in a small crowd of his Orthodox cousins in his grandfather's attic. They all leaned forward to hear the hushed voice of Eliyahu, the oldest of the group of boys who had not yet reached the age of bar mitzvah. He was going to tell them a story.

Maybe you've heard this story. Maybe you haven't. But listen closely to me now because I know the true and actual facts. I can't tell you how I know. That's my secret and I will never tell. If you tie me to a stake and burn me alive, like the great martyr Rabbi Haninah, I will still never tell how I know. That's why you can believe by me, this is the truth.

Many years ago, in this very city, lived an esteemed and learned rabbi. His name was Rabbi Yehuda ben Loew but he was known to the whole world as the Maharal. There have been many great rabbis who have lived in the Jewish Quarter of Prague. Even our Sabah is one of them. So what was so different about the Maharal, who lived here four hundred years ago?

I will tell you.

The Maharal knew secrets of the Sefer Yetzirah. So maybe Sabah wouldn't be happy if I talk to you about the Book of Creation, but if you want to hear this story, then you must know right now that there is magic. Yes, with the help of HaShem, praised be He, the Maharal performed magic and saved the Jews of Prague from complete and utter destruction.

Aryeh, stop chewing your fingers. It's not even the scary part yet.

So. It all started with a priest who hated the Jews. This priest, he told everyone that the Jews used the blood of gentile children to make matzah for Pesach. Yes, yes, I know that's disgusting. And not even kosher. But what can I say? The gentiles didn't know any better and they believed this trouble-maker priest named Thaddeus.

One day two young men came to Thaddeus and asked if the priest could attend to their younger brother who was dying. Thaddeus had a cold heart and wouldn't be bothered with peasants. He sent them away. But then he had another thought and called them back. He'd figured out an evil plan and he offered the brothers a bag of gold if they would help him carry it out. At first the brothers said no, but then they agreed on account of their poor widowed mother.

Aryeh, sit on your hands already.

Anyway, Thaddeus waited until the boy died, which didn't take long at all because he had the tuberculosis and he was coughing and gagging and spitting up blood all over the place. They buried the boy in the daytime, but in the middle of the night the brothers dug the body back up. Like a sack of potatoes they tied up the corpse, and brought it to Prague.

Now, you have to understand that Thaddeus had spies in the ghetto, gentiles who worked for the Jews, and he knew that all the Jewish mamas were busy cleaning their homes, getting ready for Passover. Thaddeus gave the corpse to one of his spies, a man by the name of Komenski, who worked at a tannery owned by a Jew name Ginzberg. Are you following me so far? Ginzberg is the Jew who owns the tannery. Komenski is the spy who works at the tannery. Good. Now listen.

Komenski cut the throat of the corpse and hid the body in the basement of the tannery. In the morning, when all the other workers were there, Komenski pretended it was a big surprise that a boy was lying there in the basement, all dead and bloody.

They called for the constable.

Komenski testified that he'd overheard Ginzberg tell his wife that they needed Christian blood to make their matzah. Another gentile testified that he saw Ginzberg sneak a large sack into the basement the night before.

Yes, yes, I know it was a lie. What can I say? They lied.

Ginzberg, of course, denied all of this, but being that

Ginzberg had only the word of his wife that he'd been home every night, the constable arrested him for murder. The only mystery remaining, according to the authorities, was who the dead body belonged to.

What? Oy veh. We know it was the boy who died of the tuberculosis. But *they* didn't. Nudniks!

Who do you think would visit the constable just then? I'll tell you. Thaddeus and the two brothers. Thaddeus said, "These gentlemen have come to me in great desperation. It seems their younger brother is missing." So the constable showed the dead body to the brothers who began to moan and wail. "Yes, yes. That's our dear brother. Oh our poor brother. Oh our poor brother is dead." The older brother said, "I sent him to the tannery to sell some skins, but he never returned. Oh woe is me!"

Yes, yes, I know. Another lie. You don't have to tell me.

All the gentiles in Prague started getting really angry, saying now there was proof that we use Christian blood to make their matzah. After that, the Jews couldn't travel alone or go out after dark because gentiles cursed them and spit on them.

You want to know when the magic comes? I'll tell you when the magic comes. But not yet.

I must tell you what the Maharal did first. He went to the king, which was a brave and daring thing to do. But he had to because this terrible slander against our people, it was putting the whole community in danger. So with his heart open and his brain filled with all he had studied, the Maharal convinced the king that the blood libel, according to the Written Law, was false. King Rudolf commanded that Jews could no longer be charged with the blood libel. This was a great feat for the Maharal and also a great credit to the king.

But in Prague, it was too late. As feathers and candles were used to sweep away the last of the leaven, Jews were beaten. As preparations were made for the Seders, houses were burned. Gentiles no longer came to their jobs in the ghetto and Jews no longer went into the city. Bigger and bigger crowds of Christians showed up at the gate, yelling and screaming and waving clubs. Rocks were hurled over the ghetto walls day and night. Trouble like you never saw.

Now is the magic part. Now I will tell you the greatest and most wondrous deed of the the Maharal. He called for his two best students and brought them, in secret, to a river. They dug clay from the bank and formed that clay into the shape of a— Mendel, can you guess? Yes, quite right. They formed the clay into the shape of a man.

The Maharal knew, you see. He knew that words could bring life. Even Rabbi Haninah, the exalted martyr, wrapped in a Torah scroll and burning at the stake, shouted to his students that he could see the letters of the Law soar upward! The Written Law. The Words of HaShem, praised be His Name. Words to learn. Words to live by, to die for. And in the secret combination known only to the Maharal, words to breathe life into a man of clay.

The Maharal taught his students the magical incantations. Seven times they circled the clay form, chanting those words. Then, in a moment as silent as this, the Maharal used a stick to carve three letters on the forehead of the clay man.

Aleph. Mem. Tav.

You know what that spells. Avrum from Warsaw who doesn't wear side-curls, even you know what that spells.

It spells Truth.

The wind swirled around and around and the moon grew brighter. The wind stopped and it got very, very quiet. If a pin dropped you could hear where it fell.

Whoosh!

This was the sound of the clay man sucking air into his nostrils. Whoosh into his nose and pheewww out of his mouth. Whoosh. Pheewww. Whoosh. Pheewww. He moved a finger. He moved an arm. And then a leg. Whoosh. Pheewww. Three meters tall, he stood up and towered over the Maharal and his two students. But he said nothing.

The Maharal ordered the golem to dress in the clothes he had brought. He ordered the creature to follow him through a secret passage into the ghetto. He ordered him to stand at the gate and defend the Jewish community.

All this the golem did without a word.

And just in time, because at that very moment a great crowd of tyrants stormed the gate, waving sticks and shovels and yelling for revenge.

The giant man took care of them. He hurled one man back over the fence. He stomped another on the ground. He broke a club in two. He smashed a head with the bully's own rock. The rest dropped their weapons and raced back to their own part of the city.

And once again, peace was restored to the Jewish quarter of Prague.

But that's not the end of the story. Did you think it was? Ha! You were wrong. What about Ginzberg? What about the golem? If you behave yourselves in shul tomorrow, I'll tell you the rest.

In the synagogue the next day, Avrum hadn't run around with the other boys. He'd stayed close by his father and stared at the ceiling, wondering about the golem in the attic.

The tinkling sounds of the upright piano echoed from the beamed ceiling. Two rows of benches and mismatched chairs flanked an imperfect center aisle. The audience trickled in. Striped uniforms. American uniforms. Small groups buzzing in a beehive of assorted languages. At floor level in the front, the orchestra was difficult to see. Prisoners comprised the band, blue stripes cleaned and pressed and faces scrubbed. A few notes of a violin blended with the drone of the growing crowd.

Natalie slid onto a bench beside Sally on the right side, close to the rear. There weren't many women here, and it was their unspoken habit to be as unobtrusive as possible.

Sally nudged her. "Welcome to Carnegie Hall, my dear. My, how it's changed."

Natalie was both excited and wary. Entertainment had been non-existent and music was limited to snippets from a single radio, coveted and controlled by Dolores, the head nurse. Even though this seemed a poor-man's concert, Natalie had washed her hair for the occasion, in a rare shower of deliciously hot water. She'd laughed when she'd shaved her legs, thinking maybe there really was a girl under there. Her hair had grown long and its waves made it impossible to style in the crisp flips and curls she had studied in the magazines that the nurses traded. Angela had helped her by pinning a neat French twist at the back. She also lent Natalie her skirt because when Natalie dug up her own she found she had grown much too thin for it.

The room filled. Officers in the front, along with camp dignitaries—former inmates who made up the International Prisoners Committee, distinguished only by a slightly elevated countenance. Natalie caught sight of him then, standing on the left, a few rows up. The boy who had come to find Avrum. She hadn't seen him since then—a few days or a week. It was hard to keep track of the time. An envelope-like garrison cap had replaced his helmet and he removed it as he sat next to another GI.

The lights dimmed and the room hushed. A sergeant in full dress uniform stood at the front and motioned with his hands for everyone to rise. In a beautiful baritone, the sergeant began the Star Spangled Banner. Although she cringed at "the bombs bursting in air," Natalie swelled with a kind of melancholy pride that made her thank God she was born in America. The sergeant's voice filled Natalie's heart to bursting as his voice rose with the final words... "o'er the land of the free and the home of the brave." A wise-cracking GI shouted "Play ball!" and then sat down quickly, embarrassed by the silence that snubbed his joke. The crowd broke into a round of tremendous applause. The smiling sergeant gave a small bow and took a seat.

The skeleton conductor stood and lifted his baton and with a swoop of his thin stick, music engulfed the hall. Natalie sat, mesmerized. She didn't know much about music but she allowed herself to become immersed in the magical conglomeration of notes and the flawless synchronization of the ragtag players.

After the orchestra played a few pieces a stoop-shouldered man took center stage. His face wore the beginnings of a white beard and his striped cap accentuated oversized ears. He steadied himself by wrapping his gnarled fingers around the back of a wooden chair and raised his face. Natalie expected a whisper. Instead, his song, edged with a peal of sorrow, rang sweet and strong. The old man closed his eyes and rocked through the melody. Natalie had never been so touched by a song. Her eyes closed and her muscles eased as if her body and soul were responding together. She allowed warm tears to flow.

Natalie clapped enthusiastically for the singer and was surprised to hear only small pockets of applause in the audience. Sally shot her a quizzical look.

Natalie's tender mood congealed into confused embarrassment. "What?" she whispered.

Sally rolled her eyes and released a long breath.

Natalie knew that look and turned away. So what if she lacked Sally's city sophistication? Natalie shrunk from Sally's silent reproach.

The band played again but the music became distant to Natalie. Her mind and her eyes turned to Daniel. He had replaced his garrison cap. Head bowed, fingers laced, he sat motionless.

The last applause faded. Chairs scraped. Feet shuffled. Voices and laughter grew louder.

"Not bad," said Sally. "Were you crying?"

"Don't be silly." Natalie wiped a cheek. "Hey, Sal. Do you mind if I run out on you?"

Sally raised an eyebrow. "Well, well, Wells. Does Little Miss Prim have a date?"

Natalie bit her lip. "I want to check on a patient."

"Sure, dear. Whatever you say. Is this a tall, dark and handsome patient?"

"Come on, Sally."

"Go ahead. I'll ask Major Dutton to walk me back. He never says no."

"Thanks, Sal."

Daniel's seat was empty. Natalie walked outside, continuing to scan the crowd, and caught sight of him turning the corner of the building. She walked quickly and caught up with him by the gate.

"Daniel!"

He and his companion, a wiry little GI, stopped and turned around.

"Er—Private Rabinowitz?"

The shorter boy's thin lips twisted into a smirk.

"I'm sorry. Do you mind if I have a word with you?"

It took a moment for Daniel's face to register recognition and Natalie touched her hair, realizing the last time he had seen her she'd been wearing a head scarf, woolen pants and boots.

"Yes, ma'am. I mean, no ma'am."

Natalie glanced at Daniel's friend.

Daniel lifted his chin in the direction of the gate. "Go on, Kopeki. I'll catch up with you later."

With his hands in his pockets, Kopeki bounced away.

Daniel stared. "Lieutenant Wells?"

"Natalie."

"Sorry. Natalie."

Natalie looked down at the ground, and then up at Daniel. "Do you mind if we walk?"

"Sure."

They fell into step.

"They moved our quarters, the nurses, into those pretty houses along the wall. In a strange way, they remind me of home."

"I know that street. It's where..."

"Where what?"

"That's how we got into the camp, the first day. Over the north wall."

It was hard for Natalie to imagine this boy in a combat situation. But they were all boys, weren't they? "I—I thought you might want to know about Avrum."

150

Daniel stopped. "Is he okay?"

"Yes, yes. He's fine. Getting better every day."

Daniel let out a slow breath and continued walking. They were following the path of the wire fence that divided the SS grounds from the prisoner's camp. Hollow and darkened guard towers loomed behind moonlit poplar trees.

Daniel didn't answer. His silence annoyed her. "Maybe it's none of my business, but you seemed so—so attached." With no response from him, her voice rose. "He's been asking for you."

They paused by a birdhouse mounted on a high pole. Natalie realized where they were and shivered. The shadow of the crematorium hovered through the grove of pine trees.

Daniel held the pole and looked up at the perfect little bird home. "A strange place for this, don't you think? Imagine paying attention to birds, to attract them, make them happy, with so many people—suffering—dying—right over there."

Natalie hugged her arms across her chest. He was making her nervous.

He cleared his throat. "It's my fault."

"What's your fault?"

"That Avrum got sick."

The statement shocked her. "He has dysentery. Everyone has dysentery. Or typhus. At least it's not typhus."

"But I gave him too much to eat." Daniel leaned on the pole and lowered his head. "Took him on a picnic. Gave him salami. He got sick after that."

Natalie relaxed her arms and took a step closer. "Daniel, it's not your fault. Dysentery comes from bacteria." She grinned and tried to catch his eye. "Not from salami."

Daniel's glance was tentative. "You're just being nice."

"No, I'm not just being nice. 'Nice' is not one of my stronger virtues. You didn't make that boy sick."

"But—"

"But what?"

"They died. Lots of them died. When we got here. From eating too much. Our rations."

Natalie rested a hand on his arm. "Daniel, look at me." Those dark eyes. So pained. So mournful. "Daniel, that's not your fault either. You couldn't possibly have known a starving man would die from eating too much. Besides, our Avrum, he wasn't starving. He'd had a few days of good, solid food. You may have given him a belly ache, but you didn't even come close to killing him. I promise."

Daniel dropped his head, ran a finger under his nose, and smiled. "Okay, I believe you."

Natalie noticed her hand on his arm and withdrew it. She had done that once before, in the hospital ward.

"I should have come to see him anyway," said Daniel. "I don't know. I guess I was afraid of finding an empty bed."

"I'm sorry I yelled."

"You didn't yell. You were just being firm." He grinned. "Lieutenant Wells."

Natalie's laugh relaxed her. "Hey, I'm not usually so bossy."

"You're not bossy." Daniel reached across to scratch his shoulder. "Thanks."

"Can we get out of here?"

Daniel straightened up and glanced at the shadow of the brick building. "This was a stupid place to end up. I wasn't thinking."

They walked towards her quarters. Now their silence was easy.

"Oh, I almost forgot." She paused. "Good news and bad."

"The bad news I could do without."

"The good news is I might have found Avrum's tallis. Did I say it right?"

Daniel nodded. "And the bad news?"

"It disappeared. Last night it was hanging on the line and this morning it was just gone. I know none of the nurses took it. I feel terrible about it. And it's a little creepy too, to think of someone sneaking around in the backyard."

"Don't worry about it."

Natalie could sense his disappointment. "I'm sorry."

"Don't be sorry. This is a strange world and strange things

happen every minute." Daniel glanced at her. "It was nice that you tried."

"So, you'll come and visit Avrum?"

"Yes, tomorrow."

"I have the day shift."

"During the day then."

Natalie relaxed into her memories of the music. "Daniel, who was that old man at the concert? What was he singing?"

"The old man? Oh. That was a cantor. He sings the prayers at shul—in a synagogue. At least he used to. Tonight he sang 'Ani Ma'amin'"

"It was so touching." She hesitated. "I'm surprised he didn't get more applause."

"Natalie, the Jews didn't applaud because the song was a prayer. The others didn't applaud because they hate the Jews."

"That can't be true."

Natalie winced at the flash of dark anger in Daniel's eyes, but when he spoke, his voice was gentle. "Do you want to know the words?"

She nodded.

"I believe with perfect faith in the coming of the Messiah. And I will wait even if the Messiah is delayed."

"The Messiah?"

"A soldier of sorts," said Daniel. "But holy. The word Messiah means anointed. When he comes the world will be united."

Daniel must have guessed the name in Natalie's thoughts. "Not a god or the son of God. Just a man."

"How do you know if this man is the Messiah?"

"You don't. Not until he's successful. First he has to fight the enemies of the Israelites and rebuild the temple. Then he can start to mend the world. He won't be recognized as the Messiah until everyone on earth lives by God's law."

"Peace on earth. Good will toward man."

"Something like that."

The withered cantor had sung with such conviction. *I believe with perfect faith in the coming of the Messiah.* She didn't know what it was like to believe with perfect faith. She hardly knew what it was like to have faith at all. How did people like the cantor and Father Rudy, people who had survived hour to hour in this stinking pit, people who had lived at the mercy of barbarians, still maintain their faith?

"Do you believe, Daniel? Do you believe the Messiah will come?" She couldn't believe she had blurted out such a personal question and held her breath for his reply.

"Yes. No. I don't know anymore."

Natalie said good-night to Daniel and walked up the path to her new quarters.

12 May

"Shabbat Shalom!" yelled Max from inside the prisoner's compound.

Daniel, doused again with DDT, hurried through the gate to shake Max's hand. "Shabbat Shalom." Daniel winced from Max's grip. His hand was still sore from the knock-out punch he'd given Red. "I showed up for your interrogation and they told me you'd been released. Insufficient evidence."

"I guess you have some pretty good connections."

"Or you do," said Daniel. "I found the dreykop who put you in there but I wasn't sure if I was convincing enough for him to make things right."

"Your connections. My connections. It doesn't matter. I'm out. Or back in here. Locked up is locked up."

"It's the typhus epidemic—"

"Save it for schlemiels who need to believe that sheit."

As if to prove Max's point, the ten deuce-and-a-halfs that had been idling in the middle of the roll call square started to roll. Max and Daniel took a few steps back to let them pass. From the back of each canvas-topped vehicle crowds of prisoners in striped hats and pants and tattered jackets laughed and waved good-bye.

"Belgians," said Max. "The whole lot of them. On their way home."

Daniel raised his voice over the racket of the rumbling trucks. "Have you made any headway with the International Committee?"

"They've had a nice break from me for a couple of days. I'll go stirs things up soon enough."

"I don't know where you get the energy."

Max shrugged. "It keeps me going."

"And the lists of the dead and the living?"

"Almost ready for publication. Got a little help from one of your rabbi chaplains. Wants his name in big print."

"Whatever it takes."

"Ahmain," said Max. "Whatever it takes."

The noise subsided as the last of the trucks exited the

compound on their journey northwest through Germany and into Belgium.

"I'm on my way to visit Avrum."

"Ah, Avrum. How's the boy doing?"

"Getting better from what I hear."

"Baruch HaShem. And blessed is God also for the disappearance of the leymener geylem."

"What stupid golem?"

"Vladik, who stuck to Avrum like icing on strudel. Never liked that Vladik. Tell the boy I wish him a speedy recovery."

Daniel passed Kopeki as he walked beneath the eagle-topped arch at the entrance to the SS compound, but backtracked. "Do you have any money?"

"Sure. How much do you want?"

"I don't know. How much do you have?"

Kopeki dug into his pocket and pulled out a roll of reichsmarks. "I finally got the hang of craps."

"Do you mind if I borrow it?"

"Okay Danny."

An impulse sent Daniel in search of the GI ward. In a room with ten beds and three patients, Daniel spotted his target propped up on a cot. His eyes were closed and a thick white bandage circled his face. Daniel read his chart, leaned his rifle against the foot of the bed and balanced his helmet on the shaft. The makeshift marker for a soldier buried in the field. Daniel sat by the patient's feet.

Daniel said a short prayer and took a deep breath. "Hey Mike."

Mike forced open sleepy eyes. Daniel guessed he was enjoying the benefits of morphine.

"My name's Danny. Finn asked me to come by and see how you were doing." Dropping the name was a test, but Mike didn't flinch. "So, how are you doing?"

Mike squinted as if to say, "How do you think?"

"Looks like that walrus did a job on you." Daniel waited to make sure this was making sense to Mike before he continued. "Fucking Krauts," he said. "I bet you had that old man locked up."

Mike puffed out a "Yeah!" and winced.

"Don't try to talk buddy. Look at it this way. It's your ticket home. You got a girl back in...?" He had concentrated mostly on the spelling of Mike's last name. Where was he from? "You got a girl back in Oregon?"

An imperceptible nod of the bandaged head.

"That's swell." Daniel forced a laugh. "Bet she wouldn't want to know about how you got your jaw broken."

He had Mike's attention now.

"Oh, don't worry, I won't spill the beans." Daniel paused. "But the thing is—you're going home—and I'm going to be stuck here for a while. That Brigitta is one pretty girl, if you catch my drift."

Daniel couldn't tell how much Mike was catching but at least his eyes were still open.

"You wouldn't mind, would you, if I took over in the Fraulein department?"

Mike waved at the clipboard and pencil on his bed stand. Daniel reached over and placed it on Mike's lap. Without looking down Mike scrawled ALL YOURS.

"Great. I wouldn't want to be stepping on anybody's toes." Sid would have been so much better at this. "Hey, I bet you'd like to bring home something nice for your girl."

Another nod.

Daniel counted out a hefty pile of reichsmarks from the roll in his pocket. "You can pick out something yourself, when you're cruising around Paris. I hear that's where they send you first." Daniel pressed the money into Mike's left hand. "Perfume, nylons, you name it."

Mike raised his eyebrows and raised his hand for a strenuous examination of the gift.

"Don't worry. It's all there," said Daniel. "There's just one thing."

Mike shifted his attention to Daniel.

"It would go a long way with—with my chances with Brigitta, if I had something to give her. Something besides money. Money makes it look bad, if you know what I mean."

Mike waited.

Daniel scratched his collarbone. "If I could get her grandfather off, I'd be her goddamn hero. I'd be set. With both of them."

Mike's eyes widened.

"By the time you're in Paris, you'll have forgotten all about them." He slid the clipboard from Mike's lap to his own. "Shopping. Drinking." Writing on Shabbos was forbidden, but Daniel bent over the clipboard with little thought of breaking the commandment. "You'll have to exchange those for francs when you get there."

Daniel read his words back to Mike. "I, PFC Michael Moduszeweski, would like to drop the charges I've made against the Dachau baker, Herr Schmidt. There has been a misunderstanding. I broke my jaw when I tripped and fell at the bakery." Daniel paused with another thought. "When this happened I was on duty and helping Herr Schmidt to resolve a potentially dangerous dispute with a customer. Respectfully..." Daniel placed the clipboard on Mike's lap and the pencil in his hand. "Lt. Chase will probably put you in for a Purple Heart."

Mike stared at Daniel.

Daniel added another four notes to the stack in Mike's hand and waited the lifetime it seemed to take for Michael Moduszeweski to sign his name.

Daniel pocketed the letter and headed to Ward Ten. In the shadows between two buildings Daniel thought he saw the face of the man who had silently challenged him when he brought Avrum back from the picnic. What had Max called him? Vladik. But the face disappeared before he could give it another thought.

"Private Rabinowitz!"

Daniel turned to watch a strange man with a beret and cracked eyeglasses waving and running towards him.

The man extended his hand, panting. "My name..." he said in English, "is Rudolf Prochazka."

Daniel shook his hand. "Do we know each other?"

"We have a friend in common. Avrum." A Slavic accent.

"I'm on my way to see him now."

"Wonderful. Wonderful. He'll be so pleased. May I join you?"

The images forced themselves to the forefront of Avrum's brain. He must have been nine or ten. When he came home from the Yiddish school, Papa was there. Avrum caught a glimpse of him sitting on the bed, crying, before Mama closed the door behind her. "Why is Papa home so early?"

Her eyes were red. "The Germans, Avrum. They've taken Czechoslovakia."

He'd heard that solemn announcement in school two weeks ago. It had made him afraid but the target of his fear was something he didn't quite comprehend. Nazis goose-stepping in newsreels. The angry mustached man. But his father home early from the university and crying, this made him more afraid than any of the outrageous stories his friends told at school.

"We haven't heard from your grandparents," said Mama.

It would be easy to make this right. "Tell Papa we'll see them soon for Pesach."

"No, my Avrumel, this year we'll have Pesach at home."

Mama removed the leaven, changed the dishes and emulated Savtah's Passover recipes as best she could. At the Seder, Papa read the account of God's signs and wonders that brought the Jews from bondage to freedom. Avrum, as the youngest (and only) child, had the privilege of chanting the Four Questions. He began with the prelude: "Mah nishtanah halailah hazeh mikol halaylot?" *Why is this night different from all other nights?* He raised his voice. *Why is it that on all other nights during the year we eat either bread or matzah...? Why is it that on all other nights we eat all kinds of herbs...?* He willed the words to fill the void. *Why is it that on all other nights we do not dip our herbs even once...? Why is it that on all other nights we eat either sitting or reclining...?* But Avrum's fervent chanting failed to charge an evening normally electrified by the din and devotion of his extended family.

The sight of Daniel walking toward him released the burden of Avrum's memories. Daniel wore a white mask and a cloth hat. Father Rudy followed.

Avrum propped himself up on his cot and smoothed his blankets. He was glad Fraylin Wells had helped him wash and given him fresh pajamas just that morning. No more lice. No more sores. And now to see that Daniel hadn't been shipped away—if it weren't for his nagging memories it could have been the best day in his life.

Daniel extended his hand. "Vos machstu?"

Avrum shook Daniels hand with all the strength he could muster. "Alevay vayter."

Daniel sat on the edge of the cot. "So far, so good? Very funny. You look well."

"I'm much better," said Avrum. "Did Father Rudy find you?"

Daniel glanced back at Rudy, standing at the foot of the bed. "*Father* Rudy?"

Rudy inclined his head. "At your service," he said in German.

"He's not one of the bad priests," continued Avrum in Yiddish. Daniel's cheeks reddened above his mask and Avrum realized his mistake. He had to remind himself life was not a storybook of good and evil. He hated himself for acting like a child. "I'm sorry, Rudy."

"Not at all, my boy," said Rudy. "You have paid me the highest compliment."

Daniel seemed distracted by his surroundings. This hospital ward offered Avrum the kind of comfort he had only dared to dream of, but Daniel's eyes reflected sorrow and pity and perhaps an inkling of disgust. "How are you, Daniel?"

"I'm fine. A little tired."

"Rudy told me you brought clothes to the barrack. I wish I'd been there."

"How could I be so thoughtless? I didn't bring you

anything."

"What do I need?" said Avrum. "Look at this." He spread his arms to show off his pajamas. "Look how strong." Avrum swung his blanket away, slid his legs over the edge of the bed and pressed his feet to the floor. He pushed his palms against the mattress and attempted to stand. Avrum cursed his shaking knees.

Daniel and Rudy hurried to his side, each clasping an elbow.

"What are you doing?" said Daniel.

"I can walk a little now," said Avrum. He didn't reveal to them that it had been Vladik who had supported him during his first halting strolls along the aisle.

Miss Wells appeared. Avrum couldn't understand what she said, but she seemed flustered, probably by the sight of her patient standing up. Vladik only came to him after Miss Wells had gone for the night.

Daniel exchanged a few words with her. Avrum happily noted the casual tone of their exchange.

"Natalie isn't very happy you're out of bed," said Daniel in Yiddish.

Avrum knew his favorite nurse only as Miss Wells. Daniel had called her Natalie. Their intimacy cheered him and gave him an extra boost of confidence. He glanced across the open ward to the sun streaming through the windows. "I want to go outside."

Miss Wells' reaction to Daniel's translation was a probing silence. Avrum had never stood in front of Miss Wells and he enjoyed having to look down to meet her stare. She pointed to the cot and Avrum didn't need words to know he'd been commanded to sit down.

Daniel watched the nurse retreat as Father Rudy chuckled.

"You know her?" Avrum asked Daniel.

"I met her the first time I came to visit you," said Daniel. "You probably don't remember."

"I remember a little. Oh Daniel." The memory spurred a wave of regret. "I lost it. The tallis you gave me."

"I know Avrum. I'm sorry about that."

Miss Wells returned. Without a word she pushed slippers on

Avrum's feet and helped him slide his arms into a bathrobe. Thin stripes of blue and white rested lightly on his shoulders. How different from the course blue stripes he'd worn for years. Avrum ran his fingers up and down the sleeve. He looked up, embarrassed to find Daniel, Rudy and Miss Wells staring with smiles pushing cheeks above their masks. Avrum smoothed the lapels of his robe and crossed his arms. He was not a child.

Daniel winked at Avrum. "The general says you can go outside for a few minutes."

Avrum pressed his palms into the cot for the second time.

"Wait," said Daniel. He took the cloth cap from his head and placed it on Avrum's. "That's better."

Daniel and Rudy helped Avrum to his feet, but before Avrum took a step he presented Miss Wells with the best salute he could muster. With a sparkle in her eyes, she brought her heels together and her fingertips to her brow.

On the bench outside, Daniel and Rudy removed their masks and Avrum adjusted his US Army cap. It was the longest walk he'd taken so far and Avrum struggled to hide his labored breathing.

"Avrum," said Daniel. "I want to ask you something."

Sunshine soaked Avrum's skin. "Okay," he said, showing off his American word.

Daniel smiled. "You're learning English."

Avrum ran through some of the phrases he knew. "Take your vitamin. Go to sleep. Good yobe. My feet are killing me. Vos heyst 'killing me'?"

"An expression. Literally, it means something's killing you, but it only means something hurts or bothers you."

To Avrum, killing was not a trivial matter. "That expression, I don't like."

"Come to think of it," said Daniel, "neither do I."

"You wanted to ask me something," said Avrum. He harbored a secret wish and hoped Daniel's question was the first step in making it come true.

"Do you think you might have some family somewhere?"

The sunlight was suddenly too bright for Avrum's eyes. He closed them and shook his head.

"There's a museum in Munich where names of missing family are posted. And your name is in Max's book."

Avrum shook his head again.

Rudy laid an arm across Avrum's shoulders. "It's something you should think about."

"I didn't mean to upset you," said Daniel.

"I was thinking," said Avrum. He opened his eyes. "I was thinking I should go to America."

Father Rudy cocked his head and Daniel dropped his chin.

"If I may," said Rudy, "although this may be a worthwhile ambition, I believe it is far too soon for a practical consideration of that particular option."

Daniel's silence cut Avrum like a knife. But what did he expect? That Daniel would pack him in a suitcase? Pass him off as a fellow soldier? No. But he had hoped at least that Daniel would want him to come to the Brooklyn he'd described with its streetcars and yeshivas and kosher salami. Was their friendship more than he'd imagined? Or perhaps he didn't understand relationships outside of the world of unpredictable horrors, where a friendship survived only as long as the friend. Or were friendships sometimes merely a mutual means for survival.

"Ah," said Rudy. "Here's our beautiful angel!"

Miss Wells smiled as she walked towards them and Avrum couldn't help but smile too. He'd never seen her without her mask, never seen her full face exposed.

Natalie plopped down on the bench next to Father Rudy with a tired sigh. She said something in English which Avrum took to be a positive comment about the weather. She bent forward to address Avrum. She asked him something that ended in "okay."

"Okay!" said Avrum and raised a thumb in the air for her.

Natalie spoke to Daniel and Rudy in English for a little while. Natalie's mouth mesmerized Avrum. He watched her lips, moving across perfectly imperfect teeth. In the ward, she either spoke with determined efficiency or directed soothing words to distressed patients. In the sunshine, slouched on the bench,

Natalie seemed, at last, complete. Real. A living and breathing woman. He became overwhelmed with fear for her. She could be hurt. She could be so terribly hurt.

Five letters were waiting for Natalie when she got back from her shift. One was from Doctor Eugene Townsend. That one she put aside. She always swore she'd throw it away unopened, but ended up reading it anyway. When she'd started dating him, she didn't know he was married. Or maybe she did and she was just fooling herself. His flirtatious attention was too hard to resist. He made her laugh. She could talk to him. He'd proclaimed his marriage to be a miserable one. It had taken her two years to realize that, despite his promises, he would never leave his wife. He wrote regularly, proclaiming his love, and she hated herself for reading his letters. She could never dispel the deep-down hope that he was writing with news of his divorce. But at this point it would be more for triumph than for love.

She'd joined the Army to get away from the double life she was leading and the lies she had to tell. The Army almost didn't take her because she was too old—all of twenty five. But they required their nurses to be single, and that she was. She'd lost her virginity to Gene, but she'd lost her innocence in the Army. The world, it seemed, was full of liars.

The remaining four letters were from her mother, who wrote on behalf of both her parents. Sometimes she got a short note from her dad. He wasn't much for writing, probably worried he'd misspell something or mess up the grammar—mistakes her mother would be quick to point out.

Natalie was torn between relishing a reading of the letters in order or digging right into the last one. Another day in the ward had eaten away her patience. She tore open the one with the most recent postmark.

March 31, 1945

My Dear Natalie,

I'm sorry you have to receive this news in a letter. There's no other way but to just say it. Your father passed away yesterday. As I wrote last, they operated to remove the cancer from his lungs, but it was too late. You're a nurse so I can't pretend to you that the end was easy. The poor man could hardly breathe.

Your friend Dr. Townsend was very attentive and that helped quite a lot. In any case, Dad is laid out nicely in his best suit and the funeral is tomorrow. I'm sure you know how much he loved you and how proud he was that you were in the Army, especially since he didn't have a son.

The ladies from the church have been so wonderful. There's someone with me all the time. Mabel took me today to buy a black dress and a hat with a veil. Dad's friends from work have dropped by too. So I don't feel alone at all.

I hope you're well dear.

Love,

Mom

I hope you're well dear. Buried tomorrow. Natalie glanced back at the date. Her father had been gone for more than a month and she hadn't even known it. Her "friend" Gene had been attentive. How dare he? And oh her poor mother. Had company. Didn't feel alone. A new dress. Natalie should have been there for her.

She no longer had a father, her dad who smiled when she came home, who talked with pride about his "little angel." Her dad who loved her. Who she loved back. So much. Gone. Gone. Never again. And she hadn't been there. She should have been there. To hold his hand. To make decisions, to make sure he had the very best care. She supposed Gene had taken care of that. Damn him. Damn the cancer. Damn the world. Maybe if she'd stayed home she would have seen it sooner, gotten him to the doctor sooner. Saved his life. It was all her fault.

Natalie's face burned and her head felt like it would burst. The tears wouldn't come though. She'd trained them too well. Now that the dyke was allowed to burst, it couldn't. Cold-hearted. That's what she thought she must be. She stood and gripped the back of the chair. Rocked it back and forth. Thumped it on the ground. Thump. Thump. Thump. Picked up the child-sized chair and threw it at the window. Glass shattered. Fragments fell across her pile of letters. She felt a rush of people in the room. They gathered around her as she examined the shards on the rug. They were almost pretty.

The top of Angela's head distracted her. Natalie didn't want Angela to pick up the letter at their feet but she couldn't seem to do anything about it.

Angela cried out. "Oh no!"

Voices whispered. Cooed. Arms held her. She let herself fall into them. But she still couldn't cry.

13 May

Daniel walked to the hospital anxious about what to say to Avrum. Getting Avrum to America would take a miracle. But it was the nature of miracles to demand the highest levels of belief and enthusiasm. Yet the flask of Daniel's passion had been drained. He knew he couldn't, physically or emotionally, help Avrum and therefore failed his own test of what it meant to be a righteous man. Just weeks ago he wondered if he'd live to see twenty. Now he wondered how he would manage a lifetime tainted by failure and doubt, cynicism and anger.

But Daniel didn't have a chance to address Avrum's desire for America.

"She's not here today," said Avrum. "Miss Wells isn't here."

"She probably has the day off."

"No. Something's wrong. You must ask one of the other nurses. Please."

Daniel found a nurse with dark eyes exposed between kerchief and mask. "Excuse me," said Daniel. "I'm looking for Lieutenant Wells. Is she here today?"

The woman pulled Daniel out of the ward and into the foyer. She untied her mask. Feeling uneasy, Daniel did the same.

Tears glazed the nurse's eyes. "I wish I could be with her now. You're her friend. I've seen you together."

Daniel's uneasiness grew. "Is she sick?"

"Her father died. Natalie got the letter last night. She wanted to come to work but Dolores, she's the head nurse. Dolores told her to stay home. The day shift is asleep by now and I hate to think of her all alone."

"You want me to go see her?"

"Oh, that would be swell. Just check in on her. Do you know where she lives?"

"Yes. But is it okay, I mean, for me to show up there?"

"Screw the rules."

Such harsh words from this petite olive-skinned girl shocked Daniel, but not enough that he didn't agree. He told Avrum the news and walked to Natalie's house. Intimidated by the front door of the nurses' quarters, Daniel walked around the back. He saw her on a wicker loveseat with her knees tucked under her chin, barefoot and in pajamas. No longer "the general."

He sat beside her.

Natalie didn't look at him. "My father died."

"I'm so sorry. May his memory be a blessing."

"I haven't cried yet."

"That's okay. You will when you're ready."

"How do you know? What if I never cry? What if I never cry again?"

Daniel brushed his fingers across the bruised knuckles on his right hand.

"I'm sorry. I shouldn't go on like this."

"It's all right. Really Natalie. I understand."

"Yes, I suppose you do."

They sat in silence for some time.

Natalie spoke first. "They buried him on April Fool's Day." She shivered. "I'm the fool. I should have been there. I should have been there when he got sick."

"Do you remember, Natalie, when I told you it was my fault that Avrum got sick?"

She nodded.

"Do you remember what you said?"

She conceded. "That it wasn't your fault." Natalie looked at him for the first time. "Tell me, Daniel, do you practice what you preach?"

"About not feeling guilty?" He smiled as he scratched his left shoulder. "No, not really."

"At least you're honest."

"Your father, he must have died during Passover. That's when the Jews celebrate their freedom from slavery and their exodus from Egypt. At the Seder, the family meal, a cup of wine is poured for Eliyahu HaNavi, Elijah the prophet." Daniel smiled. "My older cousins used to trick me by sneaking sips from Elijah's cup to prove he'd really been there." He glanced at Natalie. "Anyway Elijah was a prophet who was humble, but very wise and close to God. It's said that he's always among us in different forms, watching over us and inspiring hope. Maybe you can think of your father that way."

"I thought you didn't believe."

Daniel returned to staring at his hands. "I don't know what to believe."

Natalie tucked her hair behind her ears. "That was a beautiful story, Daniel. Thank you."

"Would you mind if I said a prayer for your father?"

She teased him. "Just in case God listens?"

He smiled. "Just in case."

"Could you say it now?"

"Now? I don't know. It's supposed to be said with at least nine others." Daniel paused. "What do you think? Does God care who's around or not?"

"Not."

Daniel stood, pulled out his small prayer book and faced the morning sun. He was about to suggest that Natalie stand but decided to let her be. He flipped through the book looking for the Memorial Prayer or the Mourner's Kaddish but stopped instead on his favorite chapter from Tehillim.

The chapter began with comfort and concluded with a mixture of hope and certainty. Daniel hadn't chosen this for Natalie's father. He'd chosen it for her. For both of them. "Would you like me to translate it?"

Disheveled hair framed Natalie's pallid face. "Please."

Daniel had never spoken nor heard this prayer in English before. He studied the Hebrew text and took one sentence at a time. "The Lord is my Shepard. I will not want. In pastures of grass he makes me lie down. Beside waters—comforting waters—He leads me. My soul, He restores. He leads me in the paths of righteousness for His Name's sake—"

Natalie interrupted Daniel's halting English with her own clear cadence. "Yea, though I walk through the valley of the shadow of death, I will fear no evil for Thou art with me. Thy rod and Thy staff they comfort me." Natalie gazed into the distance. "Thou preparest a table before me in the presence of mine enemies. Thou anointest my head with oil. My cup runneth over. Surely goodness and mercy shall follow me all the days of my life and I will dwell in the house of the Lord forever." Natalie dropped her forehead to her knees.

Daniel whispered, "Ahmain," and returned to his seat beside Natalie. "You know this."

Natalie's hair bounced across her pajama-covered legs as she nodded. "The twenty-third psalm." She tilted her head to catch Daniel's eye. "It sounded pretty in Hebrew."

"It sounded beautiful in English. I'm a little embarrassed."

Natalie brushed the bottom of her bare feet across the blades of green grass. "You've helped me, Daniel."

"I don't know how."

"I don't know how exactly either. But you've helped me in a way that no one else could." She rested her hand on his.

Daniel took her hand and held it between both of his, resting their embrace on his knee. He felt Natalie's hand warm and her body relax. The connection Daniel had accomplished through prayer had been more human than divine. But it had sufficed.

It is the time when the men and women of the daytime switch places with the men and women of the night. The woman who makes the Boy smile is not here. This is the time I have been waiting for.

I have seen the way they have gained the trust of the Boy. The woman, the soldier and the man who wears spectacles. Perhaps the Boy thinks it is these three who make his colors brighter, who have returned the pink to his cheeks and colored his eyes blue. I am tired of waiting. He is my reason. My purpose. When I take him away from them he will remember that his life depends only on me.

The men and women in masks are busy. They talk and hand

papers to each other. I sit at the edge of the Boy's bed and listen to him tell me about this one and that one. The excitement that makes his hair more golden irks me. Confuses me. It should be my delight to watch the colors of life return to the Boy. Instead—instead I remember the voice of the man with the spectacles. He claims to know what I am. I should have killed him then and be done with it. It is not my way to think, to question. An error. I do not like errors. Now that man has befriended the Boy and steals my time with him.

The Boy pauses and asks me what is the matter? Does he think these Americans are so powerful that since their arrival I have learned to speak? I indicate to the Boy to lie down on his back. I take his pillow away. He lifts his head to protest but I press his forehead. He relents and lies flat. I cross his arms across his chest gently, one at a time. The Boy looks at me, questioning me without words. This is good. The Boy must remain silent and I indicate this by pressing a finger to my lips. I release the sheet that has been tucked so neatly under the mattress.

The man in the bed beside the Boy asks me what I am doing. I glare at him in the manner I have found makes others turn away. Most others, that is. Not the colorless bubble-headed Americans who had pointed rifles at me. If the Boy only knew that, he would know to distrust them as much as I do. Men with rifles are the enemy.

I pull the edge of the sheet up and across the Boy. The Boy pushes the sheet from his face. I do not mind seeing his face one more time, but I replace the sheet. He speaks. I press a finger to the part of the sheet that covers his mouth. He sighs. Soon he will know I do this to protect him.

Stooped over the Boy, I make my way to the other side of his bed. I spy his neighbor glancing sideways at me. Another glare makes him turn his body the other way. Good.

On this side too I loosen the sheets and pull the edge up and over the Boy. He speaks again. Once more I press my finger to his lips. I do not like covering him in white. His colors are my life. But it is the only way.

I shroud the Boy as the dead are shrouded. I lift him as the dead are lifted. I carry him to the doorway. Only a few more steps. Past the busy men and women—the men and women who are used to shrouded bodies passing through the door. One of them steps aside, barely looking up. Another holds the door open for me. So easy to trick them.

The Boy asks me what is happening. His voice is distressed. My hands are not free to cover his mouth. My mouth is incapable of whispering that he must remain silent. A man approaching us looks up. He is not armed. I glare. He is startled by my power but does not move or look away. These stupid Americans are ignorant of silent threats. But my threats are not always silent.

I push past the man. He shouts. I feel eyes watching me. I walk quickly, holding tight to the Boy. I know places to hide until the darkness. I know the darkened exits in this compound. I am smarter than them. Better than them.

The Boy yells. He tells me to stop. In my arms he struggles. I try to run but the Boy kicks and punches. He slows my pace. He unravels the shroud. I feel hands on my back. I shrug them off. More hands. I lower the Boy to the ground. I turn to them and swing my arms. Men fly to the ground one after another. On the ground I see the Boy crawling towards the fallen. His colors blaze. Blue eyes. Yellow hair. Red cheeks. They make me deaf to the words he shouts at me. My vision ripples. A man helps the Boy to his feet. The boy's shouts grow louder. Like bullets, his colors shoot pain to my temples. I drown in a whirl of exploding sludge. I turn away. I must see. I must hear. I tear at the hands that hold me. I swing my fists. I run.

At first Avrum thought Vladik had been playing a game. But as Vladik had proceeded, the silent man's grip had chilled

Avrum. Avrum's trusted protector had tricked him. In a flash the accuracy of his perceptions had been turned inside out. The friend, an enemy. Avrum had been lulled into thinking he'd never have to face death again, but in those moments, at the mercy of Vladik, Avrum was afraid he would die.

Avrum scrunched down into his cot and pulled the blanket over his head. His body trembled with images of deaths he had witnessed. By beating. By stabbing. By gunshot. By hanging. By sheer exhaustion. Like Papa. He hadn't actually seen Papa die. Only woke beside the lifeless body. Watched his bunkmates drag Papa's emaciated body from the crowded sleeping shelf. The living and the dead separated only by a heartbeat; a breath. No time to cry. No time to mourn. Don't think about it. Don't remember it. Before the Americans he knew his own death was only a heartbeat, a breath, a moment away.

Think of something else. A number. 5700. A year. In the Jewish calendar, a new centennial.

When Avrum was eleven years old they welcomed Rosh Hoshanna and the sweetness of a new year filled with new beginnings. But the optimism Mama had baked into her honey cakes was not enough to prevent the impending fracture in their steadfast cycle of Jewish life. On the second day of the New Year, Germany invaded Warsaw. A week later, on the Day of Atonement, the bombs fell. On the eve of Sukkos, the first in Avrum's memory that Mama hadn't decorated the festive outdoor booth, the man in the radio declared that Warsaw had surrendered. Two days later, the man in the radio kept a mournful silence as he filled their parlor with the thundering sound of marching boots. Fifty seven hundred years and two months since Creation, Mama sewed a blue star on each of three armbands. Avrum and Papa tried them on in the parlor. When Mama looked like she was about to cry, Papa wound up the phonograph. Daa da-da-da-dum. Da-dum. Da-dum. Daa da-da-da-dum. Da-dum. Da-dum. But nobody danced. Not even to Mama's favorite waltz.

The sun had set on the town of Dachau. Daniel hesitated at the door to the bakery, peering into the darkened space. He wasn't quite clear about his true motivations for this. He stepped back. A dim light shone through the white-laced curtain on a window on the second floor. "Hello?"

A girl's voice whispered through the window. "Go away. We are closed."

"Brigitta, I need to speak to you."

The low tremble of a man's voice. "Gehen Sie weg!"

Daniel considered the command. Going away was the easier option. He had planned to give Mike's statement to Brigitta, expecting her Grandfather to still be in jail. "Herr Schmidt! Ist das Sie?" Daniel waited.

"I don't want trouble. There is trouble enough."

Daniel took a breath. "I would like to talk to you, Herr Schmidt. I might be able to help." He waited.

The shadow of a large man appeared at the side of the building and remained immobile. Daniel waited until Herr Schmitt spoke. "Commen zie."

Daniel's boots crunched on the gravel as he approached Herr Schmitt at the side door.

Daniel looked up to white hair and bushy mustache, just as he remembered from his last trip to the bakery. The buttons of a sweater strained against the baker's girth. Herr Schmitt looked Daniel up and down. "Ach so. You think I need help."

"Your English is very good, Herr Schmitt."

The walrus glared.

This mitzvah was less than pure. Daniel felt a degree of power in altering the fate of this German citizen. And he was curious. What was it like behind those white lace curtains? "May I come in?"

Herr Schmitt turned into the doorway. The wooden staircase creaked with his weight. Daniel followed at the heels of the baker's scuffed slippers. The stairway led into a living area with an overstuffed sofa and armchair softened by the amber light of two table lamps. It was a simple place. Ordinary.

Herr Schmitt motioned to the sofa. Daniel caught a glimpse of Brigitta peeking through a doorway as he removed his jacket.

Herr Schmitt lowered his body into the armchair and relaxed into the cushions. "I don't have any money."

"No, no sir. That's not why I'm here." Daniel looked around. White curtains. Flowered wallpaper. A woven rug. His eyes lingered on a photo of a happy man in a German uniform with a hand touching the shoulder of a little girl. It irked him to see an example of his mortal enemy in such a personal setting.

"My son," said Herr Schmitt. "Killed in action."

Daniel looked down. "I'm sorry."

"So am I. Did you come here to sit and stare at your hands?"

Daniel looked into the eyes of this enigmatic man. "Were you a Nazi?"

"Would you believe me if I said I wasn't?"

Daniel allowed his back to absorb the comfort of the sofa. "Probably not."

"So why would you want to help an old Nazi like me?"

"Because you helped them."

"Them. Them. Vas ist 'them'?"

Daniel remained silent.

Herr Schmitt covered his eyes with chubby fingers. "For this I thought I would be shot." Herr Schmitt dropped his hand to his lap. "Instead I am to receive this—this—vas ist verhör?"

"I don't know."

"Intero—"

"Interogation."

"Yes, this is it. And what do you wish to gain by this interrogation?"

"Something. I don't know. Nothing." Daniel pulled the folded paper out of his pocket. "This is a statement from Private Michael Moduszeweski. He decided to drop the charges against you."

Herr Schmidt took the paper from Daniel. "Decided?"

"I helped him decide."

Herr Schmidt face darkened. He leaned forward and flapped

the paper in Daniel's direction. "Brigitta! This is about Brigitta. Schwein!"

Daniel jumped to his feet. "No. This is not about Brigitta. Take it. Keep it. I'm sorry I came." He grabbed his jacked from the sofa and headed for the door.

"Wait. Come back. Sit."

Daniel hesitated.

"I am very tired. I am tired a long time." He turned his face to the interior door. "Brigitta! Bring tea. And cake." He turned to Daniel. "You will have some tea, yes?"

Daniel hesitated.

"I don't know your name."

"Daniel Rabinowitz."

"Daniel Rabinowitz, sit and have tea."

Daniel returned to the sofa and watched Herr Schmidt stroke his mustache.

"You have questions."

"Yes."

"Because you are a Jew?"

Daniel's anger flared. "Because I am a human being."

Herr Schmidt nodded.

The old man's acquiescence drained the burst of malice in Daniel's heart. A baker. A father. A grandfather. A citizen of a nation of anti-Semites. A resident of a town that harbored a concentration camp. A tired old man who risked his life to feed the weak and imprisoned. "Why did you help them?"

"Because, Daniel, like you and like me, they were human beings."

Brigitta entered. She placed a tray on the coffee table without looking at Daniel. After she poured the tea into cups, Herr Schmidt waved her away with the folded paper in his hand.

Herr Schmidt stared at the document that might keep him from going to jail for assaulting an American soldier. "This is my fault," said Herr Schmidt. "May God forgive me, I taught her to—to tease. This is the right word?"

"Flirt."

"Ja, flirt. To distract the guards so that I could give those mouths a bit of—just a tiny bit. I ruined that poor girl. And did it mean anything to them in the end? Did it save a life?"

"It meant something."

Herr Schmidt reached over and dropped the paper on the table. His chubby fingers engulfed the tea cup as he lifted the saucer from the tray to his chest. He frowned into the steaming tea.

Daniel examined the pink roses that adorned the china tea set. The question burned his mouth—the question he had wanted to ask the moment he stepped foot in France—the question that exploded in his brain when he first saw the bodies stacked against the crematorium. He had to ask it one word at a time, hoping there was an answer but knowing there would be none. "How could you let it happen? How could everyone let it happen?"

Herr Schmidt dropped his nose to the edge of the cup. The rising steam vanished into his mustache. "I'm just a poor baker. You think I know these things?"

Daniel leaned forward and dropped his face into his hands.

"Daniel."

Daniel braved the direct gaze of his host.

"Daniel, listen to me. I could give you a thousand reasons, but not one excuse."

Daniel touched the rim of his delicate teacup. He picked it up and brought the hot liquid to his mouth. "I'm sorry Herr Schmidt. I brought you this paper because I thought it was the right thing to do. I shouldn't have asked for anything in return."

"Have some cake."

"No thank you."

"You don't like cake?"

"Yes—"

"It is very good. I made it myself."

Herr Schmidt called Brigitta as Daniel took a small bite of the sweet seeded cake.

"Mr. Rabinowitz has done us a great favor, Brigitta. I would like you to thank him."

Brigitta bit her lip and curtsied. She seemed on the verge of tears. "Sank you Herr Rabinovitz."

"Sit with us Brigitta," said Herr Schmidt.

Brigitta sat on the opposite end of the sofa with her hands in her lap and her head down. "I—I am very sorry—very—" She looked at her grandfather. "Vas ist beschämt?"

"Ashamed."

"Ashamed. Ja, ashamed of how I act." She swallowed and gave Daniel a fleeting glance. "My English ist not so gut."

Daniel struggled for a reply. "Your English is—is fine."

"Grandfather taught me," said Brigitta, her head still lowered. She looked up in a spurt of excitement. "He lived in America."

Daniel turned to Herr Schmidt.

The baker took a long sip of tea. "I was not always an old man, you know."

"Zis is all right to say zis, Grandfahzer?"

"Yes," said Herr Schmidt. "After all these long years, this is all right to say."

This unexpected information heightened Daniel's curiosity.

"Grandfather vas an artist," said Brigitta.

"I do not think our guest wants to hear about my past."

"I think I do, Herr Schmidt," said Daniel.

Herr Schmidt lowered his saucer and empty cup to the table. "I have not spoken of this in many years. Brigitta kept our secret though, didn't you?"

Brigitta nodded her head. "Zey vould have put Grandfather in zat place if zey knew he teach English to me." She smiled shyly. "But I never tell."

"Yes," said Herr Schmidt, "you are a good girl."

Brigitta winced and turned her face away from Daniel.

"When I was a young man, I studied art in New York. And then I came here, to Dachau. Here there was a colony of artists. Brilliant artists. Inspired by the landscape. I painted and I painted. Never such joy in my life. Until the Great War."

"Grandfahzer vas a hero."

"Nonsense!" said Herr Schmidt. "There were heroes in

that war but I was not one of them. I cowered in the trenches, sketching birds and trees and flowers." Herr Schmidt poked his temple and raised his voice. "Verrückt in my head, pretending there was still beauty in the world." He squirmed in his chair and lowered his voice. "Excuse me, please." He paused. "After the war I returned to Dachau. I tried to paint but it was no use. I married. We had two children. Daniel, do you have children?"

"Children? No."

"They were everything to me. I found peace again by showing my children the beauty that had been to me so—how is it said?—elusive. It all changed when they built that—that place. The year Brigitta was born. And beauty was forgotten. No, not forgotten. Changed. Twisted. By a man. By a movement. I don't know." Herr Schmidt slumped into his chair and brought a hand to his forehead. "My daughter married a squirrel of a man in a fancy uniform. He took her to Berlin. My son, well my son..."

Daniel's heart went out to this man but his recent experiences quelled his sympathy. Perhaps his heart had hardened. He grabbed his jacket and stood. "I'd better go."

"Ah well," said Herr Schmidt. He pushed himself to his feet and shook Daniel's hand. "Besten Dank."

Daniel's boots crunched the gravel in front of the bakery. He heard footsteps behind him and turned.

Brigitta had followed him out. Without looking at him, she handed him a sheet of paper and fled back into the house.

Daniel turned it in the darkness until it caught the light from the window. The smudged and yellowed paper bore a sketch of a bird perched on a naked branch. Daniel stuffed the drawing in his pocket and walked along the dark road to his barracks, happy to leave the bakery behind.

Avrum and Daniel stepped out into the sunshine. Avrum hadn't felt this kind of happiness since he'd bounced in the jeep on his way out of the camp the day Daniel had taken him on a picnic. Avrum squinted at the sun and smiled at the fresh smells of springtime carried in the warm breeze.

The dark-haired nurse had helped dress him in the khaki shirt and pants, a crisp new American uniform sent by Daniel. At first he hadn't wanted the nurse's help but his hands shook from the excitement and he hadn't been able to manage the buttons. She seemed almost as excited as he was as she buttoned his shirt and buckled his belt.

Avrum stood and adjusted the envelope cap Daniel had given him. The only remnants of his past identity were the hospital slippers. Today he was a man.

Daniel guided Avrum to a wooden wheelchair with a cane seat and back.

"Oh no," said Avrum. "I'm going to walk."

"It's too far," said Daniel. "Sit."

Avrum hesitated but Daniel's gaze was firm. He eased himself into the chair and lifted his slippers onto the footrests, secretly glad that he would be treated to a ride in such a magnificent piece of furniture.

Daniel waved down the avenue and Avrum turned to see Father Rudy and another American soldier hurrying towards them. Father Rudy huffed with the weight of a boxy suitcase cradled in his arms and the small-framed soldier carried a knapsack heavy enough to bend his torso forward. Both smiled and waved. A day of happy anticipation.

Father Rudy greeted them kindly and Daniel introduced the soldier as Kopeki. Daniel wanted to take the box from Father Rudy but the priest wouldn't let it go.

"I'll take it," said Avrum. "You can put it on my lap."

Father Rudy considered this before placing the case on Avrum's knees. "It's not too heavy?"

"Not at all." Avrum ran his hands along the smooth sides. "What's in it?"

"Hmmm," said Father Rudy. "Let's make that a surprise."

Sunshine and surprises. Avrum, momentarily forgetting the self-importance imposed by his new clothes, swallowed an urge to giggle.

The four of them took up half the street as Daniel pushed Avrum along the sunny lanes. Kopeki smiled wide when he caught Avrum's eye and Avrum decided that Kopeki's good nature probably made up for what he lacked in intelligence.

They turned the corner onto a fairytale lane lined with beautiful houses and Avrum caught a strong whiff of lavender. The scent brought him back to the Warsaw parlor filled with the light of his beautiful mother. He caught his breath.

"Are you all right?" asked Father Rudy.

Avrum shook the image from his head. "Yes, of course."

"Are you worried about what to say?"

Avrum hadn't been worried at all but the question gave him an idea. "I want to say it in English."

Avrum practiced the words as they passed house after pretty house, everyone helping him get the words right. They fell into silence as Daniel slowed and turned the chair onto the walkway of a yellow house.

Natalie emerged from the doorway. She wore a buttoned shirt and a pressed skirt, black laced shoes and white socks. Avrum had never seen her legs before. He liked them.

Natalie's eyes were on Daniel as she stepped down the brick steps to greet them. Father Rudy came forward and kissed the hand she had extended. Kopeki planted his eyes on the ground as he shook Natalie's hand. When Natalie paused in front of Avrum, Father Rudy slid the box from Avrum's lap. Natalie placed her hands on her hips and smiled, obviously proud of Avrum's appearance.

"I am soorry for yoor..." Avrum had forgotten the last words. "I am sooory for yoor papa."

Natalie took Avrum's face in her hands and kissed his cheek. After she stepped back it seemed as if Father Rudy and Daniel were about to explode with laughter. Avrum's voice quivered with anger and embarrassment. "What's wrong? I said it right. Almost right."

Father Rudy patted Avrum's shoulder. "No, no, Avrum. Don't misunderstand. Your words were perfect. It's just that your face is as red as a tomato."

Anxious to maintain his dignity, Avrum planted his feet on the ground and stood up from the chair. Natalie took Avrum's arm and gave it a squeeze. She led him to the gate at the side of the house.

The green yard was sunny and bright with flowers. Benches and chairs were set up around a low table. Natalie had been expecting them of course. The dark-haired nurse had arranged it. Natalie was sad about the death of her father and they were to cheer her up. And Avrum decided he was already doing a better job of it than any of the other three.

Father Rudy put the suitcase on the table and Kopeki slid his knapsack to the ground. Natalie served sweet cold drinks with cubes of ice that tinkled against the glass.

In and out of the shadows, I followed them here. As protectors, they are as useless as pebbles in a torrent. I am the rock that will save the Boy from being swept into the muddy current. Because if his colors fade away than so will I.

I hide behind a hedge. Still watching. Still protecting. Still.

Daniel pulled Avrum aside and spoke to him in Yiddish. "Are you angry that we laughed?"

"Angry? No."

Daniel put his arm around Avrum and lowered his voice.

"It was just jealousy you know."

Avrum lifted his face to Daniel. "About what?"

"You got a kiss from our favorite nurse."

Avrum teased Daniel with a smile. "I suppose she likes me best." He lifted his chin in Natalie's direction. "But you have my permission to sit with her—for now."

Daniel gave Avrum a gentle punch on the shoulder and took his place beside Natalie on the bench.

With great flourish, Father Rudy opened the box to reveal a phonograph. Natalie gasped and brought her hands together. "How wonderful!"

Avrum stood as if in a trance and shuffled to the machine.

"We thought you'd like to have some music," said Daniel.

Natalie turned to Daniel, sitting beside her. "Where in the world...?"

"It's a long story."

"Avrum seems happy about it," said Natalie

Daniel called to Avrum. "Avrum, what do you think of our surprise?"

Avrum didn't reply.

Natalie interrupted Kopeki as he unloaded the paper-sheathed records from his knapsack. "Private Kopeki, do you have a first name?"

"Yes ma'am."

Everyone but Avrum looked to Kopeki, waiting for more. Feeling the need to emphasize each word, Daniel asked Kopeki, "What is it?"

"Oh. My first name? It's James."

"Jimmy?" asked Natalie.

"No ma'am. James."

"Pardon me," said Natalie. "James. Thank you so much for bringing the records."

"Yes ma'am. You're welcome."

"So, Kopeki," said Daniel, "why don't you pick one out so we can hear it?"

"Oh. Yeah. Sure. Just a sec." Kopeki fumbled through the discs and handed one to Father Rudy.

Father Rudy attached the handle to the side, cranked it around and reached inside the box. The rousing voice of Ella Fitzgerald dissipated into the open air.

I want to beee happy.

Kopeki turned up the volume.

But I won't beee happy.

Avrum stepped back from the sound.

Till I make yooou happy tooo.

Avrum didn't take his eyes from the Victrola.

Everyone applauded when Ella's voice faded into the scritch-scratch of the drifting needle. Even Avrum made a half-hearted attempt to push his palms together.

Father Rudy smiled at the next record and placed it gently on the turntable. The sweet sounds of a violin emanated from the little box. The priest sank into a reclining chair and set his beret and glasses on his lap. He allowed his head to fall back against the cushion of his orange hair and closed his eyes.

The next song was Kopeki's choice. A foxtrot.

Kopeki shuffled over to Natalie and cleared his throat. "I was wondering, Lieutenant. You probably don't want to. But I was wondering..."

"What is it James?" said Natalie, suppressing a grin.

"Would you like to dance?"

Natalie raised her eyebrows and thought a moment before replying. "Yes, I would. Thank you." As she stood and took Kopeki's hand she threw a small shrug of surprise to Daniel.

Kopeki straightened his back. He slipped his right hand around Natalie's waist and waited for the music. Holding Natalie at a discreet distance, Kopeki stepped into an elegant foxtrot. Natalie's eyes widened and she relaxed into the movement.

Daniel let a twinge of envy pass as he watched the pair turn and slide along the grass. Oddly enough, Daniel's focus fell to Kopeki—who had a first name. And was from Indiana or Iowa. Daniel couldn't remember which. It bothered Daniel how little he knew of James Kopeki, who at the moment was displaying a surprising abundance of grace and control.

At the song's conclusion, Kopeki led Natalie back to her seat. How beautiful she looked with the flush on her face and wisps of hair flying loose.

Father Rudy applauded. "Bravo! Bravo!"

Kopeki jogged back to the pile of vinyl discs. He picked up his head only long enough to call out to Daniel. "It's your turn to choose."

Daniel pried himself from Natalie's side and joined Kopeki, squatting down in a position that would shield Kopeki's bashful reaction from Natalie. "You're a very good dancer, Kopeki," whispered Daniel. "Excuse me. *James.*"

Kopeki elbowed Daniel. "Cut it out and pick a record."

I have seen this behavior before. Men and women together. Music and dancing. And where have I seen it? Among the enemy. German officers and pretty German women. Laughing and dancing. And when the German officers are finished laughing and dancing, what do they do? They march into the prisoner's compound smelling of drink, waving crops or pistols. Whipping the haftlings. Shooting them for sport. This drunken randomness is the greatest danger to the Boy. It is the danger over which I have the least control. A whirlpool of fear and anger swirls inside my head. I dig my fingers into the dirt, ready to spring.

Avrum's attempts to slow his rapid descent into the past were futile. He couldn't keep the faces away, even by shutting his eyes. Abba. Sabah. Cousin Eliyahu. One after the other, Avrum reached out to them, pleading with his eyes for them to save him from the fall. Bile surged in his throat. All the while Natalie turned and turned around him, animated in an endless dance, ever smiling.

185

The music stopped and the rush of Avrum's descent subsided. Natalie and her partner danced further and further away until Avrum realized he was no longer falling. The darkness lifted and he could see Natalie taking her seat on the bench. The sun illuminated the edges of Father Rudy's curls. The ground beneath Avrum became firm. He lowered himself onto the lawn. A few steps away, Daniel cranked the music box. It was all right now. Everything was all right. He pulled at the blades of grass surrounding him. This was real. He was safe.

They invaded his senses simultaneously. A waft of lavender and the tune.

Daa da-da-da-dum. Da-dum. Da-dum.

This time Avrum didn't fall. He crashed. Into the drainpipe under the sink. Mama had shoved him there. He held his aching arm and began to complain but Mama scolded him. He hated her harsh whisper. "Not a sound." He was almost ten years old and barely fit in the tiny space. Mama closed the curtains, leaving him in a cramped darkness that smelled of soap and ammonia.

The pounding on the door continued. Avrum heard his mama's voice. "Who is it?" she asked in Polish.

A muffled command. "Auftun!"

The click of the latch. Footsteps.

"What do you want?"

Mama asked this in Yiddish. A mistake. Avrum knew this from the time in the park when he'd called to his father. A group of boys turned angry faces to him and chased him. Avrum ran to Papa and they ran from the park together.

Mama should run.

"A pretty one."

Avrum knew the language well enough to understand.

"Hah," answered another. "Some of them can be very pleasing to the eye. It's part of their treachery."

"Let's see what she has hidden."

Mama's voice quavered. "Take whatever you want."

"Not to worry, liebling, we will."

Mama's gasp startled Avrum and his movement made the faintest sound. Avrum held his breath.

"Leave her for now," said the German. "Let's see what she's hiding."

Even though Avrum kept his breath shallow it still thundered in his ears. But the men didn't come into the kitchen. He heard them walking around the parlor. Avrum gathered all his courage and with a trembling finger, parted the curtains—just enough to peek with one eye. Through the legs of the kitchen table he could see a portion of the parlor. Mama's legs curved down to the pink shoes that had been a birthday surprise from Papa. Shiny black boots came into his view.

"You check the bedroom. And be thorough about it. Crafty bastards. I will see what our Fraulein is hiding in here."

Avrum released the curtain as another pair of black boots marched right past the kitchen doorway. He hugged his knees tight to his chest. Crashing sounds came from his parents' bedroom. They just wanted to steal things. A bead of sweat trickled down his temple. Soon it would be over. He peeked again through the curtain. He saw only Mama's legs. He thought they might be trembling and he fought an urge to run to her.

He heard the winding of the Victrola. But Mama was not near the Victrola.

Daa da-da-da-dum. Da-dum. Da-dum.

"Straus! I admire your taste. We'll dance!"

Mama said, "No. I—"

The boots met Mama's shoes and her heels lifted from the ground. Her knees bumped his legs. He stepped on her toes. He turned her around the floor, in and out of Avrum's view. He heard Mama crying. Tears welled in Avrum's eyes. Soon it would be over.

Boots marched back across the kitchen doorway. "What's going on?"

The waltz came to its rousing conclusion. Still in his grip, Mama now faced away from the German, her feet almost dangling between his boots. She had lost one shoe and her bare toes pointed to the ground, searching for the carpet. Mama whimpered. It was almost too much to bear. When would it be over?

The man who held Mama spoke. "Did you find anything good?"

"Jewelry. And lots of it. What about you? What have you found in here?"

"Something prettier than pearls."

Released, Mama's feet pressed into the carpet. Avrum watched her mismatched feet and wobbling legs struggle to keep their balance. Then tiny popping sounds and buttons bouncing on the floor. Avrum watched one roll right up to the kitchen doorway. When he looked into the parlor again he saw Mama's flowery blouse and white brazier collapsed on the floor, snow-capped blossoms screaming beside the deep black of Nazi boots.

"Not bad, my friend? Am I right?"

"Ach. A dirty Jewess."

"Feels clean to me."

Mama sobbed from her throat.

"Put her away and let's get on with it."

"But I haven't finished searching."

A loud rip and Mama's skirt fell around her feet. Torn panties floated to the ground. Avrum could no longer see Mama's toes. He didn't know why it was so important that he see her toes. He kept his eyes there, waiting for them to appear again. But the next thing to fall to the ground was Mama. She cradled her breasts with one hand and with the other attempted to conceal a dark triangle between her thighs.

"Please," Mama sobbed. Tears ran down her cheeks. "Please. Please."

"You see. She's asking for it."

"Don't be stupid. Who knows what kind of diseases they carry."

"Ach so."

The music started again. *Daa da-da-da-dum. Da-dum. Da-dum.* Black boots marched into the kitchen. Avrum released the curtain and covered his face with his hands. The boots clumped around the kitchen, searching. With every note of the waltz, Avrum squeezed his body tighter, compressing every centimeter of space.

The boots clumped back into the parlor. "Look what I brought you."

Avrum strained to hear above the gentle refrain of the violins. Mama's silence frightened him more than her cries. He forced his hands from his eyes. *Ba da dum—dum dum—da daa!* A slight tilt of his head revealed a smaller portion of the parlor framed by the thin fabric of the curtains. As if looking through the eye of a needle Avrum watched his mother's naked heels push her body backwards along the floor and out of his sight. The boots followed.

Ba da dum—dum dum—da daa!

And what was that? Mama's broom?

Why? What?

Mama's scream hurled the waltz into oblivion. Avrum covered his ears and clamped his eyes shut. He pressed his forehead onto the drainpipe. It hurt to breathe.

Avrum didn't know how long it was before the rush of water in the drainpipe startled him from his stupor. His body jerked and his elbow banged the inside of the cabinet. He heard the surprised exclamation of a woman. She said his name. It sounded like their neighbor, Mrs. Kowalczyk, but he couldn't look.

Avrum heard her footsteps click-clack from the room. "Mr. Loewenstein! Mr. Loewenstein! Your boy! Your boy! He's here!"

Papa's voice, high-pitched. "Avrum? Avrum is here?"

Avrum wanted to move. He wanted to tell Papa how sorry he was that Mama was dead. He wanted to tell Papa, "I wanted to save her. I'm sorry I couldn't save her. I couldn't move, Papa. Papa, it's all my fault."

Avrum heard Papa crying the words. "Baruch HaShem! Baruch HaShem!" Papa's hands extracted him. Papa's arms embraced him. "Avrum," pleaded Papa, "look at me. Please look at me."

Avrum tried to force his eyelids apart but they wouldn't

budge. He felt Papa kissing his eyes and stroking them. Avrum's lids parted to a blurred vision of Papa's red eyes and tear-stained face. He let Papa rock him like a baby.

Avrum found his voice and whispered into Papa's ear. "Mama is dead."

Papa hugged him tighter. "No, Avrum. Mama is not dead." Papa pulled Avrum by shoulders, bringing them face to face. "Look at me, Avrumel." His voice carried a hint of the authority it had once owned. "She's not dead."

"She's not dead!"

Avrum's cry startled the group relaxing in Natalie's yard. Daniel was the first to reach him. He gripped Avrum's shoulders. "What's wrong, Avrum? Avrum, look at me."

Avrum looked up with dazed eyes.

Natalie reached over Daniel to feel Avrum's forehead.

"Does he have a fever?" said Daniel

"No," said Natalie. "He's cold. And clammy. Let's get him inside."

Daniel began to lift him but Avrum struggled.

"No, no," said Avrum. "I was only saying."

Father Rudy squatted beside Avrum and adjusted his glasses. "What were you saying?"

Avrum stared at Father Rudy, perplexed. "That the priest was bad."

Father Rudy and Daniel glanced at each other.

"Avrum," said Daniel. "Will you come and sit in a chair? At least get off the ground."

Avrum looked around him. Daniel and Father Rudy pulled Avrum up and set him in the wheelchair Kopeki had brought around. Natalie placed Avrum's feet in the footrests and stood to stroke his hair.

Avrum massaged the cramped muscles in his arms and shoulders. "Why are all of you staring at me?"

"Avrum," said Daniel. "Father Rudy isn't bad. He's your friend."

Avrum's discomfort turned into frustration. "Not Father Rudy."

"Perhaps you can tell us, Avrum," said Father Rudy, "who this bad priest is."

"Thaddeus, of course. But the peasant confessed."

Daniel tried to translate all this to Natalie. The words kept sticking in his throat.

"Stop talking to her. I don't understand you."

"I'm just telling Natalie what you said. Do you know what you're saying?"

"I'm not a child." Avrum paused to regain the thread of his thoughts. "The peasant confessed that his little brother had died of the tuberculosis. The Jews hadn't killed him. Even the king believed the Jews were innocent."

"What's going on?" said Kopeki, stationed behind Avrum's wheelchair.

"Hold on," said Daniel. "I don't know yet."

"Do you mean," said Father Rudy, "King Rudolf?"

"What?" said Daniel. "You know what he's talking about?"

Avrum smiled at Father Rudy. At last, someone who understood. "Yes, King Rudolf believed the Maharal. It was the priest who was bad." Avrum studied the fracture in Father Rudy's eyeglasses. "You're a priest but you're not bad."

"I'm relieved to hear you say that," said Father Rudy.

"We should get him inside," said Natalie. "Or back to the hospital. I don't know."

"Let's all calm down," said Father Rudy. "And then Avrum will calm down too. Yes?"

"That's very rude," said Avrum, "to speak a language I can hardly understand."

"I beg your pardon," said Father Rudy. He pulled a chair beside Avrum.

Daniel sat on the bench. He reached for Natalie's hand and coaxed her to sit beside him. They rested their clasped hands between them and waited.

"You were saying?" said Father Rudy.

"What was I saying?" said Avrum.

"King Rudolf and the Maharal."

"Yes," said Avrum. "Rabbi Yehuda Ben Loew, the Maharal of Prague. While the gentiles made plans to attack the Jewish quarter of Prague he created from clay a mighty golem. When the gentiles attacked—"

Father Rudy interrupted. "The golem fought them off. He saved the Jewish community."

"That's right," said Avrum. "You know this story. Tell everyone else I'm not crazy."

"None of us think you're crazy," said Father Rudy.

Avrum rubbed his eyes. Except for a small portion of his mind that seemed to be able to weigh and measure the logic of his actions, most of his thoughts remained jumbled and confused.

"Avrum," said Father Rudy, "what happened to the golem after he saved the Jews of Prague?"

Avrum sifted through the bubbles of memory that gurgled in his brain. "The Maharal returned the golem to clay."

Father Rudy leaned closer. "Why do you think he did that?"

The gurgling in Avrum's brain subsided. Here was a question that could be attacked with a logical progression of thoughts. "The golem couldn't live among the people because—because he didn't have a soul. Not a real one anyway. The golem was brought to life by a man. HaShem made man from the dust of the earth. He breathed the breath of life into him and man became a living soul." Avrum paused. Was this from the logical part of his brain or was it from the part that had become jumbled? Using Father Rudy's welcoming face as a gauge, Avrum dared to continue. "Only HaShem can give man a true and complete soul."

"I wonder sometimes," said Father Rudy, "if this soul God has given us is a blessing or a curse."

Tears burned Avrum's cheeks. "I don't know."

Father Rudy took Avrum's hand in his. "I don't know

either. How are you feeling?"

"Tired."

Father Rudy addressed the rest of the gathering in English. "Our young friend is fatigued, but I am sure he will recover in no time at all."

Daniel spoke to Avrum softly in Yiddish. "Tell me what's wrong."

Avrum straightened up in the chair. "Nothing. I'm just tired."

Avrum looked better but Daniel felt as if an "And let us say..." had been left dangling without its "...Ahmain." He hesitated before he asked. Was the question for Avrum's benefit or his own? "Avrum, I was wondering if you wanted to tell us—if it would help you to tell us—who it was who didn't die."

"Didn't die?"

"You said, 'She's not dead.'"

Avrum pulled his knees to his chest. He covered his ears with his hands and clamped his eyes shut.

Vladik sprang. His footsteps fell quick and heavy upon the earth. He had waited too long. He should have pounced the first time the Boy had cried out. But it was not too late. He threw Kopeki to the ground and rolled the wheelchair backwards.

Shocked into battle mode, Daniel leapt to his feet. Vladik aimed a fist at Daniel's throat but Daniel slipped the punch. Vladik felt the crack of bone. Daniel dropped to the ground clutching his shoulder. Natalie flew to Daniel's side.

Father Rudy had backed away, leaving Vladik equidistant between the priest and the Boy. Vladik wanted to kill that man but the Boy was more important. He scooped Avrum from the wheelchair and ran.

Kopeki recovered himself and sprinted after them, reaching behind him for the knife sheathed at his belt. He tackled Vladik from behind and plunged the knife. The jolt of pain in Vladik's spine compromised his hold on Avrum.

Still curled in a ball, Avrum thumped on the lawn. The impact released the manic lock on Avrum's mind and muscles. Father Rudy arrived.

Kopeki's momentum forced Vladik to the ground. Kopeki, holding tight to the knife, landed on Vladik's back. Vladik emitted a howl of rage and pain and rolled on his back, pinning Kopeki to the ground. Kopeki tightened his arms around Vladik's neck but Kopeki's own breath and strength waned under Vladik's unearthly weight.

Avrum and Father Rudy looked to each other in desperation.

Vladik reached behind him and extracted the knife from his back. He twisted it into Kopeki's gut. Kopeki screamed. Avrum thrust his hands between Vladik and Kopeki, hoping to lift both Vladik and the knife from Kopeki. Avrum yelled, "Get up Vladik! Let go!" But Vladik maintained his stone-like grip. Heedless of the blood that covered his hands, Avrum joined Father Rudy. Together they pulled on Vladik's arms and shoulders. Father Rudy pounded on Vladik's head. Vladik's cap fell and Father Rudy pulled at Vladik's hair.

Avrum saw it then. Or, still questioning his sanity, thought he did. Intertwined among the sweating, dirty creases of Vladik's forehead were three Hebrew letters. Aleph, Mem, Tav spelled Emet. *Truth.* Without the Aleph it spelled Met. *Death.*

Avrum reached up to the curve of the aleph etched into Vladik's forehead. He steadied a blood-stained finger and smeared blood and sweat across the aleph, shrouding the letter that made the difference between Truth and Death.

Vladik collapsed. Avrum and Father Rudy rolled his lifeless body off of Kopeki.

"Oh dear God in heaven," cried Father Rudy. "We're too late."

By this time the nurses in the house and the doctors in the surrounding houses had been alerted. Avrum and Rudy retreated as Kopeki disappeared inside a swarm of medical personnel, many of them in pajamas.

Father Rudy's shoulders heaved in mournful sobs.

Avrum gripped the priest's arms and shook him.
Father Rudy lifted a heavy head to face Avrum.
"He's not dead."

15 May

Daniel dreamt he was back in Brooklyn. His father was sitting in his arm chair with his slippered feet propped up on the ottoman, reading a newspaper.

"Where's mom?"

He didn't look up from the paper. "They took her away."

"Took her away? Who? Where?"

His father shrugged and chuckled. "Listen to this one."

"I don't want to hear it." Daniel rushed to his bedroom and turned the room upside down searching for his rifle as his father quoted the infamous Father Coughlin. "When we get through with the Jews in America, they'll think the treatment they received in Germany was nothing." Daniel found his rifle buried under volumes of Jewish canon. He slung it over his shoulder and ran out the front door. But it wasn't Brooklyn. It was the camp. Whitey was telling him to speed up. "Whaterya doin', Danny? Sightseein'?" Daniel's rifle, more cumbersome than usual, made it difficult for him to keep up.

Daniel arrived at the naked corpses stacked like cordwood by the red brick building. The death-scented breeze grew and grew until a swirling cloud of gravel and dirt surrounded the gruesome pile. Through the dust of the tornado Daniel spied a man whose white beard and coarse robe fluttered in the wind. The man raised both arms and said, "This, says the Lord God: Come from the four winds, O breath, and breathe upon these slain, that they may live!"

Relieved and happy, Daniel watched the dead men come to life, one layer after another. The Prophet Ezekiel had prophesied over them and God had brought them to life. Daniel shouldered his leaden rifle and pointed south to show them the way to the land of Yisrael but the naked men turned their backs to Daniel and shuffled north. Still burdened by the weight of his rifle, Daniel ran to them and pushed through the crowd, recoiling at the closeness of each hollow-eyed face or press of jutting bone. His pleas for them to reverse their direction went unheeded. Daniel extracted himself from the march of the morbid and ran ahead. In the rear of the crematorium, Daniel's mother, round and merry in her baking apron, was placing a square of apple cake onto each outstretched palm. She clucked her tongue and shook her head. "Skin and bones," she said. "Skin and bones."

Daniel ran to her. "Don't feed them! If you feed them too soon they'll die!"

She continued to admonish each customer as she patiently dispensed the limitless supply of apple cake from the pan. "Skin and bones," she said. "Skin and bones."

Daniel spotted the young SS soldier in his camouflage uniform leaning against the wall by the rear stairwell, laughing. The sight of the enemy threw Daniel into the heightened mode of survival rooted in the soul of every combat soldier. He reached over his shoulder but instead of his rifle, he found himself anchored by an immense artillery gun. The strap dug deep into his shoulder. The pain grew as his anger swelled.

The camouflaged soldier laughed even louder.

"Shut up," Daniel shouted. "Shut up!"

Still laughing, the blond boy pulled out a pistol, aimed it at Daniel and pulled the trigger. Daniel fell. No longer burdened by the weight of the cannon, Daniel now suffered from the pain of the bullet in his shoulder. "Shut up! Shut up!" Daniel panted through the pain. He had to get back to his mother.

"Daniel, open your eyes."

If he opened his eyes they would all die.

"Open your eyes," Natalie insisted.

He felt her breath on his face and forced his eyelids apart. Natalie had one hand on his right shoulder and another on his cheek. "He shot me."

"No," said Natalie. "He broke your collar bone. You're in the hospital. You're going to be all right."

Daniel lifted his right hand to his left shoulder. It was bandaged all the way around and across his chest, immobilizing his left arm. He remembered. Vladik had punched him. He'd felt the bone crack.

"That must have been some dream," said Natalie.

"Where's Kopeki?"

Natalie pointed with her eyes to a section of the ward enclosed by screens. "Recovering." She massaged a spot of skin on Daniel's arm. "This will help with the pain."

Daniel felt a pinch and welcomed the dose of morphine. "Is he going to make it?"

Natalie put a hand over Daniel's. "I can't lie to you. He's lost a lot of blood. He was in surgery for hours. But the prognosis is good."

"I want to see him."

"He's sedated."

"He's strong," said Daniel. "Stronger than I thought. He'll be all right."

"And he'll go home with a purple heart."

"What about Avrum? And Father Rudy?"

"Both fine. Daniel, you must rest."

Daniel relaxed into a warm stupor and the pain subsided. "What about you?"

"Me? I'm fine."

"You're a bad liar, Lieutenant Wells."

"And you're a terrible patient, Private Rabinowitz. Go to sleep."

Overcome by drowsiness, Daniel closed his eyes. "I'm sorry this had to happen."

"If it had to happen then you shouldn't be sorry."

Avrum sat beside Daniel and studied his friend's sleeping face. Father Rudy sat at the foot of the cot and Daniel opened his eyes.

Daniel's eyes met Avrum's. "It's good to see you," he said.

"How are you?" said Avrum.

"Still breathing."

And God breathed the breath of life into Adam. "I can see

that."

"You were very brave, Avrum. You saved Kopeki's life."

Avrum prayed for Kopeki's recovery morning noon and night. He wondered if the sparks of doubt would dampen the effectiveness of his prayers.

Avrum wanted to tell Daniel that the Americans had seemed confused and flustered when Father Rudy had asked where Vladik had been buried. Was Vladik lost in the bureaucratic madness or had he simply returned to clay? Whether or not Vladik had been a man or a golem or some combination of both, Avrum couldn't help but feel responsible for Kopeki's injuries. And Daniel's too.

"Ten thousand left today," said Father Rudy. "On their way to Displaced Persons camps all over Germany."

"You should have seen all the trucks," said Avrum. "Max went with them and Dov and Moshe and Yossi too."

"What about you?"

Knowing this was the prelude to good-bye, Avrum couldn't summon the courage to answer.

"Avrum will come with me to Prague," said Father Rudy. "We might be able to find some of his family."

Daniel glanced at Avrum with a note of sadness. "Papers?" he asked Father Rudy.

"Taken care of," said Father Rudy

"When are you leaving?"

"Tomorrow the trucks will be loaded with my fellow Czechs and we will make the long-awaited journey back to our homeland."

"Avrum," said Daniel, "is this what you want?"

Avrum knew the best outcome in Prague would be to connect with a mere fragment of his family. Loss and grief would be forced on him all over again. But even a single survivor would be a thread salvaged from his family ties, cruelly severed by the demonic forces of the Third Reich. "Yes," said Avrum. "This is what I want."

"You're in good hands," said Daniel.

Hot tears stung Avrum's eyes. He lifted the recovered tallis from his lap. "We found it in Natalie's yard. Vladik must have..."

"You'll take care of it then?"

Avrum nodded and wiped the sleeve of his American uniform across his nose. "I want to tell you who didn't die."

"Avrum, I never should have asked—"

"It was my mother. She didn't die in our home in Warsaw. She died in the ghetto. When the transports began, she just—expired—as if she knew she had gone as far as she could."

"May her memory be a blessing."

"I'm doing my best to consider all of my blessings." Avrum swallowed hard. "Thank you, Daniel, for everything you've done."

"I can't see how I did much."

Avrum hardly knew how to express the depth of his feelings, turned inside out and upside down in the course of a little more than two weeks. After his father's death, Avrum had transferred the burden of his survival onto Vladik, secretly harboring the comforting illusion of mystical intervention. If Vladik had taught Avrum anything, it was that safety came with a price—the kind of price Avrum was no longer willing to pay. Although it terrified him, Avrum had no other choice but to become his own protector.

But he didn't learn this in time to keep himself from making the same mistake with Daniel. As heaven-sent as the soulful Jewish warrior had seemed, it had been unfair of Avrum to choose Daniel for his own personal messiah. Avrum didn't know how to express his regret to Daniel, or his appreciation. It was Daniel, after all, who had shown him the path to humanity. "Your friendship," said Avrum, "it meant—it means—so much to me."

Daniel pulled off the necklace draped around his neck. He fumbled, one-handed, with the clinking attachments. He isolated one of them and asked Father Rudy to detach it. Daniel swung the necklace back around his head and held the charm out to Avrum.

Avrum recognized it.

"My father gave it to me. I want you to have it."

Avrum's chest tightened. "I can't." He lowered his head. "I have nothing to give in return."

"Please, Avrum. Father Rudy, tell him to take it."

Father Rudy rested his hand on Avrum's shoulder.

Avrum pinched the skinny cylinder embossed with the Hebrew letter Shin. A tiny scroll would surely be rolled inside, inscribed with the Jewish affirmation of faith. Shema Yisrael. Adonai Eluhaynu. Adonai Echod. *Hear O Israel. The Lord is our God. The Lord is One.* When Avrum was little his mother would sit at the foot of his bed every night as he recited those words before he settled into a peaceful sleep.

Daniel extended his free hand. "I'll never forget you Avrum."

Avrum straightened his back and squeezed Daniel's hand. "Zei gezunt, Daniel."

Dazed with sorrow, Avrum rose and walked away. Outside, he tucked the miniature mezuzah into the front pocket of his shirt and silently recited the words of Moses that comprised the remainder of the prayer called the Shema.

You will love the Lord your God with all your heart, with all your soul and with all your might. And these words which I command you today will be upon your heart. You will teach them to your children, and you will speak of them when you sit in your house and when you walk on the road ...

Avrum stood on the SS boulevard busy with Americans engrossed in the process of renewal and repair. He pressed his hand over the bump the mezuzah made in his front pocket. But instead of the strength of Moses, Avrum felt the despair of the prophet Eliyahu, who had been forced into hiding, abandoned and alone. He listened, as Eliyahu had listened, for the voice of God. But through the boot-steps and the chatter and the rumble of the jeeps and the trucks, God's voice eluded him.

16 May

Daniel struggled with his clothes. It wasn't easy to dress with one hand and his shoulder ached. But Kopeki had been moaning all morning and Daniel had to get out of the ward. When their nurse disappeared behind the screen to tend to Kopeki, Daniel took the opportunity to get dressed and escape.

Daniel gave up on the shirt. He slipped his good arm into the sleeve of his field jacket and draped the other side over his immobilized left arm. At the door he almost crashed into Red. Daniel's temper rose. "What are you doing here?"

The blue and yellow remnants of a bruise covered Red's left cheek "I came to see how the little pecker's doin'."

"His name is Kopeki. James Kopeki. And he's not doing very well."

"Sorry to hear that."

"Since when do you care?"

Red raised his hands in surrender. "Take it easy, sport. I was just tryin' to make some conversation here." Red kicked the dirt at his feet. "I was thinkin' maybe I got you all wrong."

Daniel turned around. "How's that?"

"You're tougher than I thought."

Daniel considered this virtual stranger who had antagonized him since the first time Daniel had put on tefillin in Dachau. This was the man who had set up Max—either to get back at Daniel or just to punish more Jews. Daniel had no way of knowing. *Why does a dog lick his balls?* Tony had once joked. *Because he can.*

Daniel guessed Red had some need to prove himself and anti-Semitism was an easy excuse for small-minded men like him. Was a punch on the jaw all that Red needed to set things straight?

Daniel stepped around Red and marched away. He wanted to see Natalie.

Natalie had been reassigned to the penicillin team. She shared the box-like office of the Pro-station with the good-natured Corporal Nordstrom. There wasn't much of anything for them to do. The market for venereal disease seemed to have bottomed out. Dolores had sent her here for lighter duty but Natalie would much rather have been closer to Daniel. The violence that had erupted in the back yard had shaken her and she fought the urge to run and check on Daniel and Kopeki.

"I'm going out for some air, Harry."

Harry, who had been engrossed in the *Stars and Stripes*, put down the paper and looked up at her over a carton of condoms on his desk. "I'm supposed to keep an eye on you."

"Says who?"

"Just about every female in the one-two-seven."

"You mean just about every female officer, right corporal?"

Harry flicked the paper back up in front of his face. "Yes, ma'am."

Natalie smiled. She stepped out the back door and leaned on a decapitated tree that had grown too close to the building. She closed her eyes and forced herself to breathe down into her belly. If she could be with Daniel it would be so much easier. Even if she could sit with him while he slept.

Could she be in love with this boy? At nineteen, that's all Daniel was, really. Although his experience made him a man—the kind of man she didn't know could exist. Grounded and sensitive. Strong and caring. To her, he was almost other-worldly. Truly, he had come from another world—a world of city neighborhoods and Jewish customs and languages as foreign to her as the moon. Back home, before all this, she never would have considered him. She had chosen Gene, the sophisticated doctor, full of good humor and confidence.

She realized now that it wasn't Gene she had wanted. It was his world. Dinner clubs and cocktail parties and drives to Nantucket. A fantasy of "haves" developed during a lifetime of "have-nots." Their trips out of town were in the off-season when they wouldn't be seen—weekends of intimacy like snippets of a honeymoon, *to be continued*. Gene claimed he didn't love his wife, nor she him, etcetera, etcetera. The fantasy rained in pieces around her like dirt and shrapnel when she woke up one moment and realized he would never leave his wife.

The fantasy had cost her dearly. Men wanted wives who were "good girls" and "good girls" were virgins. A worldly woman at twenty-seven, Natalie found herself on the very realistic brink of spinsterhood. Unless she could keep the secret of her affair with Gene for the rest of her life. And then only if she could find a partner in the aftermath of a madness that had, in her experience, generated a decimated population of broken men.

She wanted a house and children. She liked to clean and she'd learn to cook. Was she such a miserable romantic to think she could have all that and share it with a loving, compassionate man as well?

A man like Daniel. Yes, she loved him. In this world she loved him. She loved his manner and his humor and his touch. This time she loved the man singularly— beyond the background of culture and lifestyle. But fantasies were an occupation of the past. She knew that back in the States they could never make a life together. Irony? Tragedy? Either way, it broke her heart.

It took her a few moments to realize that the voice she'd been imagining was close and real.

"Natalie," said Daniel. "The corporal said I'd find you here."

There he was, the object of her musing, telling her she looked sad.

"Not sad. Just tired." She noticed his open coat and leaned forward to button it. "You shouldn't be out of bed."

"I'm fine. Even the doc says I'm cleared for travel."

Natalie took another slow breath and forced a smile. "So you're leaving. Will they send you home?"

"I don't know yet. First I get rehab in Paris."

"Oo la la."

"With any luck this will keep me from getting shipped to the Pacific."

Natalie forced a tone of bravado. "You'll go home to a hero's welcome."

Daniel lifted his free hand in the air in mock triumph. "As if I'd won the war all by myself." Daniel slumped. "Only I'm not much of a hero."

Natalie took a step closer. "What are you talking about? You're a hero and then some."

"Come on Natalie. Don't start now."

"Start what?"

"You always call it the way you see it. That's what I—I like about you."

Natalie paced her words. "And what makes you think I've changed?"

"It's all mixed up—the kind of person I wanted to be and the kind of man I really am." Daniel adjusted his weight and spoke to the ground. "Heroes don't kill unarmed soldiers. Heroes don't feed K-rations to starving people." Daniel kicked the dirt. "Max needed help and all I could come up with was pencils and paper. And when I tried to do more, Max ended up in jail. I made Avrum sick. And Kopeki—James—I should have protected James."

At first Natalie wanted to coddle and comfort Daniel, but pretending that Daniel's imminent departure was a wonderful thing had left her too weary. Did she always call it the way she saw it? If she did, it had been a recent addition to her emotional wardrobe. She tried it, though, and it fit. "You have no right to feel sorry for yourself. Not after all the good you've done."

"What good?"

"What good? What good? Are you blind?"

Daniel stood before her, wide-eyed and motionless.

She saw him then, with an understanding that was tangible. Natalie leaned back against the tree. "You can't see it, can you?"

"See what?"

Natalie didn't know why the memory came to her then. She

told it without thinking and she told it to Daniel because she trusted him.

"For church confirmation all the girls were to wear a white dress. Long sleeves with a skirt that fell just below the knee. My parents certainly couldn't afford a store-bought dress. They couldn't even afford the fabric. So my mother made my dress from clothes we already owned. Most of it was all white, probably from a bed sheet. But she made the sleeves from one of her old dresses. A translucent white with tiny pink roses. When I tried it on I cried. I pictured all the other girls in their pretty white frocks and I was convinced that everyone would either laugh or feel sorry for me. It was the middle of the depression and I'm sure there were others who had trouble managing that ridiculous requirement, but I was thirteen and all I could think about was me and how I looked. I hurt my mother's feelings and she let me know it. I was sorry then, really sorry. That night my father sat at the edge of the bed and said, 'I wish I could have done more for you.' I didn't think much about it at the time, but when I look back..." Natalie looked into Daniel's eyes. Behind those eyes was the soul that had touched her. "But when I look back I realize that my father did everything he could for us, and more. I wish I could tell him now how good it was that he kept our family together. That he kept us from starving. That loving me was more than enough and he never should have felt inadequate because of a few pink rosebuds." Natalie wiped away a tear that had been growing in the corner of her eye. "Did that make any sense?"

"Your father loved you."

"Yes, that's part of it." Natalie blew her nose. "You're like him, Daniel, in some ways. Hard on yourself. You give more than you know you're giving."

Daniel looked confused.

"Strength. Love. Faith." How could she explain? "Do you remember that song, Daniel? 'I believe with perfect faith.' After the concert, you explained it to me. About the Messiah. That when he comes he'll set the world straight. But he's not going to know he's the Messiah, right? He'll just be a man trying to do everything right. And he's bound to make mistakes. And if the Messiah can make mistakes..."

Daniel's lips parted but he didn't speak.

"...then why can't we?"

Daniel pulled Natalie to him and pressed his lips against her forehead. She put her arms around him and sunk her face into his shoulder.

Daniel held her closer and Natalie felt his breath on her ear. "You're crying."

Natalie sniffled. "I guess I am." It felt good to cry and as long as Daniel held her she didn't worry about falling apart.

In Daniel's one-armed embrace, Natalie thanked God for all her triumphs and let Him forgive all her failures. It was sweet and it was bitter. It had happened in their last moments together but she had finally opened her heart. Did Daniel feel it too? "Can you forgive yourself, Daniel?"

"I don't know."

Daniel told Natalie he'd miss her and left quickly. He had cherished their intimacy but he found it hard to face the truth of their ultimate separation. He walked aimlessly through the camp, lost in the smell of her hair and the curve of her back. Daniel marveled at her faith in him. He found Natalie's idea of the Messiah as a fallible man interesting. Their closeness had left him in a state of loneliness and confusion. She had touched his heart as his heart was closing.

Daniel approached the rear of the crematorium and the cement staircase that lead to the basement. It was here that he had terminated the life of the green-eyed boy in SS camouflage. The abscess of hatred and fear had accumulated in one small muscle inside his right index finger and he'd pulled the trigger. Twice. But the release had been inadequate. Momentary. The abscess had burst, but not into the open. He had freed the crooked cells to roam inside his body and hook themselves into the deepest crevices of his thoughts and memories.

The green-eyed boy was most probably the newest of recruits, left behind by more experienced Nazi offenders who were closer to the truth about the imminent American occupation. The Aryan boy could have been evil or he could have been good, or brainwashed, or brave, or stupid. Perhaps the playful grin that had triggered Daniel's rage had been absent of thought rather than full of meaning. *The Simple Son. The one who did not know enough to inquire.* Daniel would never know. The infection had eaten away at his desire for intellectual enlightenment. Forever gone were the imaginary debates with dead sages. He knew too many of the answers.

With a brain forever branded by the memory, Daniel took one last mental snapshot of the place where he had committed murder, and walked away.

His infected heart understood the shadow that clung to the happiness of his return home. He would never be able to curl back into the cocoon of his youth. But like a boy who secretly clings to the blanket that had comforted him since infancy, he could preserve his vacant shell by surrendering his body to the rituals of his childhood. He would anticipate and observe the yearly cycle of holidays. He would attend the neighborhood shul.

And he would fall into the additional safety net of his father's shoe business. The infection had spread far enough into his soul to fray his connection to God, but not far enough to blind him to the travesty of completing his rabbinic education. He would rather bow to another generation of foot-focused consumers than take the chance of exposing his contaminated soul to an innocent congregation.

And so at precisely 4:02 pm on a Friday he would politely refuse to retrieve another style or size from the maze of shoe boxes in the basement because he would need half an hour to count the cash and close the shop in order to arrive home before the Shabbos candles were lit, which would happen, at that particular time of year, at exactly 4:32. He would observe

Shabbos dutifully, first with his parents and eventually with his wife. Maybe Reuven Pearlman's sister, Rachel. His mother and her group of friends would continue their matchmaking in earnest as soon as Daniel (God willing!) arrived safe at home.

In the woods surrounding the crematorium the sweet breath of pine shocked him back into place and time. The breeze ruffled the branches and the sun sprinkled dots of light on the brown carpet of fallen needles. Birds chirped and twittered.

Glory in the midst of ugliness. Growth undaunted by decay.

Daniel was reminded of a gift and pulled the forgotten paper from the pocket of his field jacket. With his free hand, he struggled to flatten the crumpled drawing of a bird. What had Herr Schmidt said? From a time when he could pretend there was still beauty in the world.

Daniel returned the paper to his pocket and studied the birdhouse that had caught his attention on his initial journey through the camp. Later on, he had walked with Natalie and without thinking, brought her to this very spot.

The finality of leaving Natalie stung the remnants of his heart. In another time, in another place they could have—Daniel stopped. Some truths could not be avoided. Yes, he loved her. But he would probably never see her again.

And then there was Tony, vivacious and warm-hearted, with whom Daniel had shared a bond unlike any he had ever experienced. Tony—Natalie—extracted from his life, but not from his memories.

How long ago had it been since he and Tony had strolled together in the relative calm between battles, exchanging jokes and memories? Daniel swallowed the knot in his throat, filled his chest with air and exhaled from his gut. He pressed the tears from his eyes and opened them to a vision of Tony.

A patch concealed Tony's right eye but his left one shone as bright as a shaft of light through azure-blue glass. Daniel couldn't help the surge of joy prompted by the sight of his steadfast friend. He focused all his energy on the apparition, willing it to remain.

Tony spoke. "Why the long face, Danny-boy?"

The voice disturbed Daniel's conscious mind, but he let

himself fall into the sweetness of the dream. "It's been a while."

"A Goddamn eternity," said Tony. "Hey, what's the difference between a pregnant lady and a light bulb?"

It was the last question Tony had put to Daniel before a random bullet had ended Tony's life. And Daniel knew the answer. He knew it in a flash but he let the bubble of sweet suspense grow between them. "You can unscrew a light bulb."

"Son of a bitch," said Tony. "You got it."

The friends laughed together until a tap on Daniel's shoulder cut the tape of Daniel's movie-reel daydream. Tony fluttered away.

A pristine American officer with a shiny silver eagle on each shoulder filled his chest with the air of unearned bravado. The inflated colonel pointed his riding crop at Daniel. "What are you laughing at, Private?" He flourished the crop and drew a crisp oval in the air. "Do you think any of this is funny?"

The spores of Daniel's anger merged into a clump around his sternum but Daniel tucked the tumor behind his heart. "No sir," he said. "No sir, I don't."

Leah poked her head into Avrum's study. Her cheeks were flushed from baking for the holiday and a wisp of white hair curled around the edge of her kerchief. "Avi, do you want some tea?"

"No, sweetness," said Avrum. "I have more work to do."

He heard her exacerbated voice as she retreated down the hallway. "Work. Work. Always working."

Usually the exaggeration of this particular complaint made him smile.

Avrum's wife of forty-two years was no stranger to work. When they met on the kibbutz she was teaching Hebrew to children; some born within the flames of Europe's hysteria but most born out of the ashes. She continued to teach through two miscarriages and two pregnancies which produced, thanks be to God, two healthy girls. Even now, with six grandchildren and a seventh on the way, Leah shared her special treatment of the aleph-bet with preschoolers and helped university students cast for truths in the sea of literature.

Avrum had his own method of fishing for truths. Some he had found and some, despite his local acclaim, remained elusive. A professor at Tel Aviv University, he had become, without much thought of owning the title, a distinguished scholar of Jewish mysticism. Leah said it was because he had a talent for living with his feet on the ground and his head in the clouds. Avrum thought of it as another of God's little miracles that he could study and teach a topic so close to his heart.

The phone call he had received a few minutes ago, however, had the effect of catching years of truths and almost-truths and outright falsehoods in a single net, so that each became indistinguishable from the other.

A reporter wanted to interview him about his experience in the "Holocaust." Years of horror for millions of people reduced to a single, hollow word. And now it seemed, fifty years later, everyone was trying to fill that word to bursting with facts and recollections of the few who had survived.

But what were the facts? His facts?

In his studies, Avrum had learned that much of the story his cousin Eli had told in their grandfather's attic had been fabricated in the early part of the twentieth century. The original golem of Jewish folklore had been created merely as a servant, and sometimes enlivened a story with comic results. The story of the avenging golem, the golem of protection and destruction brought to life by the chief rabbi in sixteenth century Prague, had been fabricated by Yudl Rosenberg, a struggling Jewish scholar who, in a clever marketing maneuver, had presented his book as a "lost manuscript."

Avrum sometimes wondered if his cousin had read the book of fiction that related the story of the blood libel and the rescue of the Jews by the Golem of Prague. If he had, their grandfather would have been displeased that Eli had been reading something other than a religious text.

When Father Rudy had taken Avrum to Prague, he had found out they were all gone—grandparents, uncles, aunts and cousins—living only in his memory, in the storybook of his mind. And sometimes it was difficult for Avrum to tell the difference between what had been real and what he had conjured.

Only Leah knew his secrets. Only Leah understood the gray line of his memory. To speak it out loud? He wasn't sure. If he spoke the truth, *his* truth about what had happened by the river when he had shaped a man of clay, he would be laughed straight out of his beloved world of academia and ridiculed at shul. But how could he tell his story if it didn't include Vladik? And once he started telling, what if he couldn't stop?

He wouldn't tell it. That was all. He dialed the reporter's number and identified himself to the young man.

"Professor Loewenstein! I'm so glad to hear from you. I was a student of yours, you know, a few years back. Golems and dybbuks. That's what I remember. What fun stuff. But really, I wanted to talk to you about something else."

"Yes, something else," said Avrum. He adjusted his kippah as he always did when he was nervous or jolted by a fleeting memory.

"Can we get together? After Yom Kippur?"

Avrum took a deep breath and closed his eyes. "I don't...," he said. "I can't... perhaps... I'll think about it," said Avrum. "I'll think about it."

"Thanks Professor. Next week then. I wish you an easy fast."

Avrum hung up the phone.

After a boisterous dinner with their growing family, Avrum and Leah retired to the back garden. Between the desert plants in the far corner Avrum and his wife had made a garden of stones. Each stone commemorated a person or a family whose lives had been shattered and whose flesh had been buried or burned in unknown places.

Avrum touched the charm he'd worn on a chain for so many years. He rolled the little mezuzah between his fingers. *Hear O Israel. The Lord is our God. The Lord is One.*

The sun descended. Leah struck a match and touched it to the wick of the single candle on the center stone. The blues and yellows of the flame, as elusive and beautiful as the souls it represented, breathed its light to the heavens. Avrum took Leah's hand.

And God was in the silence.

ACKNOWLEDGEMENTS

I have been blessed with the counsel and support of a great many friends, teachers, classmates and family members. I thank you all.

Each writer's group I have belonged to has inspired me, but I must thank the insightful writers who have shared this journey with me from beginning to end: Kathy Lang, Sikha Sinha and Sarah Weber Pearlman.

My children have been a constant source of joy and hope.

I'm sure I couldn't have completed this vast undertaking without the love and devotion I share with my husband.

I humbly thank all the survivors and veterans who were kind and brave enough to share their stories with me, including my father-in-law, Sam Levine, and my friend, Bernard Marks.

Nothing could have been learned if it were not for the authors, artists, photographers, collectors and filmmakers who have grappled with this difficult history, as well as the archivists and librarians who continue to make their efforts accessible.

SELECTED RESOURCES

LIBRARIES AND MUSEUMS

New York, NY
   Center for Jewish History
   Dorot Jewish Division of the New York Public Library
   Museum of Jewish Heritage – A Living Memorial to the Holocaust
Washington, DC
   National Museum of American Jewish Military History
   Unites States Holocaust Memorial Museum
Abilene, KS
   Dwight D. Eisenhower Presidential Library and Museum
Oklahoma City, OK
   45th Infantry Division Museum
Dachau, Germany
   Dachau Concentration Camp Memorial Site
Jerusalem, Israel
   Yad Vashem Museum

FILM

James Kent Strong
   Liberation of KZ Dachau
Greg Palmer and Scott Pearson
   The Perilous Fight: America's World War II in Color
Dane Hansen Productions
   We Were There: Jewish Liberators of Nazi Concentration Camps

MISC.

Harold Porter
   Letters to his parents from Dachau, May 7, 10, 13 & 15, 1945
   (Dwight D. Eisenhower Presidential Library)
Henry F. Staruk III
   "After the Liberation: The American Administration of the
   Concentration Camp at Dachau" (Master's Thesis, U Tenn., 2002)

BOOKS

Martin H. Abzug
GIs Remember: Liberating the Concentration Camps
Nerin E. Gun
The Day of the Americans
Harold Marcuse
Legacies of Dachau: The Uses and Abuses of a Concentration Camp, 1933-2001
Evelyn M. Monahan & Rosemary Neidel-Greenlee
And If I Perish: Frontline U.S. Army Nurses in World War II
Deborah Dash Moore
GI Jews: How World War II Changed a Generation
William L. O'Neill (ed)
Ours To Fight For: American Jewish Voices from the Second World War
Greg Palmer and Marc S. Zaid (ed)
The GI's Rabbi: World War II Letters of David Max Eichhorn
Antony Penrose (ed)
Lee Miller's War: Photographer and Correspondent with the Allies in Europe, 1944-45
Joel Sack
Dawn after Dachau
Marcus J. Smith
Dachau: The Harrowing of Hell

About the Author

 Karen Rae Levine has and MFA in Creative Writing from The New School in Manhattan. A mother of three and a former aerospace engineer, Karen's books are as varied as her interests. *All About Color Blindness: A Guide to Color Vision Deficiency for Kids (and Grown-ups Too)* earned a Mom's Choice Award as well as three independent book awards. Her first novel, *Sister Raven*, received an independent book award for Fantasy.

www.KarenRaeLevine.com

Proof